To Courtney Brown!
hope you
enjoy the book!

Frank Pynate

# THE GENE CARD

# THE GENE CARD

**FRANK PENATER**

iUniverse, Inc.
New York  Bloomington

# The Gene Card
## A Novel

*iUniverse books may be ordered through booksellers or by contacting:*

*iUniverse*
*1663 Liberty Drive*
*Bloomington, IN 47403*
*www.iuniverse.com*
*1-800-Authors (1-800-288-4677)*

*Because of the dynamic nature of the Internet, any Web addresses or links contained in this book may have changed since publication and may no longer be valid. The views expressed in this work are solely those of the author and do not necessarily reflect the views of the publisher, and the publisher hereby disclaims any responsibility for them.*

*ISBN: 978-1-4401-6143-8 (pbk)*
*ISBN: 978-1-4401-6145-2 (hc)*
*ISBN: 978-1-4401-6144-5 (ebk)*

*Printed in the United States of America*

*iUniverse rev. date: 9/14/2009*

# CONTENTS

CHAPTER 1    COUNTING THE HOURS . . . . . . . . . .1

CHAPTER 2    DARBY'S DILEMMA . . . . . . . . . . . . 11

CHAPTER 3    AN ANSWER . . . . . . . . . . . . . . . . 21

CHAPTER 4    SALES TRIP . . . . . . . . . . . . . . . . 33

CHAPTER 5    THE PATTERSON TOUCH . . . . . . . . 44

CHAPTER 6    THORN STEPS IN . . . . . . . . . . . . 53

CHAPTER 7    CAPITOL EFFORT . . . . . . . . . . . . 63

CHAPTER 8    TO THE BONE . . . . . . . . . . . . . . 73

CHAPTER 9    GOODBYE TO ALL THAT . . . . . . . . 83

CHAPTER 10    HEART TO HEART . . . . . . . . . . . . 94

CHAPTER 11    PLAN, PLAN, PLAN . . . . . . . . . . . 104

CHAPTER 12    ON THE INSIDE . . . . . . . . . . . . 118

CHAPTER 13    UNEXPECTED CONFLICT . . . . . . . 132

CHAPTER 14    CHANGE IN PLANS . . . . . . . . . . . 143

CHAPTER 15    UNDERCOVER . . . . . . . . . . . . . . 158

CHAPTER 16    LOST IN PARADISE . . . . . . . . . . . 169

CHAPTER 17    GOODBYE, HELLO . . . . . . . . . . . . 178

CHAPTER 18    RESURRECTION . . . . . . . . . . . . . 190

CHAPTER 19    LAY ON, McDUFF . . . . . . . . . . . . 204

CHAPTER 20    TOMORROW and TOMORROW . . . . . 216

# CHAPTER 1
# COUNTING THE HOURS

The tantalizing aroma of freshly brewed coffee drifted slowly through the large atrium of the Grand Diplomat Hotel in Washington D.C., accompanied by the sweet scent of fresh donuts placed out on long racks. Smartly dressed hotel busboys and bellhops scurried about, neatening up pillows, dusting furniture, picking up fallen crumbs, and keeping the luxurious room in top form in preparation for the arrival of President-elect Joseph Thorn.

He was ending his two-week, post-election vacation to hold a media conference in the swank facility. Although the meeting was not scheduled for another four hours, the hotel staff was leaving nothing to chance.

Secret Service agents had already secured the area, setting up electronic metal detectors and a sound amplification system.

Every person coming into the lobby was carefully searched. Guests at the hotel were obligated to use the rear exit—passing through screening there, too—while dignitaries entered by the picturesque front doors that overlooked the Capitol building.

Noise levels were picking up. The soft classical music playing through loudspeakers was still audible as was the hum of the air conditioning—but that would be gone soon enough. A few newsmen were already positioning their cameras and staking out sites along the entryway, looking for prime positions that would allow them to ask one question or get a comment from Thorn.

Only one man seemed disinterested in the hubbub around him. He was seated on a flowered couch on the opposite side of the atrium. Dressed in a perfectly tailored business suit and looking dignified with straight shoulders and white hair on his temples, he was intently reading the *Washington Post*. Once or twice, he glanced up at the golden clock hanging on the high wall or at the elevator that opened and closed on the other side. One older newswoman recognized him, came over, and shook hands.

He acted surprised that anyone knew who he was. A former secretary of the Department of Health and Human Services, Dr. Peter Kelly was no longer an important person in a city that judged people by their titles—not former accomplishments. A small-town emergency room doctor who had risen to great heights, he had left office a year earlier in anger and outrage. For a day or two, his complaints about the morality of fiscal decisions in the then-Nickolas Gentry Administration had gained a few headlines, but were swallowed in the ensuing election campaign coverage and then forgotten.

Now, Kelly calmly answered a few questions and realized that the reporter, Lydia Kershaw, had not taken any notes. His statements would not add to the eventual story, but she was curious about why he was there, given his animosity toward Thorn and his policies.

"That was a year ago," Kelly said slowly, as though he had rehearsed his opinions. "I am hopeful that Mr. Thorn—as president—will rethink the medical rules that have affected so many people."

He didn't say how the decisions had destroyed families, undermined the health care system, and tragically for him, prevented his own son from having children. There was no reason to say anything about that.

Kelly planned to make his statement another way.

He nervously rested his hand over the small plastic gun hidden in his coat pocket. Kershaw took the gesture as normal. Kelly was not comfortable with reporters, having had little experience with them during his years as an emergency room doctor in Pennsylvania. Even his short tenure in the Gentry cabinet had not added confidence.

He surprised himself by remaining calm. Killing Thorn was to be the last act of a desperate man—one who could see what lay ahead if Thorn imposed further measures. There was no reason why he wouldn't. His Republican Party controlled Congress and the White House. His attitude toward fiscal responsibility in health care had captured the mood of the country. His harsh measures had been treated lightly by the media. Even the tear-jerking stories about people denied medical care because of genetic anomalies had no impact.

Thorn had more cutbacks in mind. No doctor or patient was safe. Kelly knew he had to stop him.

He had not arrived at this decision on a whim. He was not spontaneous like that anyway. As a physician, Kelly was used to trying to imagine all angles. This was, he kept telling himself, just another case.

The Secret Service had already checked his credentials. Minutes earlier, he had stashed the gun in a bathroom trashcan. He waited patiently while the young agents compared his White House pass and his driver's license. Then, he went back to the bathroom and retrieved the gun previously hidden in the trashcan.

He emerged, still wringing his hands, smiling.

He hoped to be able to speak on camera and say the right things. This is the way he wanted his wife, Joan, to remember him. And his two daughters and Erik, his son. They could look at the tapes together and see him standing tall, confident, talking calmly. He also knew that close to Thorn's 3:00 PM scheduled arrival time, more reporters would be there. Many would talk to Kelly then, the way even minor athletes are swarmed over during a media frenzy. He hoped he remembered people, but knew the faces would be a blur. He was never good at recalling people—another reason why he was not a successful politician.

That had never been his goal. Ten years ago, he only wanted to reduce suffering and shunt much needed funds where they would do the most good. Instead, he felt his proposal had led to the creation of a dark monster that threatened to devour American health standards. He shuddered now to think what his simple concept had caused. He had created this monster—no one else had the right to end it.

He hoped the public would understand his action for what it was, not a random act of a crazed lunatic. Too bad he would have no chance to explain.

At first, Kelly had no doubts about the outcome. He would kill the president and be killed. That changed over time. Meticulous as ever, he researched presidential assassins. That's when he realized that there was a good chance he would survive. In fact, most people who had tried to kill a president did survive. John Wilkes Booth had escaped after gunning down Abraham Lincoln and had died in a barn fire. He could have surrendered. John Hinckley Jr., who had shot Ronald Reagan, had been sent to a mental hospital. Squeaky Fromme had missed Gerald Ford and went to jail for thirty years. Charles Guiteau didn't miss when he killed James Garfield, but he was wrestled to the ground and later executed.

No presidential assassin had ever died while killing the president. Even Lee Harvey Oswald, who murdered John Kennedy, had been shot only after being placed under arrest.

A trial didn't appeal to Kelly. This was his final act, a heroic effort to save the country. He didn't want to put his family—or himself—through any further ordeal.

He spent a lot of time online, reading up about the deaths of presidents. The hours once devoted to finding new ways to save lives had been reversed. His wife watched him and wondered about him. He didn't tell her. He couldn't. Instead, he organized research as though investigating a puzzling symptom in one of his patients.

In time, he noticed a couple of things the attempts on the president had in common. Most of the killers felt they had a good reason to act—and successful assassins used a gun.

One particular killer caught his attention: Sirhan Sirhan, who shot Robert Kennedy. That was in a crowded hotel lobby too. Sirhan had succeeded. Kennedy was tightly guarded—especially after his brother had been shot in Dallas five years earlier. Senator Kennedy had been favored to win the nomination and the election. Thorn was just one step beyond that.

Sirhan was left to rot in jail; Kelly would not be so shortsighted.

He knew who to call—his long-time friend John Patterson. The two had not talked for at least a year, but Patterson had brought him into this situation and had the tools to get him out.

Every precaution was taken. Kelly used a payphone. There weren't many left anymore, but he found one outside a gas station. He felt exposed as the October wind whipped around him. Pennsylvania was cooling in preparation for winter, but that didn't matter. The call couldn't be traced. Patterson would not be caught up in this.

Kelly wasted no words. No hello, no chatting about the family, no introduction.

"John, I need a favor," he said firmly. "I'm calling on a payphone."

Patterson hesitated. The voice registered.

"Pete," he started.

"A favor," Kelly repeated.

Patterson understood immediately. "Of course, Pete, anything."

"Do you still have contacts at CDC?"

"Yes," he answered. His response was hesitant, unsure of why he was being asked.

Kelly plunged in. "John, listen to me closely. We have an infestation of some kind of vermin. It's made my son's life hell. I need you to put me in touch with someone who can supply me with something strong enough to get rid of this vermin. Before you say no, I need you to consider how much harm this vermin has done to my family, to your family, and to this country—and who bears responsibility for unleashing this vermin."

Patterson gasped. Kelly could imagine him trying to wrap his mind around the words. He took a deep breath.

"John, I am going to try to do this with or without your help. If you choose to help me, you greatly increase my chances of succeeding. Don't let me do this and fail."

From Patterson's long silence, Kelly could tell his friend was thinking hard.

"It's a cockroach," Patterson finally said. "You have cockroaches."

"Just one big one," Kelly replied. His teeth were starting to chatter. He hoped Patterson wouldn't confuse cold with uncertainty.

"I know a guy who has experience with pesticides," Patterson said. "Let me make a call."

A week later, while an understandably confident Thorn finished up his campaign in sunny California, Patterson called Kelly back. He, too, was using a payphone, even in the chill of the Colorado mountains. The pesticide was ready.

When Kelly told his wife that he wanted to take a road trip to Atlanta, she was dumbstruck. He told her he wanted to visit an old friend from medical school. He didn't explain why he preferred to drive down to Georgia alone, but his behavior had been so distracted lately, she seemed happy just to have him out of her hair for a couple of days.

When Kelly returned from Atlanta, he was back to his old self. He jumped out of the car, burst through the door, and gave Joan a big hug and kiss.

"My, my, Dr. Kelly, it's nice to see you, too," she said and swatted him away with an oven mitt.

Later, he casually took his suitcase upstairs. Tucked inside, heavily sealed in a glass-lined tiny steel tube and encased in rubber, was a vial with 2 cc's of a derivative of an extremely potent, and ancient, African poison, curare. Bushmen would smear it on their spears. Any prey not killed by the weapon would succumb to the quick-acting poison.

The upgraded version would paralyze the victim within seconds. There was no antidote; the victim would die minutes later from the effect of the drug. Patterson's contact had even provided a delivery device—an old CIA toy—a pen into which the poison could be loaded. Simply take the pen and jab it into the victim while pushing the ballpoint activator and the needle injector would penetrate through clothing and skin to deliver the fatal fluid.

Kelly's first idea had been to stab Thorn. Then, as he ran through the scenarios, he realized that even getting close to the President-elect was going to be difficult. He would be surrounded by Secret Service. He might shake a hand through the crowd, but not one with a pen in it. Nor would there be a separate meeting later. Thorn was well aware of Kelly's distaste for him. There would be no private receptions. He had been invited to the press conference as a cynical gesture. Thorn could say, even people who disagreed with me still turn out in my support.

The pen would be for himself. He touched it absent-mindedly. What a simple, devious device. It seemed to be lying to him, as though it really were a pen.

He was getting used to telling lies and getting lied to. He hoped Joan would forgive him for his final one.

Two days earlier, he had casually mentioned at dinner that he had received an invitation to the new president's news conference and that he was thinking about attending.

His wife paused mid-bite and stared.

"Why would you do that?" she managed.

He shrugged as if he had not devoted any thought to the idea.

"I considered it. You know how upset I've been with what happened. Still, I haven't been back to D.C. for a long time. I did manage to make a few friends during my time there. Most of them will be at the reception afterward."

"Some friends," she snorted.

The discussion ended, but she saw him packing.

"You're taking your gun?" she asked innocently.

He took a deep breath. Did she know? She couldn't.

"Do you think I should?" he finally asked.

"D.C. isn't any safer than it was when we lived there," she replied.

He nodded.

"You know best," he said. "I'll take it."

He had bought the gun for protection while living in the nation's capitol. It was still registered—he always followed the rules—although that didn't matter. Since it was plastic, he could carry it on the plane if necessary. But, that would not be the case now. On the plane, he was a nobody. The need for it wasn't there.

She dropped him off at the airport in silence. She hugged him for a long time.

"Joan, what's wrong? I'll be back in a couple of days."

Kelly tried hard to sound reassuring. Joan pulled back and stared at him, still beautiful even through her tears.

"Nothing," she said.

He looked hard at her. Her thoughts were obvious.

"Honey, I'm not having an affair."

"You've just been so distracted lately."

"God, Joan, no! That's the last thing on my mind." This, at least, was true.

"Oh, Pete. I'm sorry. It's just not like you to go off to Atlanta and now Washington. You're a small-town doctor—even if you spent time in government."

"I just feel restless," he said.

"Do you think you should talk to someone?" she asked.

He could see the worry in her eyes. It hadn't gone away.

Smiling through another lie, Kelly promised to talk to a therapist when he returned. "If you think that would help."

"Will you really?"

"Yes," he lied smoothly.

She managed a weak smile. "Things will get better," he told her and kissed her again.

"When you get back," she said and stepped away.

"When I get back," he agreed—a final lie he would have to live with.

"By the way," she added as she climbed into the driver's seat. He leaned over to hear her above the beep of horns and the roar of traffic. "The only time I'm going to go out of my way to be in close proximity to Joe Thorn is when I get drunk at his funeral."

Smiling, he stepped away from the curb. He was going to miss her.

She didn't look back.

As though completing a cycle, he had made reservations at the same Grand Diplomat he had stayed in when he first started working in Washington. He felt as though a giant gear had been slowly revolving over the past ten years. Notch by notch, it was getting closer to clicking back into place.

Kelly took a taxi straight to his hotel, cursorily watched some TV, and tried to sleep. He wanted desperately to see Erik one last time, but couldn't. One person already knew what he was planning to do. Two might be fatal. Erik would have to figure it out himself. His father had failed his son and he had to make things right.

Kelly couldn't sleep, but forced himself to lie in bed with his eyes closed, his heart racing until his wake-up call arrived.

Now, just hours from destiny, he sat on the couch in the lobby. Around him, people milled and talked. Thorn would pass this way en route to the conference room. There would be no pool of reporters. Thorn wanted to give even small media outlets a chance to talk to him.

He was so obliging with that oily smile of his.

Kelly knew his only chance to get close was here—amid the flurry of bodies—as Thorn stopped to acknowledge those lined up to greet him. A pen had no chance. A gun in the hands of an innocent-looking former government official would be the only opportunity.

Watching the minute hand move slowly across the clock's face, Kelly was determined not to fail. Tens of millions of people—many of whom had no idea why—depended on him. Thousands, maybe more, had already died. Kelly was determined to stop that grim count. He must succeed. He would succeed.

So, amid the rising tumult, awash in the strong scents of coffee and donuts, cocooned in the quiet of his own thoughts, Kelly waited.

# CHAPTER 2
# DARBY'S DILEMMA

Mechanically, Kelly took a pen from his pocket—being careful to have two—and calmly folded the newspaper to expose the crossword puzzle. He did the puzzle every day. Joan knew not to disturb him during that exercise. He always started in the right corner, not the left, and worked his way across. Each clue was examined carefully and then answered. The process took time—which was exactly what he needed to fill.

Today, Kelly struggled. He realized that the answers should be obvious, especially in the *Post* puzzle that was not as complex as the more-famous version in the *New York Times*. Finally, he just gave up. He put the newspaper carefully on the coffee table in front of him.

Several minutes passed. A few more people had gathered inside the lofty atrium. The murmur of voices was getting louder.

The light musical background could scarcely be heard over the rising din. Coffee cups clinked together as people gathered around the urns.

In the corner, nesting like wasps, Secret Service agents, hands against their ears, listened to instructions and watched the crowd. Kelly could feel eyes sweeping across him, the way a searchlight scans the sky.

His heart pumped slightly faster. He could feel sweat beginning to bead under his collar. He was annoyed at himself for getting agitated with so much time left. He sat up straight and began to take deep breaths, forcing himself to concentrate on his breathing. It was a self-meditation trick he had learned in medical school when the amount of knowledge that had to be crammed into his brain seemed overwhelming. Patterson had shown him how to focus on something in the distance or internal—a painting, a heartbeat, anything—and to feel the tension ease away. Kelly had scoffed, but the approach worked.

Everything seemed so formulaic and organized. Each floor exactly twelve feet above the floor below. Hanging plants draped perfectly.

*Had it been ten years already?* He analyzed the scene. *It seemed longer. How had things moved so fast?* In his orderly mind, everything seemed a jumble as he tried to figure out what had happened. It was, he realized, quite a puzzle.

He could imagine himself back in the emergency room of St. Michael's Hospital, a place he never expected to see again. It must have been 4:00 PM, Kelly saw a couple of nurses hurrying down the open corridor. They seemed on some urgent task, but he knew better. For some reason, things had quieted this afternoon. A woman giving birth was safely in obstetrics. A young man with a broken leg sustained in an overly exuberant tag football game had been sent off to orthopedics. Only twenty-eight of the forty-seven rooms in the hospital were occupied and no one was sitting in the ER waiting room.

Kelly let himself relax. Nurses behind the central desk were typing and checking files. He could hear the soft pad of shoes on the tile. The thin odor of disinfectants, usually masked by the tension of the moment, sifted across him. Things were so quiet that he could hear the clock ticking.

"Doctor?" one of the younger nurses spoke. She smiled at him.

"Yes?"

Kelly enjoyed the camaraderie with the staff. They genuinely seemed to like him—despite his insistence of strict adherence to rules.

"Sore?"

He shrugged. She was sweet and pretty, reminding him of his youngest daughter, Rachel. It was nice to have a person only as old as his daughter care about him, he thought.

"It's age, sir," she said quickly, teasing him.

He managed a weak grin. Maybe she was right. After twenty-five years in the emergency room, he was beginning to feel aches in his feet, neck, and back that stuck around well beyond quitting time. His fiftieth birthday early in the year hadn't encouraged him to think he would feel better soon. He hoped that his massage therapist would have an hour free later in the week.

He looked around. If he worked in an office, he could be checking the news online or maybe writing down all the medical stories he had collected over the years. Patterson had done that. The book was an easy read with no sex and few anecdotes, but he had gotten it published.

*There were a lot of things to write about. What about all the money wasted in a small hospital with duplicate equipment? Or the lack of homecare that might save some people from journeying to a hospital or ending up in a substandard nursing home?* The more he thought about a book, the more excited Kelly became. He could talk about the whole question of Medicare and the consistently late payments to doctors. *How about the control insurance companies were exerting on medical treatment? That would be a couple of chapters.*

He grinned to himself. A book? His old high school English teachers were going to start chortling if they saw anything published with his name on it. After all the rewriting he had been forced to do? The whole idea was silly. However, he enjoyed the feeling. A man couldn't be serious all the time.

He smiled absent-mindedly at the young nurse. She gave him a puzzled look. Kelly understood what that meant and found the quizzical expression even more humorous. He shook his head. No, he told her silently, he had no interest. She just happened to be in his line of vision.

There was no time for further idle thoughts. The loudspeaker clicked. He was sensitive to that sound and sat up even before hearing Matt Jefferson's voice.

"Class one respiratory. E.T.A. two minutes."

Kelly sped over to the intake desk where Jefferson was writing down information being supplied over the phone by the paramedic. Kelly knew at a glance what was happening, as though someone had splashed cold water in his face.

Wilbur Darby was returning.

Jefferson and Kelly briefly exchanged quick looks. No words were necessary. The old man was a regular. His lungs were failing. He could barely breathe after a lifetime as a coal miner in the Pennsylvania underground and another decade sitting at home smoking cigarettes. He was tough, hardened by the long hours underground. Still, there was only so much his body could take. When his struggles for breath got to be too much, the only alternative was to send him to the emergency room.

Outside, the siren grew closer. Kelly ordered two nurses to join him, although, he knew they knew the procedure. It helped to have someone in charge. Jefferson started filling out the paperwork. It was really only a matter of copying the previous ER record and changing the date. Darby had been there the day before and three times last week.

Seemingly seconds later, the ambulance doors swung open and an EMT wheeled in Darby on a gurney. Sweating and blue around the lips, Darby gurgled. Bubbles of saliva gathered on his lips and he barely moved as he struggled to inhale and exhale.

As nurses gathered, Kelly quickly yanked open Darby's shirt and applied the stethoscope to the old man's sweat drenched chest. He heard barely a whisper of air passing through the lungs. His heartbeat was irregular. The man's skin was cold and clammy. His drawn, gaunt face was too emaciated for the oxygen mask to fit properly. His pale blue eyes were open, but saw nothing. He smelled of death.

"Where's John?" Kelly asked, looking around for Darby's eldest son.

A retired pharmacist, he usually accompanied his father. John was supposed to have filled out a "Do Not Resuscitate" form. With it, Kelly could stop any meaningless, heroic effort to save the old man so he could gasp for air for one more day. Without one, both his conscience and his medical oath obligated him to try to save Wilbur.

"Don't know," the EMT said. He was chewing gum laconically.

*Maybe, this time,* Kelly thought, *no one at the nursing home had contacted the son. Maybe the younger Darby was away on business.* Kelly couldn't wait.

"Find him," he ordered Jefferson, shouting now as a hospital orderly wheeled the gurney away from the waiting room. Darby was routed into an open room. The blue curtains hung around him like a shroud. Nurses quickly hooked up a heart monitor and an EKG was attached to his sweaty chest. Kelly watched. The quiet time meant more hands eager to help—too many as far as Kelly was concerned.

He weighed the options. He needed John Darby to approve radical measures, but waiting was not an option. Everyone expected him to try something. The ventilator was the only choice. Darby could not breathe on his own; every second wasted meant more of his brain was dying. The insanity of putting a tube in this dying patient and placing him on a ventilator was clearly evident, but there would be no other option. Kelly could not stand there and watch Darby die without an official "Do Not Resuscitate" from the family. The old miner might accept that fate, but the hospital attorney—and Darby's children—might not be so forgiving.

A nurse supplied the needed IV meds to relax and then paralyze Darby. When the breathing ceased and his muscles went limp, Kelly gingerly guided the tube into the fragile trachea and the ventilator took over the work of breathing. Stepping back, he watched as the old man's chest rose and fell smoothly, and his oxygen saturation began to rise.

Everyone seemed to relax. The young nurse, jovial so recently, was upset. Beads of sweat gathered on her forehead above her mask. She shot a worried look at Kelly.

Suddenly, the EKG monitor began beeping rapidly—though Darby was finally getting enough oxygen, his proud heart had had enough. Action in the room briskly started at Kelly's orders. The nurse closest to the defibrillator called out "all clear" and hit the button. Some 360 joules of electricity shot through the old man's body. It rose and fell involuntarily—bowing like the top of the cave that Darby once labored under.

Kelly could see the energy failing to revive the patient. He called for Lidocaine, a heart rhythm drug that, in high doses, may help increase the effect of the defibrillator. It worked. Darby's heartbeat became regular.

For a moment, everyone watched the old man struggle to live.

"Good job," the young nurse whispered to Kelly. He paternally patted her shoulder.

"Old men aren't completely useless," he assured her with a grin.

Later, Kelly met with Darby's son John and his wife, Kate, in his office at the hospital. They had finally been reached at a friend's house via cell phone and rushed over. A thin, short man, John was not the kind to mince words. Moreover, he had spent years counseling local customers at his pharmacy. He had no illusions.

Kelly greeted them warmly. "You know the situation," he said. Both Darbys nodded. They looked ashen, as if already prepared to hear the worst.

"We were able to stabilize him."

Kate looked quickly at her husband. "That's good, isn't it?"

He nodded.

"For how long?"

Kelly had no answer. "He's old. He's sick. I don't know how much time he has left."

Neither of them showed any hint of surprise. They whispered something to each other.

"What's next, Pete?" John finally asked. The informality came from years of contact and professional courtesy. Many of Kelly's patients went to John's pharmacy. He knew almost as much about medical treatment as any doctor.

"That will have to be your decision, John. He may need to stay on a ventilator," Kelly told him, "but I'm not so sure he would want that. He can't tell me, so you have to make the call."

John took a deep breath. His wife put her hand over his. "My father is not really living. He just exists. He can't do anything without getting completely exhausted and he is always short of breath. He won't even eat most of the time. I don't even talk to him because he doesn't have enough air to answer me back."

He paused. His words hung in the air. In the silence, Kelly could hear the wheeze of the air conditioner and the click of the wall clock as it moved ahead one minute.

"What would you do, Pete?" John asked.

Kelly carefully formulated his answer. His own father had become rapidly demented over a short period of time shortly after his eighty-ninth birthday. No explanation was found, despite a lengthy evaluation by one of Pete's friends. When the progressive dementia got to the point that his father would no longer eat or drink, Pete had to make a decision. Should he put a feeding tube in, or just keep his father comfortable? He chose the latter and—although it was a difficult and emotional decision—Pete never regretted what he did. Peter's father had lived a long and healthy life and had no desire to be kept alive if he did not have his faculties about him. And he had told his son just that.

That was the answer he now gave John and Kate. They nodded and shook hands. There was nothing more to say.

John paused by the door. "You'd think there would be some other way to do things than run to the emergency room all the time," he said to his wife. "Why the hell does my father have to go through that at the end of his life, being prodded and pried and wrenched around?"

"We didn't have any choice," Kelly interjected softly. "We needed a DNR."

Darby turned around. "We filled one out," he said.

Kelly's stomach dropped. "John … I don't know what to say. We didn't know. When we weren't able to reach you, we had to make an instant decision or lose him."

"I filed it with the nursing home," he said.

"I'll get a copy," Kelly said.

"I guess it doesn't matter now," Darby said as he closed the door behind him.

Kelly sat down wearily. Instead of the peaceful, dignified death that his family had hoped for him, Wilbur Darby continued to suffer—only now he was in worse shape than ever. Kelly criticized himself: he had increased Darby's pain and he had let down the family. His own head throbbed with a combination of frustration and sadness.

He had little time to think about it. Another case followed. A father had tried to rescue the family cat from a tree and had fallen. Cuts and bruises seemed the probable diagnosis, but Kelly ordered more tests for any internal hemorrhaging. The cat, of course, was fine and had descended with little fuss.

Amazingly, Wilbur Darby got better, too. He soon was

breathing on his own and eager to leave the hospital. Kelly wondered how long before the sirens heralded Darby's return.

He was still trying to come up with a solution to the basic dilemma: an aged, dying patient would be far better off in familiar surroundings. However, how would that patient get proper care?

Kelly had no solution. This was not like coming up with a diagnosis and treatment. He had experience for that. He was good at taking academic tests, studying lab results, reading X-rays and the like. Creativity was not his forte. His ability lay in implementing a concept, not creating it in the first place. No one, however, had a proposal he could put into effect.

The real problem was that Darby had been brought to the hospital in the first place. There had to be a way to keep him in the nursing home and bring any necessary equipment to him. The defibrillator was portable. So was the EKG machine. A nurse could do the work without a doctor present. Nurses were well trained and, in many cases, better versed than physicians in situations such as this.

Kelly took out a piece of paper and began to create a schematic: patient, hospital, nursing home, nurses, medical equipment. After a few minutes, though, he was too tired to continue. He would talk it over with Joan, who, as a former hospital nurse, might have some helpful opinions.

She was usually better at coming up with concepts, but not this time. Joan ran through the scenarios: Not helping the patient was unacceptable. To do only a little seemed worse. Nursing homes and private homes were ill-equipped to handle such serious crises.

For Kelly, time to focus on the problem vanished almost as soon as John Darby closed the office door. Case after case suddenly flooded into the ER, as though everyone had been waiting for the first one to break the logjam.

There seemed an endless parade of ancient souls with broken bodies coming to him for physical salvation. Their eyes panicked with the fear of death, pleading for some miracle to be wrought as their bodies struggled to die. They were knocking on heaven's gate, and he would do his damnedest to drag them back down to earth—to his ER. They might go on for another day, or week, or month, until they would be back, knocking again.

There were always new, more expensive drugs, tests, treatments—new tricks for old diseases—but in the end, the diseases always won. The problem was clear, but the solution was still out of Kelly's grasp, obscured by morals, ethics, and unrealistic societal expectations.

Every time he struggled through a case, his heart hurt, his brain agonized, his palms sweated, and the knot grew bigger in his stomach.

He would grimly do his job and struggle to revive his unwilling patient. When he succeeded, the doting family would be relieved that Granny would live another day. And when Granny was well enough to be discharged, she would go back again to the nursing home, to her semi-private room with the drab curtain separating the two beds. Perhaps she would stare at the ceiling while her mind wandered to who knows where. She would wait for the next time her brain misfired or her heart decided that it didn't want to pump anymore. Then, fluid would pour back into her lungs and she will be rushed back to the hospital where the whole drama will play out again.

Each time, he wished for the creativity to find a solution. If the patient died, Kelly was almost relieved not to have them endure more of the agony. Yet, time after time, Kelly forced himself to do what he knew wasn't right, wasting the hospital's resources and the patient's money, and most importantly, denying the patient the right to a dignified, painless death.

Somehow, an equation balancing costs against morality and ethics did not seem to compute.

Exactly seven days later, Wilbur Darby came back. This time, he did not roll out the front door in a wheelchair several days later.

# CHAPTER 3
# AN ANSWER

Something buzzed in Kelly's suit pocket. His cell phone. He answered it automatically.

"Hi, hon," Joan said cheerily. "How's it going?"

He glanced at the clock. Still close to two and a half hours to go before Thorn was due to appear. He told her that in a low voice. He didn't like to share conversations—a habit reinforced by the normal privacy between a doctor and patient.

"Enjoying yourself?" she asked teasingly. "See any old friends?"

"Not many," he admitted.

"That's because Thorn is not exactly a draw," she said.

"He's the president now," Kelly countered.

"God help us," Joan said. "Have a Valium or something. You'll need it when he comes by. By the way, CNN is covering the conference live. Wave at the camera or something so I can see you."

"Oh," Kelly said softly as he closed the phone, "you'll know I'm here."

He thought back to Wilbur Darby. Who knew the death of that old man would lead to this?

As Wilbur Darby struggled to breathe, Kelly plowed through his regular cases for another week. Most were simple enough: sprains, rashes, and the like. A surge of flu kept everyone hopping. Often, however, if he didn't know what the problem was in the first two minutes of his evaluation, he knew he wasn't going to figure it out in the ER. Of course, the blood work, X-rays, and other medical tests had to be done to develop a diagnosis and to satisfy the "standard of care" that doctors are expected to live by. Here the rules were constantly shifting—largely affected by insurance companies and what they would or would not cover. Kelly knew what outrage would follow if he decided to admit a patient that the insurance people wanted treated as an outpatient.

Then, there were the other patients—the ones like Darby.

The next day, four beds in the ER were taken up with elderly admissions and the floor was not ready to bring them up. The fluorescent lighting mercilessly illuminated the pale, sickly faces of the ancient souls lying in their tiny cubicles. A pasty woman in her nineties suffered from rectal bleeding. The nurses had already changed her bed twice, but the stench still wafted through the rooms. The monitor in the next room was constantly clanging because the patient's heart rate was forty beats per minute, and nobody had reset the alarm parameters. The patient didn't mind since he was deaf.

The psychiatric quiet room was occupied with a violent paranoid schizophrenic in four-way leather restraints. Unfortunately, the major sedatives that had been administered had not yet kicked in and he was screaming obscenities at the top of his lungs. The elderly patients waiting for admission, however, were all so hard of hearing that they were blissfully ignorant.

Into this confusion rolled Mary McGill, sent over from the nursing home adjacent to the hospital. Kelly saw her coming and shook his head sadly. In tow behind her hospital bed were two elderly daughters, themselves not far from nursing home placement. McGill was ninety-eight years old and had managed to outlive four of her eight children. Her tiny frame seemed encased in the hospital bed, as though she had become one with it. Her thin hair, sweaty with fever, barely covered her withered head. The eyes had become too big for the emaciated face, but there was no fear in them.

Kelly bent over the old woman in a familiar pose, using a light to peer into her eyes. The back of her eyes were white with a telltale tinge of yellow slowly seeping in. McGill was still living, but barely.

Kelly's stethoscope revealed the rest of the story. McGill was in respiratory failure, likely from aspiration pneumonia. There was nothing he could do short of putting her on a ventilator and have the machine breathe for her. Her daughters hovered nearby. Kelly had talked to them about a month earlier when their mother had suffered a stroke that left her with difficulty swallowing. The daughters correctly decided not to put a feeding tube in, but had not mentally prepared themselves for the pneumonia that would inevitably do her in.

Kelly asked the nurses to make her comfortable and led the two daughters to his office.

There was no easy way to address the situation. Kelly folded his hands in front of him, looked somberly at the two women, and told them the truth: their mother was comfortable, but she was dying.

"I can't fix her this time," he said.

They looked at each other. Elsie, the spokeswoman of the duo, wanted to argue, as if getting Kelly to change his mind would somehow cure her mother. He explained as succinctly as he could. Wanda listened; Elsie continued her objections. Her mother seemed so alert just a day or two ago. She even sipped some soup and ate minced chicken. Maybe there was some new medicine or operation that could help her?

Kelly shook his head, "I don't think it would be in her best interest to do anything more."

Elsie shook her head. "I know my mother," she said. "She's a fighter."

Kelly stood up. "She has to be to have lived this long. I wish there was something left to do, but, I'm sorry, there really isn't," he said. "I am out of options. You both agreed last month that you didn't want any "machines" for Mary. You need to let her go now."

Less than an hour later, McGill died peacefully with her two surviving daughters and the parish priest by her side. Kelly heard the quiet sobs. How sad, he thought. Didn't this proud woman and her daughters deserve to share a more private, dignified death than in an ER with only a curtain separating their solemn grief from the pervasive odor, patients wailing, doctors barking orders, and nurses bitching about the weak coffee?

As if having a veil lifted, Kelly began to notice how many ER patients were elderly with chest pain, congestive heart failure, chronic bronchitis and/or emphysema, severe infections, complications of diabetes or "changes in mental status." They were all just barely clinging to the bitter stub of their life. Kelly had to tell the families that no one ever really gets "better" from these diseases—they only get worse. Most listened. Still, many of these distraught sons and daughters—anxieties on their faces and hopes in their hearts—were looking for a long-term fix, if not an outright, miraculous cure.

Kelly wondered if he was only noticing these older patients now or if there really were more older and more infirm Americans in the Lehigh Valley. Maybe, he decided, it was both.

Every time Kelly ordered a test or X-ray or CAT scan, an insane image flickered through his thoughts. He would imagine the entire American economy being devoured by healthcare costs, a sort of strange Pac-Man image gulping down bundles of dollars. This Pac-Man was old with a wrinkled brow despite the voracious appetite.

He couldn't help but look around. Even with young nurses, the ones in his ER, the country didn't have enough young healthy people to pay the bills and to work in nursing homes to take care of all the elderly and infirm. The entire society could come crashing down in a torrent of bandages, bedpans, and feeding tubes. This absurd scenario haunted him. He knew that to some small extent, that very process was now unfolding in his tiny corner of Pennsylvania—and he was contributing to it. The bar was always being set a little higher for the "standard of care" with every new test, CAT scan, MRI or miracle drug that came out, and there was no end in sight for technical development and improvements in medical treatments—it was solely a matter of more money. What happened when the money ran out?

Even when he looked at it as a cold mathematical formula, the situation made little sense. Kelly didn't pretend to be an economist, but it didn't take a genius to figure out that financing the last few days or weeks of a dying patient's life was costing society many billions of dollars for no apparent benefit to anyone. It seemed to him that granting people comfortable, dignified deaths was more important than squeezing out every possible minute of survival.

He even argued the previous day with Dr. Cleveland, his colleague in the ER. No, he wasn't planning to become a Dr. Kevorkian. This wasn't euthanasia, but rather the natural process of death taking place in as comfortable and peaceful a setting as possible. Cleveland had his doubts anything like that could be worked out.

Kelly did, too. At least, he hadn't stumbled on any plausible solution. However, the unease continued to grow inside him, especially since all the equations refused to add up to an answer.

Each night, he would talk with Joan about his concerns and then doodle over his increasingly indecipherable plan. It was going nowhere and taking him for the ride.

She watched him come through the door after the Darby funeral. It was low-key and quiet. The old man had suffered a long time. Everyone was relieved his agony was over. The few other retired miners Darby knew here in Allentown—a couple of surviving friends and a distant cousin or two—commemorated his simple life with few words. There weren't many like him left in the Lehigh Valley, an area settled by the tough Irish, Germans and Poles who once lived most of their lives underground, saying few words and expecting less. The minister had little to say either.

Kelly went because of his relationship with John, who thanked him, and then John asked if it would be all right to drop by the house. Kelly figured John wanted to talk about some patients and agreed, although with some trepidation.

What if he wanted to talk about the DNR plan and the way it was overlooked? Kelly wasn't looking forward to that conversation.

Dinner was already on the table when he arrived home: roast chicken without the skin, small salad, light Italian dressing, and green beans without butter. Kelly noted the healthy approach. Joan was always sensible and watching out for him.

He felt particularly tired, weighed down by heavy thoughts and long hours. His shoulders were slumped and he hung up his raincoat with little energy.

Joan watched him wash his hands and sit down at the table. With their three children grown and away, it was just the two of them. Tonight, she thought, it was probably a good thing.

"Everything all right?" she asked gently. Kelly picked at his food, moving around the green beans like a chess player.

"It was sad."

"Funerals are."

"John Darby wants to talk to me."

Joan looked puzzled. Her husband usually didn't worry about the patient's family. He never second-guessed himself. Whatever decision was made in the ER was the best one at the time. There was no point going back.

"It'll be all right."

She hesitated. She knew he'd pick up on the cue—no matter how tired he was. He raised his eyebrows and looked at her. She managed a coy look.

"It's Rachel," she said.

He shook his head. Their youngest daughter was spoiled and flighty, so unlike either Erik or Diane. Erik was now a lawyer and Diane was in pre-med at the University of Pennsylvania. She was still undecided about which specialty to follow. Rachel was a freshman at Temple University, and befitting the school nickname, was something of a night owl.

"She called," Joan continued.

"Money?" Kelly asked, taking a small bite of lettuce. The thought of sending more money to Rachel, who had no concept of a budget despite multiple conversations, distracted him from his lack of appetite.

"No." Joan took a deep breath. "She was almost expelled."

Kelly stared at his wife. He didn't like to show emotion, but shock filled his face. One of his children? He expected good behavior. They knew that. He expected them to make the proper decision when facing moral questions. They knew that, too. They practiced that every day of their lives at home. Rachel was the most rebellious, but, nevertheless, she knew better. He hoped she was not using drugs. That would be awful.

He closed his eyes and waited for Joan to tell the story. It was bad, but not horrible. Rachel had been caught with a copy of a psychology test answer sheet. She had been failing the class and was desperate. The professor, at least, decided to analyze her decision to use the stolen material and decided that she was compensating for something in her family life.

"This is one time being blamed had a positive effect," Joan noted.

"Sure," Kelly answered, "but I doubt we'll be honored guests at Parents' Day."

As a result of his conclusion, the professor allowed Rachel

a second chance. She managed to eke out a C on the exam and nothing went on her transcript except the final grade.

Still, Kelly realized, this was a serious matter. Beyond the grade was the matter of ethical behavior. She was taking a shortcut. She wouldn't learn anything except that the answer to question twelve was C, for example. That wasn't why her parents were paying tuition at an expensive, academically renowned university.

"We need to talk to her," he said.

"I did."

Kelly nodded. "Then, I'll reinforce the lesson," he said.

He still played with his food.

"Upset about Rachel?" Joan tried. He shook his head. "John Darby?" Another shake.

"Thinking of doing something else? You're too young to retire."

"Maybe we need a dog," Kelly said absent-mindedly.

"You know neither of us is home enough," Joan commented. "Besides, the kids would be upset. They didn't have a dog. They leave and we get one."

"Seems like a fair exchange."

"Anything besides the dog?" Joan tried.

Kelly shrugged. "I had another pointless resuscitation today—someone who should have had a peaceful death at home. Instead, she died in the ER."

"I'm sorry," Joan said.

"So am I," Kelly replied.

She heard the thoughts nestled between his few words. A former hospital nurse who now ran her own home-nursing business, Joan knew doctors well. Too many of them kept their thoughts inside. Her husband was no different. Maybe that's how he managed to survive all the turmoil of medicine. The joy of helping someone heal was always muted by the reality of someone's death—someone who could not be helped despite all the knowledge and technology.

Joan smiled. "I'm sure you'll think of something," she said.

He looked at her with sadness. "Someone has to."

John Darby knocked on the door around 9:00 PM. By then, Kelly had talked to his daughter. She was contrite, crying. Her tears had always watered down her father's disappointment. He projected a stern attitude but had little resolve with his daughters. He lectured her anyway. Ethics were so important, he told her. What is a person without them? What is society?

"I know, I know," she repeated.

She knew better than that. He hoped she listened anyway.

Darby seemed more sincere. He was certainly more somber. He smiled at Joan, shook hands with Kelly, and accepted an invitation for a glass of red wine. Joan always kept harder liquor around, but that was for guests who were serious about their alcohol intake. A nice glass of wine was plenty for everyone else. There was some scotch, too; her husband only sipped that on special occasions—such as before he was forced to fly somewhere.

The trio chatted for a moment. Joan offered her condolences and left. Darby nodded. For a few minutes after moving into the living room, he and Kelly talked about Wilbur and how life had changed in the area. The old mines were closed or barely operating. That was no place to work anyway, they agreed.

"We all want to stay above ground as long as possible," Kelly noted.

John nodded with a small smile. Balding with thick glasses, he was invariably pleasant and polite. Townspeople trusted him; he exuded such a positive feeling.

"I was thinking about what happened with my father," he began.

Kelly felt a chill creeping up his back. Had John come to complain? He learned forward. The old chair gave a slight groan as if mimicking Kelly's inner thoughts.

"And I remember something you said," John continued. He

put his goblet down on the coffee table with a soft clink. The room was very quiet. Nearby, Joan was typing away on the computer. That was the only real sound in the house. "You wanted to help my father end his life with dignity."

Kelly nodded. He, too, put down his drink. Maybe he should have opted for the scotch.

John looked at him. "Pete, why do so many people come to the pharmacy instead of the doctor's office?"

That was an easy question. "You don't charge them," Kelly answered.

John nodded. "I also give them medical advice, too," he continued.

That was no secret. It really wasn't a problem. Pharmacists knew drugs, interactions, and treatments. They couldn't diagnosis or write prescriptions, but they could recommend over-the-counter remedies and did so with enthusiasm.

"Sometimes, they never see a doctor at all," John added. "I thought that maybe something could be done in the same vein for patients like my father."

"Send them to pharmacists?" Kelly thought aloud.

John gave a slight laugh. "Not exactly," he said. "What if a system could be worked out where chronically ill people could get help without going anywhere?" he proposed.

"I don't follow."

John nodded. "I am thinking of it this way. People who are sick at home, or even in personal care homes or nursing homes, would contact their primary-care physician, or his representative, before calling an ambulance. Then, maybe a nurse or physician's assistant would check out the guy. If a ride to the ER was necessary, then off they'd go. If not, the patient would stay put."

He looked up hopefully.

Kelly sat back.

"It would be kind of like seeing a pharmacist and getting help without going to the doctor," John added.

"Even at two o'clock in the morning?" Kelly asked. "As I

recall, pharmacists don't keep bankers' hours, but you did close the shop around nine at night."

"Good point," John said. "Such a system would have to be available around the clock—and the response time would need to be pretty much immediate. I haven't figured out the details yet. But there must be some rational alternative to the countless trips to the ER by chronically ill people every time something goes wrong with them. I know my father didn't want to go. And I'm pretty sure that the patients would be better off at home if they could get the right treatment."

The approach was intriguing. However, Kelly was too tired to think it through carefully. He asked Joan to join them. She came in and sat down on the couch. John went through the idea again. Joan nodded. Kelly wondered what her reaction would be. She digested the concept carefully.

"There would need to be more than one doctor involved," she noted.

John looked puzzled.

"When a person goes to a nursing home," Kelly quickly explained, "another doctor often takes over from the primary-care physician. That doctor may have never seen the patient before. End-of-life issues just don't seem to be a priority for these doctors."

"Well, that's really dumb," John said. "How can you fix it?"

Kelly shrugged. "If I were king, everything would be fixed."

"Then there's the question of the Do Not Resuscitate form. Not everyone has one. Your father did," Joan said, "but without one, a doctor would face some real legal issues if he didn't examine and treat his patient, but sent a physician's assistant instead."

John shook his head. "That could be handled. Perhaps the State Medical Society could help get a law passed requiring everyone over a certain age to have a living will. Those that want to go to the ER then could."

"You think the Legislature could pass a law requiring a living will for folks in nursing homes?" Kelly asked. Using a political approach had not occurred to him.

Joan considered the legality of the issue. "I would say that it would be reasonable to require a living will when a patient enters a nursing home. However, that doesn't mean that they would all come into your ER as a DNR."

"I don't think everyone should be a DNR," Kelly said, "but there are too many that should be and aren't. I like John's idea."

"Well, don't do anything radical," Joan cautioned. "You don't need a malpractice suit."

"Thank God for insurance," he said.

Joan went back to work.

"What do you think?" John asked.

"It's worth pursuing," Kelly told him.

It just might work: people could get diagnosed and treated without running up the huge cost of using an ambulance, emergency room, nurses, and physicians. Maybe the price of training enough physician's assistants could be balanced by the reduction in medical expenses and hospital admissions on the other end.

In fact, Kelly did some quick mental arithmetic: patients—and Medicare—this scheme might save a ton of cash.

That's when he had an original idea. He had no concept where it came from. He stood up.

"You know what?" Kelly asked. "We should call this the Darby Plan."

John grinned.

"The Wilbur Darby Plan," he countered.

They shook hands on it.

# CHAPTER 4
# SALES TRIP

"Sir, sir," someone said with cold efficiency.

Kelly looked up. A young Secret Service agent was staring directly at him. He could only have been a foot away. Kelly could even see a small razor nick on the otherwise smooth jaw. A cord hung down from his right ear and ran down the back of his white shirt. His collar was worn—as though chafed by a constantly rigid neck.

Kelly nodded. His throat felt very tight.

"You'll have to move, sir." The agent's eyes were slate gray and cold.

"All right," Kelly said slowly. *Where did the agent want him to go? Why?*

He stood up. Swiftly, the agent swung the chair back against the wall. Kelly looked around. All the furniture had been moved away from the entryway. Behind him, chairs, tables, and couches were being carted through the back door. A hotel manager, clearly identified by his frazzled look, was watching with increasing alarm as his coiffured atrium was being professionally dismantled.

The agents were busily ignoring him and clearing much of the room simultaneously.

After a moment watching the confusion, Kelly wandered over to the front desk. "What's the problem?" he asked casually.

"Someone called in a death threat," the young man behind the counter said with professional disinterest without looking up. "Who would want to shoot the president? He hasn't even been sworn in yet."

"You never know," Kelly murmured.

He moved over to a corner. There, leaning against the wall, he watched the parade of furniture. The agents were very good. His mind, though, was focused on what the desk clerk had said. Someone else wanted to shoot Thorn. That made sense. The man must have alienated a lot of people en route to the White House.

If he had only known, he could have taken care of Thorn in Colorado so many years ago. It was like meeting Adolf Hitler before that madman became German chancellor.

Of course, Kelly had no way of knowing what Thorn would turn out to be. The whole thing seemed so innocent at the time. Thinking back, Kelly realized it had been his idea to go west. Joan had hinted at a vacation several times, but no place seemed promising. They had been on several cruises, but Joan thought the food wasn't very healthy on board, and Kelly found it hard to relax whenever a four-hundred-pound cruiser wandered by. He kept thinking of ER visits and how the gurney could possibly endure such a weight.

The various beaches were nice, but, then, so was the sand in Sea Isle City—and it was a lot closer to home.

Neither liked gambling, so Atlantic City was out. Las Vegas held no allure. Rachel was the skier, not her parents, so mountains offered no special inducements, not even the nearby Poconos. They would rent a cabin there occasionally, but only in warm weather. They did go to a massive flea market in Berwick, although it hardly could be the "world's largest" despite its entrance sign.

In the end, typically after pawing through stacks of brochures and exasperating their travel agent-friend, they would revisit Philadelphia, drive up to New York, or troll for bluefish in Cape Cod Bay. They would rent a rustic cabin in Eastham: Kelly would relax and battle with voracious green flies while Joan would obsessively call her office. Eventually, they would return pretty much as frazzled as they left.

This time, Kelly suggested a visit to Colorado. He wanted to discuss the Wilbur Darby Plan with John Patterson. The two had communicated regularly since med school. This was a perfect topic to chew over, especially now that Patterson had some political clout.

Joan arched an eyebrow at him. "Mountains? Isn't there enough snow in Pennsylvania for you?" she asked.

"I have my heart set on making snow angels in something that isn't already black with soot," he replied.

"You'll have to fly," she noted.

"Just pack the scotch," Kelly told her.

Joan was delighted to agree. She said the usual things about getting away from the office—although she never actually got too far away for some kind of contact. Mostly, though, she was happy her husband would take a break. In all the years in the ER, Kelly rarely missed any time.

A quick call to John and Terri Patterson made it easier. The couple had recently completed construction of their new house and were eager to show it off. Kelly realized that he already knew something about the home, built on the side of a mountain with a "breath-taking view of eagles' nests and a first-aid center for overzealous skiers," as Patterson put it in a recent e-mail.

The two men exchanged regular communication. They had met at Jefferson Medical College after spending the first two years in the usual classrooms and laboratory study. Students did not see a patient until the third year anyway. The first two years were nothing short of grueling, with thousands of pages of printed notes to be memorized and regurgitated back on tests. The seemingly unending hours of studying material seemed utterly pointless—millions of details in biochemistry, anatomy, physiology, and pharmacology that nobody could begin to imagine could help any doctor actually treat a single patient.

Few students spent much time socializing and rarely spent a lot of time meeting each other, except in some kind of self-induced haze. To achieve that end, some students opted for marijuana—this was the 1970s after all. Others preferred more traditional methods. Doc Watson's Pub was the student hot spot in those days. Situated conveniently on Eleventh Street, directly across from the library and the student classroom building, the place was a magnet for thirsty, exhausted students.

After a particularly vexing pathology exam, the usual crew of bleary-eyed med students gathered in the back of the dark, smoky bar to compare notes. The conversation had been loud and angry. Dr. Lukas Aponte, chairman of the Pathology Department, had promised the test would be a ball-breaker, and he was right. The three hundred obtuse questions—focusing on some of the most obscure information—bewildered almost everyone. Everyone in the class struggled to complete the exam in the allotted time, including Kelly.

He staggered from the classroom and managed to find his way to Doc's. After a brief chat with classmates—and the sickening realization that all of them had probably failed—he meandered to a booth and sat down with a plop. Another medical student was already there and, based on the number of empty mugs, well on his way to achieving the desired catatonic state.

Kelly was not a big drinker. He preferred to drown his sorrow in remorse rather than liquid. Instead, he merely pushed and groped at his beer mug, as though he had forgotten how to use his hands.

"You're supposed to drink it," commented the tall, thin young man seated across from him.

"Damn," Kelly said. "There's always some new rule. I hope it's not on the next test."

"Want me to show you how?" the young man continued. "I'm getting a bit dry. I've only had four so far."

"No, that's all right. You can make a contribution to society some other way," Kelly said, sipping the bitter concoction.

"Is there another way?" his companion asked. "At least this gal seems to understand what's necessary," he indicated the waitress carrying a tray full of foamy steins toward them.

Kelly waved her off, but his booth-mate helped himself.

The young man burped loudly and wiped his mouth. "You got a name?"

"Kelly. Pete."

"Kelly Pete? Kind of a funny name, don't you think?"

Kelly was too tired to protest. "I'm still back in school, sir," he said.

"Right. Kelly Pete, I am Patterson, John," the other student announced. He offered a hand, still wet from the frosty side of his mug. They shook, cementing what fast became a strong friendship.

Patterson was a talker; he could spin a conversation out of nothing. Kelly preferred listening, which, being with Patterson, meant he could practice that skill a lot. Kelly lived at home and drove to medical school, while Patterson lived on campus. Shyer, Kelly needed an "in" to the parties on campus; Patterson needed the occasional use of a car. They were driven to become friends, they often told other students.

After graduation in 1975, they headed to their chosen residency appointments—Kelly to Family Practice in Allentown and Patterson to Internal Medicine at Harrisburg Polyclinic. They exchanged phone calls, attended each other's weddings, and kept in touch even when Patterson, drawn for his love of skiing, headed to Colorado. To Kelly's children, Patterson was Uncle John.

"Looking forward to seeing John again?" Joan asked, nudging her husband.

"I'm looking forward to a drink," Kelly replied, peering over the edge of the plane window. He wasn't even in the air, and he was already getting queasy. None of that would have happened if he hadn't gone on that darn whale-watching trip. He and Joan had honeymooned in Cape Cod—although it was a year after they got married—and she thought it would be great fun to take a ride in the North Atlantic on a fishing boat. Who was going to argue with a bride? About ten minutes away from Provincetown, Kelly began to feel nauseous, which he blamed on a snack of roasted peanuts. Not until he headed below and saw so many other passengers looking as green as him did he make the proper diagnosis of seasickness.

From that point on, every kind of ride with any hint of undulation unhinged his stomach. He needed a thirty-minute timeout to recover from a trip through Splash Mountain's three waterfalls at Disney World. The first one, a mere bump in the watery concourse, was enough to convince him that Joan's belief, reinforced by the children, that he could handle the attraction was completely incorrect. The final plunge left him a very strange color. His family enjoyed two more long waits and subsequent splashdowns before he recovered enough to wobble off with them.

He steeled himself for the plane ride. Then, no one cared much about security. Alleghany had not morphed into US Air and the whole process had a gentle, reassuring aura—at least, while on the ground.

A decade later, when coming to Washington, Kelly had to endure all the security checks and long waits. He had dutifully taken off his shoes and belt, watched with disinterest as security guards shunted off an aged woman with a cane for a full search, and carefully retrieved his wallet and keys from the little basket.

The plastic gun had been fine and unnoticed in his luggage. But, as he observed, the flying public was now safe from little old ladies.

On that first journey to Denver, he followed Joan aboard and threw himself into his seat. Joan refused to sit by a window, so he was forced to assume that dreaded position overlooking the many busy workers guiding the crafts, but who, Kelly noted, never seemed to get on a plane.

He braced himself for the rush down the runway, the bump of the landing gear being stowed inside the plane, and the sense of lift. His stomach immediately plummeted on its own. He gripped the seat tightly, trying to focus on some distant spot. A magazine stuffed into the back of the seat in front of him featured some lofty view of clouds. That, he decided, was no help. He did not look out the window. Two air pockets in succession were not welcomed. He didn't even hear the pro forma safety announcements, but stared mindlessly at some spot on the armrest. Slowly, he began to relax.

A few minutes later, a buoyant flight attendant deposited a tiny bottle of Glenfiddich in front of him next to a plastic cup full of ice. Glancing over at Joan, who was watching him expectantly with a sparkle in her eyes, Kelly shrugged. He twisted open the little bottle of scotch, emptied it into his glass, smiled, and raised it to Joan in a toast. She chuckled and raised her own plastic glass of wine to him.

She seemed distracted. He felt better after a sip of the amber liquid and asked what she was doing. She had her portable computer out and waved away his concern. Still, he could see her focused on something and frowning. He glanced over her arm and saw a list of her clients.

Someone was text messaging her. She wrote back furiously and stared at the names again.

"Shoot," she muttered, which was about her most serious profanity. She had been saltier while in college and early in their marriage, but when Erik repeated at school something inappropriate he heard at home, she cut back on the cursing. Still, for Kelly, even something as mild as that was proof something was wrong.

Joan explained hastily. Her office manager, Leslie Kneedson, seemed to have messed up. Somehow, a patient had not been assigned a nurse.

"I know I included him on my list," she said. "But he's not here."

She spun the computer around for Kelly to look at. "See if I'm missing something. Look for a Sol Langerbrunner."

Kelly complied. No, he reported soon after, that name wasn't on the list.

"He's got to be in my e-mail or somewhere," Joan decided. "I know I did it."

She fired off a still message to Kneedson, muttering about how many times the office manager had made mistakes and that maybe it was time to change. Kelly didn't listen. His wife often made such comments, but never followed through. Training a new employee was not worth the aggravation.

After calmly working her way through miles of e-mails, she sat back in her seat, frustrated and annoyed. She would have to double-check when they landed in Dallas before transferring to the Denver flight.

"Think about something important instead," Kelly suggested. He raised his cup to the attendant going by. "Excuse me miss, could I just get one more Glenfiddich over here?"

Sipping slowly, he wondered what would have happened if he had followed Patterson's path. While Kelly entered into emergency room work, happy to contribute to society and not worry about maintaining his own office, his friend rapidly realized that he was not cut out for office practice, dealing with blood sugars and irritable bowel syndrome. Upon completion of his residency, he got a job in Denver working for a small group of emergency physicians who had contracts with several hospitals in the Denver and Colorado Springs area.

In short order, he maneuvered himself into a position of prestige by joining the Colorado chapter of the American College of Emergency Physicians. His wife was a Realtor, a profession guaranteed to fill up the back account in a booming market. Not that money was a problem for Patterson, who had inherited millions. While she showed off homes, Patterson demonstrated a skill to talk his way into higher and higher circles. He was elected president of the Colorado ACEP and started giving advice on medical issues to Governor Gentry.

His timing could not have been better. That very winter, skiers had begun to develop a mysterious illness that threatened to curtail the season in Aspen, Vail, and other resorts along the Rockies. Gentry had watched tourist dollars head for Vermont and New Hampshire and panicked. Naturally, he had wanted to be seen as doing something, but not be trapped into actually making a decision. His chief of staff, Thorn, had suggested that Patterson become the spokesman for the investigation.

That had suited the Pennsylvania native perfectly. He talked to the media with ease, born of years of smooth-talking professors, hot dates, and his parents. Patterson was the son of a wealthy business leader and his status-conscious wife. The silver spoon and the microphone were easily exchanged.

Kelly had remembered seeing several news reports that had featured his old classmate as state officials busily tracked down the culprit. He once sent a clipping to Patterson after a story appeared in the *Philadelphia Inquirer*. Patterson noted that he now had forty copies and sent a laminated version back for Kelly's living room.

The two men had discussed the case. Kelly had suggested that Patterson look into Legionnaire's Disease, a respiratory illness first spotted in Philadelphia in 1976. He had been pleasantly surprised when studies by the Centers for Disease Control found evidence of a form of the bacterium, called *Legionella pneumophila,* in the mist machines, humidifiers, and whirlpool spas enjoyed by skiers seeking warmth away from the slopes.

Backed by the studies, Patterson made the diagnosis and got the resorts closed and cleaned—outraging a few owners concerned more about lost income than the health of customers. At Thorn's suggestion, Gentry talked the state legislature into refunding some of the costs to the now-mollified owners, ensuring not only the governor's re-election, but also Patterson's status in the governor's mansion.

"I was just in the right place at the right time with the biggest mouth," Patterson had cheerily written to Kelly. He hadn't said a word about Kelly's suggestion. Kelly didn't expect credit anyway. He could have been wrong, too.

Now, however, maybe Patterson would return the favor. Kelly needed some help getting the Wilbur Darby Plan off the ground. He wanted to run a test of the Wilbur Darby Plan, something small and, no doubt, expensive. The Pennsylvania Legislature, notoriously tight, was not likely to proffer the funds for the experiment. However, maybe Patterson—if he liked the idea— could persuade the Colorado lawmakers to spring for the bucks. If the governor thought this would further enhance his prestige, he'd sign on, too.

The small glass of scotch provided a warm underpinning to that scenario. Kelly drifted off to sleep, sure his friend would help.

Next to him, Joan struggled to remember whether or not she had handled one last task before she left. The frustration gnawed at her. Why couldn't she find Langerbrunner's name? Could Kneedson accidentally have deleted it? She wished she were in her office and could check through the files there. Paper had a place—even in the computer age.

She glanced at her resting husband. Maybe she should have ordered a scotch, too.

The trip was largely uneventful until Dallas. That's when Joan was finally able to contact her office. She got off the cell phone with a dark shadow over her face.

"Shoot," she said. Kelly listened. Somehow, in the rush of

packing, getting a taxi to the airport, and handling the flurry of assignments for her secretary and office manager, Langerbrunner had been overlooked. No nurse had shown up at his house. His daughter had called, very upset.

Kneedson had immediately handled the situation by getting a nurse to the home, but the daughter was not appeased. She had missed work and been thoroughly inconvenienced. She also refused to believe Joan had gone on vacation.

Kneedson and Joan exchanged several anxious calls during the layover. Joan tried to reach Langerbrunner's daughter with no success. She left a short message of apology with a promise to get back to her after reaching Denver.

Upset, Joan told Kelly what happened. He told her he was sorry. There wasn't anything else to say.

"Offer to give her free service for a week," Kelly suggested a few minutes later.

She nodded. That seemed like a possible solution. She resolved to put the idea out of her mind until reaching Denver. She was on vacation. On the second leg of the trip, however, she did have that scotch.

# CHAPTER 5
# THE PATTERSON TOUCH

Ten years ago, when he met them at the airport, Patterson was still talkative, but now the wrinkles around his eyes were deep. His hair was gray with little of the light brown that once caught in the Pennsylvania wind. It was still wispy, but lacked the bounce—the flair—that led coeds to ask Kelly to introduce them to his friend. He looked wise and, perhaps, a bit more worldly. The young man Kelly remembered from medical school, the outgoing talker, the master of the social situation, seemed to have devolved into a more serious bureaucrat. That, Kelly decided, was one of the curses of politics.

Patterson's spiel started as soon as the couples met. The airport was huge: largest in the United States, Patterson crowed, fifty-three square miles. It could hold Philadelphia International Airport, Dulles and, probably, JFK without straining the fences, he insisted. It really was big. Their gate was in Concourse C, which meant an underground train ride to the terminal. The line of people waiting to go through security seemed to stretch back endlessly.

Fortunately, Kelly recognized Patterson immediately among those awaiting incoming passengers. With all the luggage carousels, Kelly had no idea where to go. Patterson had no such problem and happily expounded on the number of flyers now frequenting DIA.

Once outside and bundled into a large, black Mercedes, he quickly pointed out all the parks as they drove by. More than two hundred, he insisted. Manhattan could nestle into all the open land. And the sun, he continued, gesturing toward the clear skies, Denver has more than three hundred days a year of sunshine. Snow was a minor inconvenience. The Mile High City was simply the garden spot of the Western world.

"I wasn't thinking of moving," Kelly told him, reassured by his friend's familiar patter.

"Too bad," Patterson told him. "We could really use a good man out here. We've got lots of doctors and hospitals; but with your experience and skill, Pete, old boy, you'd really clean up."

*Probably the garbage,* Kelly thought.

"In fact, you might get my job," Patterson continued while the wives talked in low voices in the back of the Mercedes. Kelly glanced at him.

"Retiring?"

"No," Patterson laughed. "Not me. Nick is thinking of running for president. I might get a chance for some big post in Washington."

"And leave all this?" Kelly teased. "Actually, you deserve to get one. After all, you took care of that health problem for him," Kelly said.

Patterson shrugged. "The microbiologists did all the work. I was just the mouthpiece. That was last year, anyway. Politics is all about what you've done for me lately."

That seemed like a perfect opening for Kelly to raise the Wilbur Darby Plan. He hadn't intended to rush in so quickly, but if Patterson needed a new idea, he was willing to bounce one off of him. However, Joan interrupted.

"Pete," she said, tapping him on the shoulder. "Terri thinks I should just admit the mistake and refund Mr. Langerbrunner's fee."

Patterson asked for an explanation. Joan filled him in, including how the patient's daughter was so angry. Her voice was actually shaking. She was not used to making mistakes. Kelly felt sorry for her.

"That's an easy one," Patterson said. "You have a staff. Blame one of them. Tell the biddy that you've fired the incompetent fool and are sure this will never happen again. Don't refund money. You'll get a reputation for handing out cash. The next time, someone will raise a stink even if nothing's wrong just to get some cash back."

"Pete?" Joan asked plaintively, putting her hand on his right shoulder.

He didn't say anything. Patterson had a point. People did take advantage of any weakness, but, still, a mistake had been made. Joan was honest; her business had a reputation for fairness. She only had a two-person staff. Joan really couldn't blame Kneedson, or the secretary, Claire Burle. They had been with her for years.

"Joan," he finally said. "I know you'll do what's best."

Her hand slipped off his shoulder. "You're right," she said plaintively.

Patterson smiled broadly. "There's always a way to get out of anything," he said. "Do you want me to talk to Langerbrunner? I could say I'm your attorney. The family wouldn't know."

"Thanks," Joan answered quickly, "but no."

Patterson quickly changed the subject. Dinner was on the itinerary. They were going to a fancy restaurant in downtown Denver. Maybe the next day, Monday, they could go into the statehouse and meet the governor and his chief aide, Joe Thorn.

"He's a real go-getter," Patterson said.

Kelly had no idea then how Thorn would affect his life. How could he? This was like when he first met Joan, then a nurse at a clinic. He had gone there on an interview, didn't like the job, but was intrigued by the pretty brunette who came walking by him several times while he waited for the personnel director.

"A single doctor?" she teased him later. "What girl in her right mind wouldn't be interested?"

"There is that sanity aspect," he noted.

"It wasn't temporary," she said. "I'm still crazy about you."

At the time they met, he had no idea they would be married or share more than thirty years together. Somehow, though, he knew they belonged together.

Patterson opted for an elegant dinner in the Broker Restaurant on 17th Street, which was built inside the vault of an old bank. Money clearly was not a concern, Kelly noted, surveying the luminous cherry wood siding and antiques inside the restaurant. Patterson simply grabbed the bill, using his government-issued credit card to pay for the meal.

"We're talking business, right?' he crowed.

The foursome then headed back to the new house. Kelly didn't say much. He focused mentally on the Wilbur Darby Plan, trying to imagine what objections Patterson could raise and what would be valid answers. He hardly noticed as Patterson shifted the car into four-wheel drive and headed up a steep two-lane road past other ample residences toward a house sitting on what looked like a massive ledge. Diesel smoke billowed from the back of the straining car, quickly dissipating in the clear air.

Built halfway up a high hill, with a dramatic view of the mountains visible from the front porch and as a backdrop in the back, the home almost cantilevered away from the ground. A thick, rocky base seemed to be the only reason it didn't roll down the hillside. A large veranda stretched halfway around the house, a perfect setting for enjoying a star-lit night and the distant black edge of the Rockies. With his feet on solid ground, Kelly's stomach relaxed, but his mind still grappled with the conflicting ideas circulating through it.

The lights of Denver were gleaming in the distance while the moon rolled across the mountains as if trying to avoid being punctured by a crag. Here and there, a large bird would suddenly flit through the night sky.

Kelly glanced over at Patterson, standing out on the front porch. His feet on the wooden railing, a glass of bourbon in his hand, Patterson resembled one of those country squires who never tilled an inch of soil, but chatted about agriculture with the assurance of a veteran farmer.

"I sure miss those days with patients, checking temperatures, patting behinds," Patterson was saying.

"Gerontology is most of what we do anymore," Kelly noted. "All I see are older patients these days. It's like the whole country suddenly aged."

Patterson looked at him. "Don't you know Pennsylvania has the second highest percentage of elderly in the country?" he asked. "In a few years, you might surpass Florida."

"I had no idea," Kelly said. No wonder the ER was overloaded with geriatric cases.

"It's happening all over," Patterson continued. "People are living longer. That's why Social Security and Medicare are going broke. Now, with medical technology what it is, old people and their diseases are big business."

He took a gulp of bourbon.

"That's my job—keeping track of those kinds of statistics," Patterson said. "What do you think keeps them in Pennsylvania? It sure as hell isn't the weather." He took another sip. "The big thing I'm studying is Medicare. How can we cut the costs without slicing service?"

"What do you think?" Kelly asked.

"Hey, you're the one who told me you had an idea. My job is to pooh-pooh it and then sell it to the governor."

Kelly was glad Patterson didn't want to wait. He was ready

anyway, and the words spilled out of him. He carefully explained how the idea developed. He talked about Wilbur Darby, and how his son had come up with an approach. Basically, he told Patterson, who was leaning back in his rocking chair as if on the verge of falling asleep, every Medicare recipient would have a designated primary physician. The patient—or family member—calls the doctor or the doctor's physician extender, who knows the patient and can figure out if a visit to the ER was necessary. Most weren't.

Then, a physician's assistant, a nurse practitioner, or even the doctor could stop by the house.

"Of course, if it really was an emergency, the ambulance would be sent as usual," Kelly concluded.

"As a doctor, I can say I wouldn't want all that extra work," Patterson noted. "Calls, home visits. That's asking a lot of anyone."

Kelly had considered that. Every primary care doctor who gets Medicare payments would need to have a physician extender, either a physician assistant or nurse practitioner, working with them. The physician extender would handle the home visits and emergency responses, he explained.

"Sounds expensive," Patterson drawled. Kelly wondered if his friend was channeling the governor or really meant it.

No, he countered. "Pay the primary care doctor enough money to more than cover the costs of the physician extender and it will work. The doctor will have less hospital work and his home visits will be covered. If the physician doesn't practice hospital medicine, he will maintain better control over his own patients, instead of having a second doctor taking care of them during the hospitalization and, possibly, controlling their care. The elderly patients will be getting better, more consistent care than ever—and the doctor will actually have less work to do."

Patterson pondered that approach. "Where will all the money come from?"

Kelly opened his hands. "From all the saved hospitalizations, of course," he said.

Taking another sip, Patterson stood up and walked inside the house. Kelly watched him. Was that a sign of interest or a broad hint to change the topic? Patterson also had a habit of thinking on his feet. That was his explanation for poor initial academic results despite his obvious intelligence.

"Don't show too much talent," he once told Kelly. "Get an A on the first test and the prof expects that on every test. Get a C or D and when you do a little better on the next one, the prof thinks he's a damn genius who really taught you something. You end up with an A doing half the work."

That approach seemed to work. *Didn't he always come up with a high GPA at the end of the semester?* Kelly thought. *Patterson even got one of the two A's that semester in that blasted pathology course. Dr. Aponte practically made him the class mascot.*

A few minutes later, Patterson came back out on the porch with some grapes in a bowl. He placed them on the nearby table and munched a few while still thinking. Kelly joined him.

"You realize this would change the entire medical system in the country. How would we ever get doctors to accept such a radical departure from business-as-usual?" Patterson finally asked. "All the primary-care physicians in the country would need to be in the program for it to work."

"You don't think they'll buy the idea of getting more money for less work?" Kelly wondered aloud.

"Sure," Patterson said sourly, "right after we get the insurance companies to sign off on it. They call the shots."

"Pull out the big guns," Kelly suggested.

"Howitzers?" Patterson asked facetiously. "Mortars won't be powerful enough."

He took a deep breath. "I need to sell this thing," he said audibly to himself. "For starters, it needs a new name." He thought for a moment. Kelly watched him. What was wrong with the Wilbur Darby Plan? "The Gentry Innovative Medical Plan,"

Patterson recited slowly. "GIMP. You need to have the plan spell out something or the media doesn't like it."

"No," Kelly said quickly. "I agreed with John Darby that we'd name it after his dad."

Patterson looked at him. "Forget that," he said. "I've got to sell it in Colorado. I've got to tell it to a governor who's not so great at remembering names—especially of people who live in another state. He knows his own name. If you want to get it past his desk, you'll need a name he can accept. His own."

Sitting back, Kelly stared off in the distance. Sitting more than a mile above sea level did cause him shortness of breath—or maybe it was the sudden awareness that whatever proposal became law was not likely to resemble anything familiar. On the other hand, there was a small chance that even something pawed over by politicians could actually be beneficial. What did a name matter anyway?

He brushed aside the memory of shaking hands with John Darby.

"Call it what you want," he said.

"Thanks," Patterson said. "I will."

He finished his drink. "By the way, now you can write the trip off as a business expense." Kelly cocked an eye at him. "We talked business. That's all it takes. Every meal, every place we go now comes right off the income tax."

That night, in bed, Kelly told Joan about the conversation and expressed his disappointment about the name change.

"He knows what works," she said.

Kelly nodded. Patterson certainly did. The idea was too good to fight over what to call it. If the plan worked, anyone interested could learn about its origin.

"I am really happy that the plan, by any name, may have a chance, Pete," she said. "You should be proud of yourself."

Her voice was strained. In the brief light coming in through the window and the illuminated face of the clock by the bed, he could see her hair spread across the pillow and the troubled expression in her eyes.

"Do John's ethics bother you?" she asked.

"He's always been a bit fast and loose."

She nodded. "Perfect for politics."

She seemed lost in thought. Kelly realized that Patterson's ethics weren't what concerned her.

"Have you decided what to do about your patient?" he asked quietly, finding and taking her hand.

"No," she said. "I just know that I will have to take care of it."

"John made a suggestion."

Joan shook her head. "I can't do that. It would be easier to blame Claire or Leslie, but that wouldn't be right. Sometimes, you have to stand up and admit you were wrong. I'll talk to Langerbrunner's daughter tomorrow. This is something I have to take care of—no one else."

Those words continued to echo in Kelly's mind a decade later.

# CHAPTER 6
# THORN STEPS IN

Monday morning, he shaved carefully, clipped his nasal hair—
the bane of older men—and joined Patterson for the commute
to Denver and the statehouse. The road back was just as tortuous,
but the view made up for the trauma of the descent.

The building surprised him. Visible from throughout
downtown Denver, it featured a gold-covered dome that towered
close to two hundred feet above the building.

Patterson parked in a small lot set aside for government
officials in a spot featuring his name on a sign. The security guard
at the gate gave a friendly salute. Patterson dutifully returned it.

They climbed the stairs toward the statehouse as Patterson
cheerfully waved, smiled, and occasionally gave a mock salute to
other employees. To Kelly, the statehouse resembled the Capitol

in Washington, but the more ornate features were a sort of one-upmanship.

The building featured Colorado white granite; large pillars at each entrance supported a ceramic-style roof. Pillars along the west entrance were topped with carved stone statues depicting Denver's bygone Wild West era. Its passing wasn't lamented until later folks, buried in sleaze, began to look back at that rambunctious time with fond nostalgia. To emphasize the historical links, the architect added nineteenth century light posts around the grounds and next to the tall entrance doors embedded with copper and glass.

"That's twenty-four karat gold up there," Patterson pointed at the gleaming yellow dome.

Despite their size, the front doors opened easily. A lone guard stood on the side, looking bored. He nodded at Patterson and touched the brim of his uniform hat. Patterson called him by name and asked him if everything was all right. The guard answered, but Patterson didn't listen to the response.

The two men walked across mauve-colored concrete in the atrium to the other side. Light burst through stained-glass windows and off brass used as highlights. The walls featured oil paintings of every American president, each looking out on passersby with bemused disinterest.

Patterson pointed out the various large rooms: House Gallery and Senate Gallery. He led Kelly into one. More stained glass and gleaming brass awaited. The seats looked very comfortable. The legislature was not in session.

"That explains why the air conditioning seems so cool," Patterson said. "No hot air."

State offices extended down another corridor. Kelly could hear his shoes echo down the hard flooring. He felt like he was following himself.

Patterson passed through a wooden door into an office marked with the governor's name in golf leaf. A young woman behind a desk looked up and smiled.

"Hello, sweetheart," Patterson chortled. He introduced Kelly to Pam Albright, his "one true love" and the governor's secretary. "When do you think the big guy will be in?"

Albright shrugged. "He doesn't have an appointment until one," she said.

"Great. Let him know I'd like to see him after lunch."

"He's golfing in some charity tournament," Albright said. "That's his appointment."

"Pete, are you still a 10-handicapper?" Patterson asked. Kelly started to protest that he couldn't hit a golf ball with a shovel and had no idea what a handicap was, unless it referred to his lack of interest in the sport. Patterson put a finger to his lips.

"Sign us up, Pam," he said. "We'll surprise St. Nick at the course."

With that, he waved goodbye and ushered Kelly out. "The old man usually doesn't get to work in the morning. He's too busy with late-night card games."

With that, he was off to glad-hand anyone else who came too close to avoid him. Actually, everyone seemed genuinely happy to see him. Patterson inquired about health, spouses, children, and even pets. He seemed to know everyone and everything about them.

The last man they met was thin and tall with dark, close-cropped hair and a fixed smile. He could have been a Marine out of uniform with broad shoulders and a firm stride coming toward them. He exuded confidence and his handshake was firm. He grasped one hand and used his other to grip the wrist as if real contact mattered to him.

"Joe Thorn," Patterson said, "the man behind the governor."

Kelly retrieved his hand from the iron vise.

"The governor's his own man," Thorn said with a voice that featured a whiff of insincerity.

"If you want something done around here," Patterson continued, "Joe's the man to do it."

Thorn looked at Kelly. His dark, piercing eyes were cool and direct. "What do you want done?" he asked.

Patterson gave a small laugh. "He's not a lobbyist, Joe," he protested. "We were just talking about a way to save the government a few billion dollars in medical care."

Thorn didn't lose an ounce of intensity or even hesitate. "Tell me about it," he said.

Kelly never had a chance. Patterson ran through a brief scenario, describing how costs could be sliced "by billions" by using physician extenders. Thorn listened. Kelly was struck by how much his friend had absorbed the previous night while feigning disinterest. On the other hand, Thorn was completely focused as if nothing else mattered.

"This is your idea?" Thorn asked Kelly.

"It's all his," Patterson said, patting Kelly's arm. "He's the guy who suggested we look at Legionnaire's Disease. I told you about him."

Thorn continued to gaze openly at Kelly. "The governor should hear about this. We're trying to cut the budget. This might give us a way to save some important programs. How long are you in town?"

"Until Friday," Patterson answered.

"Can you be here around 2:00 PM tomorrow?" Thorn continued, seemingly unaffected by Patterson's continual answers and Kelly's silence.

Kelly nodded.

"Sounds great," Patterson said. "I'll have him here."

"Good," Thorn said. He thrust out his hand. The two men shook. Abruptly, Thorn turned and walked away. Kelly could feel the pressure on his hand long after Thorn disappeared from view, the way a sound echoes endlessly through an empty canyon.

"That man gets things done," Patterson marveled.

"You know," Kelly said softly, "I could have answered for myself."

"You need to worry about your golf game," Patterson said happily. "I'll handle Thorn."

They were on the links just before 1:00 PM. The governor was holding court in Pinehurst Country Club's clubhouse and surrounded by a variety of men dressed in brightly colored golfing attire. Kelly felt out of place with a simple Polo shirt and pants. One of the members of the governor's entourage wore a red-and-black checkered cloth tam with a large red ball on top over a white and green shirt and bright lime-colored slacks. Another was dressed in knickers; and a third had on a multi-colored shirt that looked as if an abstract artist had finally gone crazy. The governor was more sedate with a Colorado Rockies baseball cap, an orange Denver Bronco shirt, and blue Denver Nuggets pants. A driver rested between his legs with the grip poking him in the chest.

He was puffing on a thick cigar, which he removed to say hello to Patterson. The governor seemed genuinely pleased to see him.

"This fellow may get me into the White House," Gentry said, standing and patting Patterson on the back.

Kelly saw Gentry was on the short side, maybe five feet eight, a bit stocky, with thick, close-cropped hair. His eyes were dark and seemed to be set deep in his head. His mouth, encircled by fleshy lips, seemed too large for his face. It gave him a friendly appearance—more of a genial neighbor than a head of state. Then, his commanding baritone voice quickly established him as the center of attention. All of his mannerisms were practiced and purposeful. He was a strong presence, despite his stature. However, he did not compare to Thorn, who was like concrete to the governor's malleable façade.

"Golf much, Kelly?" the governor boomed. "Pat, here, can really blast 'em. He's been telling me all last week that you are twice the golfer he is."

"That's what is so sad, sir," Patterson interrupted before Kelly could protest. "Hurt his wrist." Everyone looked at Kelly's right wrist. Kelly began to rub it. "He got into a driving contest with Davis Love III and, wouldn't you know it, sprained his wrist. Hit one 315 yards before that though."

"Too bad," the governor said.

"He'll just ride along," Patterson assured the governor. "Anything for charity."

"Maybe you can give me tips," Gentry suggested to Kelly. "I've been trying to get rid of a slice."

"I'll see what I can do," Kelly mumbled.

"What about what you showed me?" Patterson jumped in. He grabbed the governor's driver. "Remember, Pete? You said to hold that right hand even on the side of the club. That way, the club comes straight through the ball and the right hand doesn't overpower the left."

"Exactly," Kelly mumbled. "I didn't think you heard me."

The governor grabbed the club. "I'll try it." He fumbled with the club. Everyone backed away as if expecting Gentry to swing. He didn't. "Thanks," he said. "I can't wait to try it out."

With that, he led his entourage out of the clubhouse to the first tee. Someone checked. The governor was up next. He selected three others to play with him—two Republican state senators, and Patterson.

Patterson got a cart while Kelly and Gentry exchanged small talk. Kelly quickly discovered the governor did not have a long attention span and had very little interest in anything other than himself. He was glib and genial but not very deep. He seemed authoritative in his manner, the way he carried himself, even the firmness of his voice. Yet, something was missing.

On the opening hole, he naturally assumed honors and teed off first. He marched across the tee with a determined stride and placed the ball exactly midway between the markers. Eying the fairway, he readied himself and took a mighty swing, but the ball toppled only a few feet forward before stopping in the thick grass.

"At least it was straight," Patterson noted.

"You fellows don't mind if I take a mulligan?" Gentry asked while already placing a new ball on the tee. Everyone chorused approval. Gentry set up, wagged his club and his rear end, and cocked his head. A mighty swing and the ball arced nicely almost straight up and straight down maybe forty yards ahead. The women's tee was more in danger than the distant green.

Gentry stared at the feeble effort. "It's a start," he said grimly. He grabbed his cigar and puffed furiously as the rest of his foursome teed off. They all easily surpassed him, although Patterson delivered a massive slice.

"In the woods," the governor announced with obvious glee.

A few minutes later, Kelly watched Gentry pick up his ball and drop it close to where one of his partners hit his drive. No one said anything. Kelly knew his knowledge of golf was limited, but was pretty sure that moving the ball by hand was not in the rulebook.

The entire eighteen holes were played that way, with little interest in the actual score. The governor posted a dubious eighty-four, which he probably reached by nine holes. Patterson had a more honest eighty-six, losing on the last hole by misplaying three shots, including two in a greenside sand trap. Gentry loudly counted each stroke and was exuberant at his apparent victory.

"It's how you play the game," Patterson told Kelly later. "I don't care about golf. I care about his support for GIMP. He's primed for tomorrow."

The two men spent the night gathering information via the Internet on medical care and costs. Kelly was amazed how easily Patterson navigated through various sites and somehow knew exactly where to look. For him, computers were an alien breed sent to conquer humans. He let his secretary handle the inputting, while he used his computer for e-mail. It seemed more benign that way. Patterson, however, demonstrated just how valuable the device could be.

Thorn welcomed them to the meeting. He introduced them to William Rosario, secretary of Health and Human Services.

He happened to be in town—Thorn said—and wanted to learn more about the plan Patterson had proposed. They sat in plush chairs in a semicircle facing Gentry.

Thorn stood to the governor's right. He explained the program, pointing out carefully how much money the system could save without cutting health care. Kelly was impressed as Gentry carefully took a lot of notes. He was covering a scratch pad with neat, precise writing.

At the same time, Rosario was interested. He listened intently, occasionally putting comments into a hand-held tape recorder. Once or twice, he asked a few questions, none probing. Thorn did the answering. He only looked at Patterson once for help. It was quickly supplied.

Kelly felt like a bookend, holding up the sides with little else to do. He watched the clock hands move. Thorn took fifteen minutes to outline the program. The discussion that followed took only a few minutes more. He couldn't believe how quickly decisions of this magnitude were made.

"I think I could come up with money for a pilot," Rosario finally said thoughtfully. "How much would you think you'd need?"

"$10 million," Kelly jumped in, glad to have the opportunity to contribute. He had done a preliminary budget and had a good idea what a small pilot plan would cost.

"$100 million," Thorn quickly amended. His voice smothered Kelly's suggestion. He smiled. "Our friend from Connecticut is a doctor. He doesn't understand the finances."

"Pennsylvania," Kelly murmured.

"That's all: $100 million? I thought this was going to run into real money," Rosario noted cheerfully. "I'll get a check to you next week to get you started and then apply for funding in the usual way. We have some seed money in the stem cell research fund just sitting around. I'm sure we can spin a connection."

The governor looked up from his writing. "I don't like the name GIMP," he said. "It has a bad connotation. I came up with this." He held up his pad and read, "Gentry Assistance and Improvement Alternative Medical Plan. GAIAMP."

He smiled triumphantly.

Thorn and Patterson clapped. "That's amazing," Thorn said. "I just wonder if the reporters could grasp the meaning. You know how they really mess things up. What if we gave it a nickname? The Gentry Plan. No reporter could get confused with that. The real name can be on the bill in Congress after the pilot project."

The governor pondered the concept.

"It might work," he finally said.

Rosario sat up. "I'm going to need someone to oversee this in Washington, Governor. Is there anyone you could recommend?"

"John Patterson," Thorn said quickly. "Don't you think so, Governor?"

Gentry beamed. "Absolutely. What do you think, John?"

Patterson seemed surprised, although Kelly wondered whether his friend was acting. "I hadn't thought about leaving Colorado," he said.

Gentry, Thorn, and Rosario only needed a few seconds to convince him.

After Rosario left, Thorn patted Gentry on the back. "Sir, that was masterful," he said. "We got some extra cash, and you've got a leg up on a presidential bid. You may want to announce now, using the Gentry Plan as the main issue. Voters are going to be impressed with someone who has a plan to save money while improving medical care."

Gentry held up a hand of caution. "Let's be sure this works. I don't want my name and reputation riding on a proposal that flops," he said.

Everyone looked at Kelly. He felt his voice catch in his throat. "It'll work," he managed. "If it's done right."

"John," Thorn said, taking Patterson's sleeve. "This is up to you. You'll be the governor's front man in Washington. You make this work, and Governor Gentry will become the next president."

Later, back on the porch, Patterson sipped his drink and stared off into the distance. Inside the house, Terri and Joan were discussing the sudden, dramatic turn of events. The men could hear the excited voices. Kelly had already expressed his congratulations. He was glad not to leave his small town for Washington, D.C. Let Patterson go. He had the bonhomie and the knowledge to make this work.

Patterson was in a thoughtful mood as he sat on the porch.

"You know," he told Kelly, "the horizon is only about twenty-two miles away. That's all. But, sometimes, you feel you could see forever."

Kelly looked. From his perspective, everything looked downhill. That could be good or very, very bad.

# CHAPTER 7
# CAPITOL EFFORT

It had been very hurly-burly those first few years, although the process only picked up speed with time. While Kelly returned home from that initial visit to Denver feeling as though he had accomplished something, Patterson had headed for Washington, D.C. soon after. He regularly called Kelly as the weeks went by.

Neither thought anything was really going to happen, despite Rosario's promise. They both realized that fiscal commitments made in private offices had a way of melting in the open air. Still, Kelly kept a silent hope that, somehow, the Darby-Gentry Plan would be strong enough to endure.

After finding a condominium in the capitol, Patterson had even golfed once with the secretary, but Rosario never said a word about the cash or the project. Patterson made sure to lose, although, he told Kelly, it was very difficult. In a monumental display of ineptness, Rosario somehow managed to play worse than Gentry.

If losing on the links was Patterson's design to break into Rosario's inner circle, it didn't work. He never bothered to introduce Patterson to the president or to any other cabinet officials. Patterson felt as though he were assigned some secret mission that would be denied as soon as anyone found out about it. He took to wearing a trench coat and trying to appear nefarious. No one reacted. In Washington, eccentric people typically are already in prominent positions. The rest aren't worth noticing.

While waiting, Patterson chose a small hospital in Colorado Springs as the primary test site. About 9 percent of the city was sixty-five years old or older, a high percentage for the Boulder State, which did not attract or retain many senior citizens. A series of meetings were held with doctors to explain the plan. They were more amenable when bonuses were added to the fee schedule. Kelly even flew in once to help provide some of the details. Patterson passed himself off as a working doctor, which helped his credibility. Kelly didn't correct the impression. The program outweighed such considerations.

The next part was arranging for the physician assistants. Patterson could have turned to the University of Denver's College of Medicine, but chose instead to affiliate with Eton Technical Institute in Aurora, Colorado's third largest city. It was located south of the airport and offered Physician Assistant degrees. He also worked out an agreement with National American University in Denver, which also had Physician Assistant training.

Both were for-profit schools with long histories of shifting owners and names. Kelly wondered at the skill level and experience, but Patterson was positive it would work and be inexpensive, too.

In fact, students eventually signed up for the program as a kind of internship and even paid for the privilege. They were supervised by professors and teachers from the University of Colorado's HSC School of Nursing, contracted through a home-nursing business run by the niece of the Republican majority leader in the Colorado state senate.

When approval finally arrived to start, Patterson's secretary, Kate Watson, put away her romance novels and began doing some typing. Short and stocky, she radiated an aura of confidence and efficiency. Patterson had quickly learned to depend on her.

With his duties picking up, Patterson actually had a reason to show up at the office. He discarded the Mata Hari look and went for the conventional suit and tie. That made him almost invisible, but Rosario was friendlier. Thorn even called him from Denver and added encouragement. Everyone knew what was riding on this project.

To everyone's delight, the Gentry Plan worked. Costs were minimal. Patients who did not need to be rushed to an emergency room stayed home. Patients who needed immediate help got it. Patterson's accountant began to note a significant drop in costs compared to the previous year.

Kelly watched it unfold with undisguised delight. Everything was going so well at home, the hospital, and with the program. He told Darby what happened to the plan's name. As expected, the retired pharmacist didn't care. He just wanted the program to succeed.

Kelly could only smile through the long hours in the ER. He even arranged for his own team of physician assistants to follow up on calls to his emergency room. He paid the initial expense, but the hospital reimbursed him as its costs fell. He went home happy, fulfilled, and excited about the future.

His family shared some of that joy. Joan had worked past her client problem with an abject and honest apology. Her business continued to thrive, aided by the success of a homegrown version of the Gentry Plan. Local families needed nursing at home, rather than relying on the hospital's staff. There was still plenty of work for the hospital, but these were the real emergencies.

The rest of the family was flourishing, too. Erik had accepted a position as an attorney with the American Civil Liberties Union.

Diane graduated and moved to Columbus to start medical school at Ohio State University. She wanted to be a surgeon. And Rachel had settled down. She had boosted her GPA and was focused on becoming an anthropologist, although her parents weren't exactly clear why that field caught her interest. Rachel wasn't sure either, but really didn't care. Apparently, several cute boys were also majoring in the subject area. They got to do fieldwork together, she told her mother with breathless excitement.

Joan decided that her husband didn't need to know that.

Within three months of the nationwide rollout of the program, the savings from the Gentry Plan were obvious. Rosario held a press conference to announce its success and to boost Gentry, the "man who developed" the program. Soon after, the governor announced his decision to run for president.

"What I did to cut medical costs without cutting medical care, I will do to the rest of the bloated federal budget," he promised. Thorn quickly distributed a thick list of Gentry's Colorado accomplishments, some of which caught the local media by surprise since they were generally thought to be the work of the previous governor. Nevertheless, to voters overly burdened by taxes, Gentry became the frontrunner almost overnight.

Everything happened so quickly.

Within a year, Patterson was running a burgeoning program to train physicians' assistants and nurse practitioners, convincing doctors to participate and inform the public. He still kept in touch with Kelly, but their conversations were more limited as time went on.

Kelly didn't bother him. Instead, he kept news clippings and monitored the progress. He enjoyed watching from afar as his plan became the cornerstone of Gentry's victory in the fall election a year later. The Democrats could offer nothing to counter the way Gentry's medical cost cutting had succeeded. In fact, the results were a clear landslide, sweeping not only Gentry, but also his Colorado staff and auxiliaries such as Patterson into office. Rosario stayed, too—a holdover who held on.

Terri Patterson moved to Washington to be with her husband, regretfully leaving their beautiful home on the hillside. The Kellys came to the inauguration as special guests, but felt overwhelmed by the crowds and fanfare. As a result, they spent most of their time consoling Terri who was already homesick and rapidly becoming disenchanted with the demands of the Capitol social life. She thought about continuing to work as a Realtor, but didn't know the market well enough.

After that, the two families retained little contact. In fact, after Gentry was elected, the two men barely talked. That changed in March; as Gentry charmed newsmen with his golf game and poker outings, Patterson was named assistant secretary of Health and Human Services.

"The first doctor," Chief of Staff Thorn announced grandly, "to hold that position and evidence of President Gentry's commitment to improving medical treatment in this country."

After the brief swearing-in ceremony, Thorn was more direct. The job's requirement, Thorn told him, was to come up with a new idea to save additional money. "We promised the voters more savings," Thorn reminded Patterson. "It's time to deliver."

"Maybe we could cut military spending," Patterson suggested. "One tank for …"

Thorn glowered at him and stopped him cold. "For that, I'd talk to the military brass. I'm talking to you."

Patterson was in Pennsylvania the next day. Kelly had no comments but sensed his friend just needed to vent.

"Maybe John Darby has another idea," Patterson suggested facetiously.

They were sitting in the living room of the Kelly's two-story home. His view through the window was of more homes. The vistas of Colorado had been replaced by rooftops and the rolling hills of the Blue Mountains. The scene was suburban and restful, not isolated and untamed. The environment seemed to infect their mood.

"I could always go back to Colorado," Patterson mused.

Kelly knew better. His friend was enamored with the bright lights and attention. Despite his laid-back approach at the moment, his voice was animated; his eyes radiated a glow. Patterson was at home in the limelight.

They chatted aimlessly until some new thoughts began to emerge. The initial plan, now known universally as GP, had guaranteed assistance for elderly patients who would be better off being treated at home. What if, Patterson thought aloud, a physician extender responded to almost every emergency call?

Kelly pondered that: Increasing medical attention on the spot should decrease ER visits and overall costs. EMTs were well trained and competent, but their main effort was to stabilize their patients and hurry them to the hospital. Physician extenders, on the other hand, could determine if such an extreme step was necessary. Many victims may be able to go home after some relatively minor medical attention.

Hospitals are the most expensive element of medical care, Kelly noted. The less they are used—except when truly required—the less the government and insurance companies would have to pay.

Patterson asked him to collect data to underpin the claim of additional savings. His colleagues agreed to help—for a small fee. For six months, Kelly and his partners kept statistics proving that the two-pronged approach did not compromise health care, but did slice costs. A person calling 911 got a visit from a nurse and physician extender first, both of whom could provide immediate care. If the ambulance was needed, it arrived after initial treatment had already been administered.

Everyone won.

It also had side benefits: Kelly's ER was quieter now; more nurses were traveling to patients rather than waiting at the hospital for them to show up. The most important person in health care became the dispatcher. Of course, home healthcare providers such as Joan found demand exploding.

The statistical support was all Patterson needed to hear. The

Patterson Corollary to the Gentry Plan, he told Thorn seven months later, could save millions, even billions, more. Thorn quickly changed the name, placing his own on it.

The details were surprisingly simple: the same physician extenders already serving the elderly would now respond to 911 calls and contact ambulances as needed. In the St, Michaels catchment area alone, Kelly reported, ambulance runs were down almost 60 percent.

Insurance company executives had taken to sending large bouquets of flowers, fresh fruit, and wine to St. Michael's Hospital almost on a daily basis.

Naturally, the new program's success led to a press conference and additional pilot projects. The Thorn Plan was a huge success. Gentry wondered why his name was not on this program, but agreed, as Thorn explained, that there couldn't be two plans with the same name. In time, the Gentry Plan faded away, replaced by the Thorn Plan.

The Thorn Plan began to include a new element: nurses and physician extenders going to the homes of elderly patients prior to emergency calls. They could check on medicine, determine status, discuss treatment plans with doctors, and use preventative approaches rather than simply respond. That was Thorn's innovation. He noted that sending nurses and physician extenders on emergency calls had reduced costs. Why not go a step further?

The secret to success, he told Patterson, was writing regulations that guaranteed medical facilities had to participate or lose funding. He turned that chore over to a rising star named Kevin Delacourt, a young man with a law degree, medical training, and high aspirations.

Delacourt's proposed regulations included a mandatory "Do Not Resuscitate" clause. It also absolved the nurses and physician extenders from any lawsuits resulting from their actions or lack of them.

The term "do not resuscitate" initially meant no CPR or

machines, but as time went by, the DNR concept began to expand to exclude expensive medications and certain on-going treatments, such as renal dialysis.

Patterson read the rules over very carefully. The phrase "Withholding of treatment" was troubling. Would this give the physician extenders carte blanche to end treatment? He was sure no one would be so callous, but that possibility existed.

Delacourt also created treatment guidelines that encouraged "limited" medical involvement and banned "heroic" measures. Moreover, physicians were instructed to keep medicine to a minimum. Medicare rules correlated to these new requirements, which were quickly adopted.

It didn't take long for the savings to start to show up. Still, Patterson was concerned. He asked Kelly to keep an eye on elderly patients in his area. Kelly did, but saw nothing wrong. His nurses were well trained. They made regular rounds. Most of them were very happy. They had the opportunity to provide hands-on care, something often missing in hospital routines. Nursing schools were delighted, too. Applications were soaring. For the first time, nurses felt as though they were being treated on par with doctors.

As a result, Kelly noted no change in the life expectancy of older residents in his community. On the other hand, Patterson realized, preliminary figures from around the country weren't as pleasant. In some areas, such as retirement communities like Delray Beach, Florida, and Sun City, Arizona, deaths skyrocketed among older residents. Life expectancies dropped as much as two years compared with statistics from the previous five years.

People in their eighties could not expect many more years of life, he realized, but, nevertheless, fewer were making it to ninety or one hundred. At one time, people older than eighty were the fastest growing segment of the population. Not anymore. The change was abrupt.

Patterson brought the anomaly to Thorn's attention, but he icily dismissed any concern. "We're talking about rescuing

Medicare," Thorn pointed out. "Look at it this way: a few, very sick, very old people may die, but they were going to anyway. Why prolong their agony?"

"That's euthanasia," Kelly said in a low, hard voice after Patterson called him. He did not shout when losing his temper; he lowered his voice and spoke through gritted teeth.

"No," Patterson said, talking quickly. His voice sounded almost tinny over the phone line. "You said people should die with dignity at home. That's all the Thorn Plan is doing."

"But we promised everyone the same medical care they would have gotten at a hospital. Benign neglect isn't care," Kelly argued.

"I think you are getting too sensitive," Patterson suggested. "Look, I'll get your name onto something."

"It's not the name, John," Kelly said sharply.

"You can count on me," Patterson insisted, "I'll take care of it. Americans need to know who they can credit for such incredible progress in medical treatment."

"John," Kelly tried to interrupt.

"That's what friends are for," Patterson said. "And, don't worry, I won't tell anyone that your wife has benefited from your plan. That's our secret." He hung up quickly before Kelly could respond and called his secretary into his office. He asked her to buy an engraved plaque to award Dr. Peter Kelly.

"Make it fancy," he said. "For America's Premier Emergency Room Physician. Call it the HHS Award of Excellence."

Watson nodded. "I know a few others who deserve recognition," she said.

"Good," Patterson said. "Make up a batch of them. Just change the reason each time."

After Patterson hung up on him, Kelly held the phone receiver for a long time. Finally, as the phone beeped urgently, he put it on the cradle. Any happiness he had felt dissipated. His stomach churning, he lay down in his bedroom, trying to think of some solution.

"I think it's time to stop trying to work with John," Joan suggested later.

Kelly didn't answer immediately. Would Patterson actually tell the media how Joan's business had blossomed since the Thorn Plan went into effect? Would reporters believe there was a connection? He shuddered.

"I'll try to work with him," he finally said. "Maybe he'll listen to reason."

Later, he realized that it was the first lie he had told his wife in all their years of marriage.

# CHAPTER 8
# TO THE BONE

When Patterson's call ended so abruptly, a chill went up Kelly's spine, followed by the realization that Patterson knew about Joan's ancillary success. That meant Thorn did, too. Patterson might have a few scruples left, despite his sinister imprecation, but Kelly had no illusions about Thorn. And, in truth, Joan's business was doing well. She had gone from a two-person office to a staff of fourteen responsible for coordinating the actions of more than one hundred nurses and an equal number of physician assistants. She had an office now in a high-rise building downtown, a prestigious locale. Income was well over $2 million a year, with profits around 12 percent. By any standard, the Thorn Plan had been a real boon for her.

Kelly could imagine the embarrassment if her success was presented in the wrong way. She would be mortified; he would be humiliated. How could he insist that the original plan was designed to save money when, obviously, it had boosted the family income in such a grand manner? That could hardly be a coincidence.

He could see the headlines, especially in his own community. Neighbors would stare at him. Friends would shun him. He knew how that worked; politicians running against the administration would cite Kelly as evidence of corruption. He'd be the butt of jokes on late-night talk shows.

Kelly sat by the phone for a long time, growing increasingly disconsolate. It would not matter if the Thorn Plan had worked and saved the government a lot of money while reportedly maintaining the health of citizens. The focus would be on this very personal side issue. He shuddered.

Of course, nothing would happen if no one found out. Would Patterson be so callous and tell the media? Kelly tried to picture his friend. In that image, Patterson's face was placid, smiling, his eyes twinkling. That was in medical school. Now, he was cooler, more calculating. He loved being surrounded by reporters and having his every word noted and analyzed. Kelly shook his head. Patterson wouldn't say anything directly. He'd hint, nudge, and—if necessary—shove some reporter in the right direction. The media would look like heroes, uncovering corruption. Patterson would never get his hands dirty. Besides, he'd come up with some spiel to soothe his conscience. But even if he wouldn't do anything, Thorn would.

Kelly could see the scenario play out. Patterson would deny everything as the news stories began to dissect Kelly's life. The abyss loomed in front of him.

There was only one thing he could do. He would swallow any distaste and continue to communicate with Patterson. He would pretend to be content as disgust gnawed at him. What choice did he have? As long as Patterson—and Thorn—felt he was still supporting their plans, they would not jettison him. As soon as he spoke out, they would ruin him.

For several days, he was quiet, going to work, seeing patients, and trying to avoid any hint of unrest. That approach was bound to fail and did. The emotion had to seep out. He started snapping at his colleagues in the ER. Even the pretty young nurse stopped smiling at him.

Joan watched her husband grow more morose. He didn't talk much normally about his feelings. Now, he was communicating even less. She suggested getting away, a change of scenery. He simply nodded. There was no escape, he knew. Still, he felt guilty. He wanted to say something to Joan, but what could he tell her? She'd be appalled. There was no way she would understand. How could she? She had built a business; that's all. The repercussions of his efforts would seem bizarre—a penguin flapping its small wings in Patagonia and creating a tsunami that swamped Samoa.

In virtual silence, they drove to their new cottage on Lake Ariel, a quiet, secluded little piece of heaven in the Pocono Mountains. The two-bedroom lake house had been purchased with their expanding income. While the children were living at home, they had occasionally gone there in the summer as a weekend getaway, renting a cabin. Now, they owned a house there. Kelly had been delighted by the purchase. Now, he viewed the second home as a visible symbol of a coming disaster.

He sat on the porch, his back to the house, staring into the woods that spread to the north. On the west side was the lake, cool with waves gently lapping the shore. Arriving in the middle of October, he tried to relax amid trees aflame in their fall glory. The afternoon was crisp and clear, but he could not warm up. The beauty of the scenery could not enliven his dour thoughts. He had no idea what to do. Joan was not going to sell the business, not after years of hard work to build it to this point. Besides, how could he explain why she had to get out without sounding either paranoid or insane? He stared out at the mountain lake, shimmering in the afternoon sun, and prayed for an inspiration.

The only idea that eventually bubbled through his troubled mind was to get advice. Maybe a lawyer. Who knew if he had inadvertently violated some conflict-of-interest provision or some AMA precept? The family attorney would be no help. Alan Watterson was good with wills and home purchases. This item seemed beyond his expertise.

Kelly spent a few minutes mentally running through a roster of possible attorneys he could call on. He knew only a few. There was the lawyer who had survived a heart attack and credited Kelly for prompt diagnosis and reaction. What was his name? Schmidt? Schmiditer? Kelly went inside and looked him up in the phone book. He had a big ad: Schmidt. Kelly's heart sank. He was a divorce attorney. Joan would never understand that.

Naturally, he had met a few malpractice attorneys at the hospital, but they hardly seemed the right choices. They were certainly avaricious enough, diabolical and downright unscrupulous, but their specialties prepared them for broad attacks, not the subtlety needed in this situation. This was not an ambulance chase.

Back on the porch, away from Joan, who was making a blueberry pie, he flipped through the pages of attorneys in the Allentown phonebook, marveling at the volume. As far as he could tell, there had been some kind of coup and lawyers had infested the region in flu-like numbers. However, none of the names were familiar. Nor did he feel comfortable with calling a stranger. He was not going to ask any medical friends for a recommendation either. He did not want any of his colleagues to think malpractice, which would be the first thought that came to mind if he approached any of them. On the other hand, he couldn't explain the problem to a friend. That, too, could lead to embarrassing questions and even more embarrassing answers.

After scanning the listings of lawyers and not feeling comfortable with any of the names there, Kelly closed the phonebook. Some of these attorneys were bigwigs in the Allentown area. They'd file this juicy tidbit for later use in some political campaign. He needed someone committed to the family.

Someone he could count on to keep his mouth shut. Someone who would honor client-attorney privilege.

A moment later, he realized the answer: Erik. Of course. His son would keep the situation quiet. The idea of confiding in his eldest child was jarring, but, Kelly rationalized, Erik was a grown man, a full-fledged attorney. Joan had always wanted her children to become a doctor, lawyer, dentist, and psychiatrist. That way, all the basic needs were covered. At least, the lawyer was in place. Diane was on her way to becoming a doctor. They'd have to skip the psychiatry thing given Rachel's predilections. Maybe she'd grow fond of teeth, which did have a place in anthropology.

Kelly went back inside. Joan was upstairs, using the computer set up in the spare bedroom. He grabbed the kitchen phone and called his son. Erik was in the office, which was a relief. Nevertheless, Kelly stumbled over what to say. He didn't want Joan to overhear and had a hard time getting Erik to understand the urgency.

"Big problem?" Erik finally asked after his father mumbled a brief introduction.

"I can't explain on the phone," Kelly whispered.

Erik pressed, but Kelly declined to elaborate. He wanted to, but preferred to see Erik's reaction, read his eyes, and see if he really comprehended the situation. Erik finally agreed to drive up that weekend.

Impatiently, Kelly waited. He told Joan that he had invited Erik to join them. She was happy her eldest child was coming by. She didn't ask why, although Kelly saw the question in her eyes. He didn't tell her. Instead, he went outside to sit in the sun, admire the scenery, and run through conversations in his mind. What could Erik tell him? Kelly did not know.

Tall, thin, and outgoing, with a smile and a joke always at the ready, Erik had moved to Baltimore to live with some friends after college graduation to work as a juvenile probation officer. After four years of knocking around in the slums of Baltimore and logging considerable time in the courtroom defending his clients and explaining their inexplicable behavior, Erik realized that, though his commitment to public service was undiminished, he had spent enough time in the trenches. He applied to law school and was accepted by the University of Baltimore Law School, eventually graduating near the top of his class. An avid fisherman, he was overjoyed when his parents purchased the cabin.

He arrived around 10:00 PM. Tired from the trip, he chatted about family matters: he announced that he was finally engaged and would bring his fiancé, Julie, around as soon as possible. His parents had met her twice before and were happy with his decision. Joan decided Erik had visited to tell them the news. That was a relief to her. Given her husband's mood, she had thought something was wrong. They celebrated with a round of drinks and a nice dinner at a local restaurant that served as the way station for inept fishermen.

Throughout dinner, they talked about how everyone was doing. Kelly only had a few words to add to Joan's detailed account of the success of her business. When Erik looked expectantly at his father, Kelly shook his head. Tomorrow, he mouthed. Erik nodded.

By nine o'clock the following morning, Kelly was back on the porch, gazing out at his son on the lake. The young man resembled a hunched silhouette on a silver sliver, illuminated by the rising sun. His pole shone like a strand of a spider's web, swaying only slightly in the light breeze. Pretending nothing troubled him, Kelly allowed himself to be slowly hypnotized by the twinkling of rays playing off the ripples on the water's surface. Erik returned to shore soon enough to break the reverie.

He joined his father on the porch, sitting down with a thud on the top step. "I don't know what it is with this lake. Everybody else seems to catch fish but me," he moaned.

"Maybe they have something against lawyers," Kelly teased. "You know what would happen if all the lawyers were placed end to end under the Pacific Ocean from San Francisco to China?"

"No," Erik admitted.

"No one would mind," Kelly said with a laugh.

"You just aren't happy with malpractice suits," Erik countered. "Good thing I'm not specializing in that area."

They sat quietly, broken only by the hum of a passing insect and the chirps of robins and mockingbirds.

"How is your new job with the ACLU going?" Kelly asked, groping for an opening.

Erik squirmed a little. "Okay, I guess," he said. "The pay is crap, but I'm getting experience and opportunities that I wouldn't readily get in the private sector. As a matter of fact, I'm getting involved with something you know about."

Kelly sat up and cocked an eye at his son.

"We've been looking into The Thorn Program. Health and Human Services makes a lot of decisions that affect millions of people every day—lots of opportunity for human rights abuses. We have to keep an eye on that."

"Found anything?" Kelly asked faintly. Was he too late?

Erik smiled, swallowing the secret. "Enough to know not to say anything," he said, standing up. "I could use a can of soda."

Kelly watched his son head inside the cabin. He had to unburden himself.

Erik spent a few minutes chatting with his mother and lamenting his lack of fishing prowess. Actually, his limited skills were a family source of amusement. On one occasion, while in Atlantic City, he had eagerly tossed a line on a pier crowded with fishermen busily pulling in bluefish. Instead of dinner, Erik hooked a shark and had to cut his line. He didn't catch anything else and ended up disconsolately munching on bluefish purchased from a fish store. Another time, he manfully stood in the cold surf and fished all day, collecting only a sunburn and disappointing the egrets who gathered around his empty creel.

The hope was he'd do a better job catching clients.

Finally, in the late afternoon, Pete asked Erik to go for a walk. Joan watched them for a moment through the living room window. She was glad. Maybe they'd have a pre-marriage man-to-man talk. Her husband had been a good partner. He could share his expertise with their son. She was also glad to see how they had finally bonded. For years, her husband was inevitably working late and focused on his career while Erik had meandered through school. He was smart, but indifferent, infected with high ideals and low energy to achieve them. Both parents had been frustrated, even more so when Diane came along and turned into a buzz saw who quickly surpassed her brother academically. They tried not to compare the children, but the difference in grades and achievement was obvious. Nevertheless, Erik finally matured, cut his multi-colored locks, got rid of the facial ornaments, including one very painful-looking tongue stud, and began to succeed.

Now, father and son seemed to be comfortable in their roles. Delighted, Joan wiped her hands on a towel and headed back to her computer. There was always work to do, even on vacation.

Kelly and his son meandered into a nest of pine trees along a path worn bare from years of hiking boots and bicycles. As they walked slowly through the darkening shadows, Kelly finally explained what was happening. Erik listened. Kelly saw his son for the first time not as his child, but as a companion, even a friend. It was a strange transition.

"Does Mom know?" Erik asked. Kelly shook his head.

"I can't tell her," he admitted.

Erik stared off into the distance, digesting everything his father told him. "Mr. Patterson really said that?" he asked.

"Yes."

Erik took a deep breath. That was what was really bothering his father: his friend had turned on him. He stopped and played with pine needles for a moment. The only sound was his shoes digging softly into the soil. "Dad, you didn't break any law," he said slowly, "but there is the appearance of impropriety."

Kelly nodded. That part he was sure of.

"What am I supposed to do?" he asked. "I feel like I'm being blackmailed."

"In a way, you are," Erik told him. "But, there's no money

involved. Mr. Patterson didn't demand anything. In fact, he said he wouldn't tell anyone."

"Then I can't do anything?" Kelly felt so helpless. His voice sagged.

"Not really," Erik said. "Maybe Mr. Patterson will retire. That would remove the threat. You are still friends, aren't you?"

Kelly shrugged. "I don't know."

"Do you think he discussed this with anyone else?"

"I don't know that either."

*Yes,* Kelly told himself, *he did. Thorn would know. Thorn knew everything. In fact, Thorn may have told Patterson.* He brightened: that was a thought. He could see Thorn informing Patterson about the apparent conflict of interest. Patterson would have blanched. He would have defended Kelly. Thorn wouldn't have listened. That's what happened. Patterson was being blackmailed by Thorn. Of course, Patterson had no choice. If his friend was exposed, he would be forced to resign. Instantly, Kelly felt much better. Patterson was warning him, not threatening.

Erik was watching the emotions play out on his father's face. "Are you all right?" he finally asked.

"I feel much better," Kelly said, patting his son on the back. "Let's go see what Mom caught at the fish store."

Two days later, from the quiet of his hospital office, he called Patterson. His friend sounded irritated and tense. Kelly tried to thank him for showing concern, but Patterson wasn't interested.

"You have to hear the latest," he said. Kelly felt a chill sweep over him. Now what? "It's Thorn's newest idea," Patterson continued, lowering his voice.

"I'm not sure I want to know," Kelly said.

"It's the greatest idea since sliced bread," Patterson said sprightly, cheering up with surprising speed. Someone else was in the office; Kelly heard some noises in the background. He waited. A door closed.

"I'd better discuss this privately," Patterson finally said.

"We still have a guest room," Kelly invited.

"There's a conference in Philly I need to attend. I didn't think about going before, but there's so much to learn at a conference. Let me see." He ruffled through papers. "Here it is: 'Sewage and the Future.' How could I think of missing something like that?"

"I could meet you there," Kelly suggested. "We really have to worry about hazardous waste disposal at a hospital."

Patterson agreed to pay for Kelly's entry fee.

Joan was nonplussed. A conference? Since when? Her husband wouldn't go to medical meetings—even after he was appointed to the hospital board. When he was forced to attend a gathering, all he did was mutter about inane presentations, lousy food, and obnoxious visitors who talked incessantly without saying anything. On the other hand, he really did need to get away. Something was definitely bothering him. Philadelphia was nearby. Besides, she thought, maybe he'd learn something at the conference. He seemed cheerful about going. That was a positive. Who knew that sewage could lift his spirits so much?

# CHAPTER 9
# GOODBYE TO ALL THAT

Patterson clearly was concerned enough to leave Washington and meet in Philadelphia. Maybe he figured his office was bugged, Kelly considered. Then, too, he thought, maybe Patterson was setting him up. See if Kelly is on our side. That's what Thorn might have wanted to know. Would Patterson do that? Kelly knew he would. Patterson would fulfill his job.

Kelly resolved to maintain silence as much as possible. What Patterson didn't say could be as important as anything he said.

Patterson had booked Kelly into a Comfort Inn, which relied more on a name than actual amenities. He waited in a line while a single harried clerk checked in guests with surprising disinterest and snail-like efficiency. Two other clerks hovered in the background, occasionally poking heads out seemingly to count the number of people in the line. Neither made any effort to help.

When it was Kelly's turn, he discovered quickly that the government was as efficient as ever. No reservation had been made for him or, at least, none had been confirmed with the Comfort Inn computer. Rather than further delay those mumbling behind him, Kelly produced a credit card and finally was given a key to his room, which was small, but efficient. He did get a nice view of Broad Street, which was overrun with vehicles day and night. Honking seemed to be a popular past time in the City of Brotherly Love, and Kelly expected his sleep to be punctuated with many prime examples that evening.

He dialed Patterson's cell phone. No one answered, but seemingly seconds later, a black limousine pulled up in front of the Comfort Inn. The front desk clerk deigned to let Kelly know about fifteen minutes after the limousine arrived.

Kelly climbed in and was whisked to the Ritz-Carlton on the Avenue of the Arts. He recognized the hotel's tower, having seen it when he and Joan took the kids to Independence Hall just a few blocks away.

The driver opened the door for him. He stepped out. No one seemed to notice the limousine. He decided that popular local athletes might cause a stir, but arriving dignitaries were too commonplace for more than a disinterested sniff by passersby. Philadelphians are notoriously egalitarian anyway. They degrade friend and foe with equal vigor.

The Ritz Carlton's front entrance featured huge columns, as though some architect had decided to build a Greek temple inside the facility. People milled around in the usual disorderly manner, but Kelly could see several men in suits who clearly looked out of place. They were unabashedly staring at him. He checked at the front desk for Patterson's room. The clerk openly signaled one of the men. He walked over.

"Dr. Kelly?" Kelly nodded. "Come with me," the man said officiously. They walked to the elevator. One was reserved for the penthouse. The doors opened as soon as the button was pushed. Dignitaries didn't have to wait.

Once inside, the man carefully searched Kelly, running a small metal detector over his clothes.

Kelly was scanned again exiting the elevator and when he crossed into the room, with its shimmering curtains, broad atrium, and luxurious furnishings.

"I must be in the wrong place—you can't be this important," he teased Patterson as they shook hands. "Is there always this much security or have they already identified me as a threat?"

Shaking his head, Patterson was strangely somber. "It's the Washington mystique. Nobody trusts anybody in or out of the Capitol."

He guided Kelly to the porch and closed the sliding glass door behind them. Below, tiny figures and numerous cars dodged each other in a chaotic frenzy. Clouds covered the sun, adding a gray tinge to the somber mood. Agents remained a few yards away on each side of the terrace with their backs to the two men.

Kelly could feel the chill in the air. Whatever humor had once enlivened Patterson's face was gone. His skin was gray; his eyes, dull.

"Talk quietly," he said.

Kelly glanced back at the agents. Were they listening? He nodded his head.

"Tell me about the sewer problem," he suggested. Patterson gave a wan smile.

"It's worse than you think," he said.

"I try not to think," Kelly told him. "Sewage is something no one really thinks about."

Patterson said alarming stats were rolling into his office. Good doctors, like Kelly, were checking on the nurses and physician extenders making sure that patients calling for emergency help were getting proper care. But, not all doctors were so concerned. Worse, many had outsourced emergency responses to newly emerging businesses that now sent independent nurses and physician assistants.

While the law that created the Thorn Plan required that

nursing firms be licensed, no provision insisted that employees be properly trained or licensed. That was, Thorn had said, understood. Not to these newly minted businesses that took advantage of the loophole to hire unqualified and disinterested staff. Many of the newcomers had little training or had been "educated" in schools that had popped up to fill the need.

Kelly could hear the despair in Patterson's voice as he whispered the information. He also didn't need any detailed explanation of what was happening: People who could be helped were dying needlessly. Their families didn't know. They trusted doctors. Most people did. They believed nurses who came to the door in professional attire. They listened with sadness to physician assistants. And, they helplessly watched their relatives die. That picture was clearly painted in the silence between Patterson's words.

"We're saving so much money," Patterson said with a sarcastic laugh. He glanced over his shoulder as though someone would overhear.

"It is really sewage," Kelly said sadly. "What can we do?"

"It gets worse," Patterson said. Kelly felt sick to his stomach. What could be worse?

In a low, shaky voice, Patterson continued. Thorn was looking into a new area. Several years before, Congress had approved a law preventing discrimination against people who may show markers for various illnesses in their DNA. Thorn was no doctor, Patterson noted, but came across the information while reading through past issues of the *Congressional Record.* Kelly shuddered at the image of anyone poring over the tedious *Congressional Record* in spare time.

Thorn decided that if people with markers in their blood for a disease could be prevented from having children, then the number of cases of afflicted babies would fall—as would the associated costs. Preventive medicine, he called it.

"That's awful," Kelly said. He, too, took a quick look around him. "What a sewage problem."

He didn't have to say anything else. Again, both men understood. This was eugenics, the attempt to create a higher type of human. The Nazis had fomented the concept, but modern genetics had made aspects of it possible. Such testing would break up relationships: would a woman want to marry a man who had markers for diabetes, multiple sclerosis, Parkinson's, or other genetically transferable diseases? Or vice versa?

"What would happen if a couple still decided to go ahead and get married?" he asked.

Patterson shrugged. "No government health care benefits for their afflicted children," he said coldly. "by law."

Kelly slumped back in his chair. This was worse. The Thorn Program could be rescued with more oversight and by the insistence on better certification. On the other hand, nothing could help ease the pain of this new idea.

"Congress won't go along, will it?" he asked.

Patterson was noncommittal. "It's just an idea being floated, but a lot of people are impressed," he said.

"Impressed!"

"They see this as a way to eliminate Down's syndrome and many other birth defects, as well as a variety of diseases," Patterson said.

"Like smallpox?" Kelly murmured. Were the Congressmen thinking about the effort to eradicate smallpox, a once-deadly disease? The United Nations led the charge, which involved isolating victims from the rest of the population to reduce infection, then inoculating everyone who might catch the disease. The process took years, but succeeded. DNA testing promised to speed up the elimination of diseases: no children, no future carriers.

"*Brave New World*," Patterson said grimly, referring to a novel that described a future world that classified people based on genetics.

"*Gattaca*," Kelly added, recalling a little-known movie where genetic testing was used to separate the "haves" from the "have-nots."

"I wonder if Thorn is a fan of that movie," Patterson thought aloud.

"He's not a fan of research," Kelly said. "DNA testing isn't that accurate."

"Yet."

"The genetic markers don't always indicate a child will get a particular disease anyway," Patterson continued. He didn't explain further, but Kelly knew. Lay people thought that one male gene lined up with one female gene: the dominant one then decided the various characteristics of the offspring. But, it wasn't that simple: multiple genes connected from each side. That way, even if both parents carried markers for something as deadly as Tay-Sachs disease, their child still may not have it.

Moreover, scientists were still unsure if environment had an impact. Could a marker be activated in a certain environmental situation—such as acute stress or a virus—while remaining benign in another?

They sat in silence, conjuring up what kind of future lay ahead of them. Kelly had a knot in his stomack. He also was not sure yet he could trust Patterson.

"I'm not done," Patterson said.

Gentry was so popular, he said softly, that a small movement had started to eliminate the Constitutional prohibition against a president serving more than two full terms. Congress had passed the amendment after Franklin Roosevelt's four terms in office.

"Gentry wants to stay on as president?" Kelly asked.

Patterson shook his head. "Hardly," he said. At first, the conversation about any new amendment was muted, he explained. Some hints reached his office, but he rarely heard much until the media made it a front-page story. Katie Watson, on the other hand, remained fully informed. She told him.

The first strong signal was a *Time* magazine article that carried a recap of the Twenty-second Amendment and how it was born as a kind of historical review. Then, last week, Colorado's Republican senator, Jayson Hardesty, submitted a bill to repeal the Twenty-second Amendment, but the new bill excludes the current sitting president from taking advantage of the amendment.

Again, Patterson didn't explain further. Since Thorn was already the presumptive Republican presidential nominee, the repeal would directly benefit him.

The idea did make Kelly sick.

The fact that a Colorado congressman had proposed the repeal made sense, since Gentry was from that state. However, the change would benefit Thorn, who listed his permanent address as Wyoming. That was curious.

"I know Hardesty," Patterson continued. "He and his wife live in our Denver neighborhood." The couples often ate barbeques together, although camaraderie had fallen off in recent months.

"He grew up really poor, but supposedly got a scholarship to some "prestigious" school," Patterson reported. "I remember he said he was really lucky even to get into such a fine college."

He recalled Hardesty in the statehouse, but was not impressed with his journalism skills. "He's a better politician," Patterson said.

"Did he know Thorn?" Kelly asked.

"Sure, who could avoid him?" Patterson said. "They used to go to the horse races together. Thorn loves gambling, but won't lower himself to play poker. He likes the bluebloods at the track."

He stood up and walked back inside the room. Kelly watched him go. Gone was the bounce in his walk. His shoulders were bent. He almost shuffled. He came back a moment later with a file in hand.

"More sewage," Patterson said as he shut the door behind him.

He sat down and opened the file. It contained background on Hardesty with handwritten notes on the borders of newspaper clippings and printouts from computer sites. Wordlessly, Patterson passed it over to Kelly.

Kelly was not surprised to find the man had a colorful background. Hardesty had graduated from the Dr. John Brinkley Journalism Institute in his home state of Idaho. The notes indicated the school did not endure long nor could claim any special graduates. Hardesty then turned up at the Arvada *Mile High News*, not exactly the acme of Colorado media, despite its name. Someone had put an exclamation mark next to the newspaper's name.

From there, Hardesty gravitated to Denver and was a sports reporter at the *Denver Post*. Soon after, he oozed into the news section. Kelly found himself reading some vintage Hardesty stories. Many were from the front page and clearly showed some inside information. Unfortunately, Hardesty seemed addicted to the words "unnamed source" and "highly placed administration official." Still, based on follow-up stories, he was very accurate.

Gentry was often mentioned, both before he was elected governor and afterward. His name was underlined in the stories. The accounts were highly complimentary. Gentry was the star: "rising higher in popularity than the tallest peak in the Cascades and threatening to surpass the Rockies in local public support," to quote one obsequious Hardesty report. Thorn also earned an occasional line or two, but usually in a perfunctory manner. He was limited to "special assistant to the governor" or "governor's chief troubleshooter."

Hardesty then became spokesman for Gentry during his first term as governor. When Gentry ran for his second term, the journalist tagged along. The stories containing the information came from *Denver Post* archives.

"You've been busy," Kelly said.

"Sewage keeps rising," Patterson noted laconically.

Photos showed Gentry, his arm around Hardesty, standing on various daises during the campaigns. The two men seemed inseparable. In fact, Gentry even called Hardesty his "protégé" on several occasions. Both men won their respective elections easily.

Hardesty had been in Congress ever since.

His proudest accomplishment to date, he said on a printout from his site, was introducing the Thorn Plan to Congress.

Kelly closed the file thoughtfully and handed it back. Patterson took it back inside. Then, Kelly heard a whirring noise. It lasted only a few moments.

"Portable shredder," Patterson explained on his return.

Kelly thought about what he had read. *The congressman had found a meal ticket. Could someone like Thorn have been involved? Could he have planned that far in advance?*

The answer was obvious. Hardesty had bet his future on Thorn. Now, the erstwhile reporter was paying off. Thorn was only fifty-two; if the Twenty-second amendment was repealed, he could be president for a long time. No, Kelly reflected. He *would* be president. In fact, if everything worked out, Thorn could become an American emperor, the new czar of politics.

"The idea of unlimited presidential terms has long percolated through American politics," Patterson said. "If Republicans could have gotten the law approved in his day, Reagan would have been nominated for a third term. Some Democrats were hoping Clinton would stay in office until his personal peccadilloes undermined that idea. There was even some thought that a Democrat would run with Clinton as vice president in 2000, win the election and then resign so Clinton could take office again, bypassing the amendment."

Kelly listened. Thorn was made of sterner stuff. That's why he was trying to have his crony get the amendment repealed. He wouldn't even have to say anything. Let Hardesty do the talking for him. He could even deny any interest. The man was so slick. "Tricky" Dick Nixon could have learned a lot from Thorn.

"Now what?" Kelly finally asked.

Patterson clasped his hands. The skin turned white. He

seemed ready to leap over the balcony wall. His whole body was leaning that way.

"I don't know," he finally said. He gulped air. "He wants to call this DNA brain storm The Patterson Plan."

Silence again dominated, broken only by the distant echoes of the cacophony from below.

"You can't stay in office," Kelly told him. "This is unethical, immoral, and contrary to everything you and I learned in medical school. If you stay, you'll be endorsing the program."

"I can't look at Thorn anymore," Patterson went on in a broken voice. "His voice sickens me. His tone, his condescending manner, even his flat Western accent. Reporters seemed almost deferential, asking soft questions, allowing him to avoid direct confrontation. I want to shout at them through the television. One time, I gripped the armrest of the chair and actually tore it in frustration."

He was staring at the concrete flooring.

"It's hard to walk away, isn't it?" Kelly said.

"I put my whole life into getting here. Now look at me," Patterson said.

He stared off into the distance. "I told the ACLU," he finally admitted. Kelly took a deep breath. Was that what Erik meant? He said the ACLU was keeping an eye on the Thorn Plan.

"I know Thorn's going to be nominated to be vice president," Patterson continued. "Then president."

Kelly nodded. Thorn had been embraced by Gentry, the gentle, beloved overseer of the United States. The occasional scandal that every administration was heir to had not touched the ex-governor. Instead, reporters found scapegoats. Gentry continued his card playing, golfing, and bonhomie meetings with other world leaders while awash in waves of support. The national debt was high, but that was Congress' fault. Wars continued unabated, but the president couldn't get the Pentagon to change its evil ways. And so on. There was an answer for everything. Gentry didn't even break a sweat in news conferences. His permanent smile became a fixture on the television and computer screens—an embodiment of the high hopes and lofty self-confidence of the people he led.

Thorn was something else. He radiated cold. His dark eyes had none of the light that enlivened Gentry. He seemed to foreshadow a harsher, more intense leadership—more intellectual, less fun. Yet, he stood alone with Gentry's mantle draped securely across his shoulders.

Kelly reached over and put a hand on Patterson's arm.

"Maybe we need to put in pipes to handle the sewage," he said. "The shit can only rise so far."

Patterson nodded slowly.

Kelly did not give any further explanation. He could only hope that some brave legislator would stand up to Thorn. If not, the only solution may lay in his hands.

There were no words to express that thought. None were needed.

# CHAPTER 10
# HEART TO HEART

How depressed Patterson was that day in Philadelphia. In just a couple of years in national politics, he had gone from an ebullient go-getter with a mischievous sense of humor to a morose man seemingly beaten down by the world. Kelly never thought that would have been possible. Even in moments of dark despair, such as when some onerous test loomed in medical school and the previous night's party threatened bad results, Patterson was always upbeat and convinced of his own infallibility.

Joan had even been taken by him during his occasional visits to the Kelly household. Patterson probably appreciated her cheery disposition. He grew up in a very different environment. As a youngster, he invariably fought with his father, a dour fellow who rarely saw a glint of light in the darkness of everyday events. Patterson, an only child, inherited his mother's chipper view of life, which clashed inevitably against his father's rocky moods. Unfortunately, his mother died when John was still a child and he had to battle his father alone. Weldon Patterson was wealthy and ran a plumbing supply chain founded by his father. Wealthy and class-conscious, he paid for his only son's education and had little time for amusements. He never married again either, nor could he understand his son's propensity to see the sun shining when a storm always loomed before them.

After all, tomorrow, a recession could undermine the business. Or some competitor could appear—a Wal-Mart of plumbing— to undermine sales. Maybe a bookkeeper would embezzle money, or the government agents would demand unwarranted back taxes, or a customer would sue, draining millions for lawyer fees. Wendell Patterson saw each abyss looming before him and struggled to stay on the straight and narrow amid the pitfalls.

Patterson simply could not let such ominous predictions envelop him, even when his father died. At the funeral, he had the organist play "On the Sunny Side of the Street," claiming it was his father's favorite song. "I know dad is in heaven singing along," he mischievously told the friends, family members, and company employees who attended.

By then, Joan had introduced Patterson to Terri Gerhardt, her roommate in nursing school. They double-dated several times; then Terri and Patterson became a twosome. Patterson was the one who told jokes, supplied the transportation, picked out the finest wine, and generally enjoyed life to the fullest.

That part of him, Kelly was sure, was gone forever.

Patterson resigned upon his return to Washington. Kelly knew he would. Kelly hadn't made an overt recommendation for that abrupt action, but was positive Patterson had read between the lines. In truth, he had little choice. Patterson may enjoy the finer things in life, but had no stomach for the rough-and-tumble life of a politician.

The announcement of his decision had been brief, befitting a little-known assistant secretary of Health and Human Services.

His boss, Rosario, had said a few nice things, although the brief report on FOX seemed garbled. Kelly stumbled over it while looking for a real news program and couldn't decipher the cryptic comment about Patterson's "commitment to human health and longstanding effort to boost American Medicine." He supposed Rosario let someone else write the political obituary and, as usual, got tangled up in the recitation.

Kelly called Patterson as soon as he heard the news. Terri said that her husband had been out with the dogs, wandering around the hills near their home. She didn't sound upset. Patterson, too, was naturally upbeat.

"Good advice, fellah," he boomed. "I quit, and I feel a hell of a lot better."

He had no idea what he would do next. There were no openings in Colorado state government for him, although his positive reputation still lingered. Two governors had come and gone after Gentry. The latest, a Democrat, had little use for a former advisor to his Republican predecessor. Patterson had no desire to return to private practice, something he had never enjoyed. He didn't want to sit around the house either.

"Something will turn up," he announced. "Otherwise, I'll just sit around and bother Terri. That'll keep me busy."

Actually, the duo now had more time for social activities and cultural events. The recent real estate downturn had hurt Terri's business, as had her frequent absences to visit her husband in Washington. So, she threatened to take her husband to every new art show in town, Patterson reported with obvious dismay.

Money was not a problem. They had ample savings and investments. Patterson's inheritance from his father saw to that. He had sold the plumbing supply business long ago, which guaranteed no financial strain. They also had no children, cutting expenses even more.

Terri expected land sales to pick up anyway. Colorado, she commented, was not likely to be affected by global warming.

After all, Patterson added cheerfully, she could sell some of the homes here as future waterfront property.

For Kelly, the conversation had been a relief. He hoped his friend could recover quickly from the debacle. He seemed to have. Instead of moping or sounding bitter, he quickly severed all ties to politics and sent amusing e-mails about Thorn and current issues. He only chortled when, in a final divorce act, Patterson's name had been removed from the DNA-related plan presented in Congress by none other than Senator Hardesty. Instead, it was now named for Rosario.

While Patterson lolled about on his mountainside retreat, Kelly watched what was happening in Washington with interest. He became a faithful viewer of C-Span, listening to debates on The Rosario Plan, which had evolved into a very controversial issue. One thing was obvious: Thorn had latched onto an idea that could pass superficial observations, the standard approach by most Congressmen and voters.

Hardesty gave speech after speech lauding DNA testing. It would change health care in the United States and, at the same time, save billions in American health care dollars, he insisted. Current DNA screening allowed doctors to predict the likelihood of diabetes, premature heart disease, cystic fibrosis, some psychoses, Alzheimer's, and a number of other, long-term, chronic, costly diseases. With proper planning, Hardesty told the nearly empty House of Representatives, these diseases might be eliminated altogether.

Kelly listened with rising anger. The Rosario Plan was horrible, he told anyone who would listen. It would destroy lives. He realized his bitter comments were being tossed into empty air. He knew that Thorn's mind, once it had settled on an idea, had the tenacity of a weasel. It would dig and pry until he got what he was after.

Two weeks after the bill hit Congress and was assigned, as expected, to the House Labor, Health and Human Services, and Education (LHHS) Appropriations Subcommittee, the one

Hardesty served on, Kelly was called by Thorn at the hospital. Kelly had just taken care of a dislocated shoulder in a budding shortstop who had tumbled across a low railing when his secretary told him Thorn was on the line.

He went into his office and closed the door. For a moment, he watched the light on his phone blink. Finally, he picked up. Thorn was then connected.

In some ways, Kelly had expected to hear from him. Without Patterson, Thorn needed medical input. He knew Kelly well enough. He also knew of his involvement in earlier, successful medical schemes. On the other hand, Kelly had hoped his name would not pop into Thorn's mind.

"Dr. Kelly," Thorn said without a preamble. "I need to pick your brain a bit."

"You're welcome to whatever's left of it," Kelly responded grimly.

Thorn barreled on without a moment's pause. "As you probably know," he said, "Congress is now discussing a bill that would use DNA to help eliminate disease. I need as much information as possible to be sure this bill is best for the American people."

Kelly started to say something sarcastic, but stopped himself. Thorn would shrug off any comment like that. Besides, he wondered, hadn't anyone done any research before making the proposal? He was sure Thorn must have. That man didn't take anything for granted. As Kelly pondered that thought, he wondered what Thorn's ulterior motive was. It definitely wasn't the need for more information.

Instead, Kelly said that while he studied genetics in college, he couldn't offer much assistance. He suggested Thorn contact Dr. John McKittrick, professor of genetics at Thomas Jefferson University in Philadelphia and Kelly's former medical school colleague.

McKittrick was not much help either. As the professor relayed the conversation to Kelly later, he told Thorn that science was "an awfully long way from understanding how the entire mechanism functions, to say nothing of tinkering with it."

"Did he ask about using DNA to predict and eliminate diseases?" Kelly probed.

McKittrick said Thorn did. "I informed him that we are years—perhaps decades—away from any practical application of this knowledge. Our current research techniques are very costly."

"What did he say?"

"He offered to throw a ton of money into research," McKittrick said. "That's a positive. Genetics hasn't attracted as much government funding as, say, AIDS or cancer research. What we really need is someone to oversee this kind of program, someone with an understanding and ethics to make sure the research is used properly."

He didn't offer any suggestions, but Kelly understood the implication. This could be a way to control government intrusion into medicine. If he were in charge, he could stand up to Thorn. Patterson was a lightweight: brilliant, politically savvy, and energetic, but lacking in a commitment to ethical standards. Moreover, he was not used to running anything like an ER. The lobbying consortium Patterson had headed before signing on with Gentry was built on compromise. In a hospital, doctors learned to stand up and speak out for what they believed was right. Patterson would have remained silent even when something outrageous was proposed. He would have looked for a compromise solution, Kelly realized. He would not.

Kelly had never considered working in government before, but on an issue as important as this one, he had to consider it. He and Joan talked about the possibility. She dismissed the idea as idle thoughts of a small-town doctor being drawn to the bright lights of politics. He was not so sure.

Gentry hopped on the bandwagon in his State of the Union address that January. Kelly rarely listened to such speeches, knowing they were self-serving and rarely dealt with the state of anything, at least realistically. They were perfect for promoting brainstorms and seeing if anyone was willing to endorse them. This speech was focused on healthcare. Kelly could almost hear Thorn's voice in every sentence.

"My fellow Americans," Gentry said in his genial way, "what if we were able to eliminate many of the most costly and devastating diseases that plague our society? Just think how much needless suffering and how many billions of dollars could be saved if we no longer had diabetes, or schizophrenia, or Alzheimer's, just to name a few. This is not some idle dream. Today, we currently have the technology to screen for a few markers of mostly rare diseases through DNA analysis. If we spent the money and did the research, I believe we could identify the people whose offspring were likely to become schizophrenics or diabetics, or any number of other widespread diseases. With proper planning, those diseases could be completely eradicated."

Applause from both sides of the aisle interrupted him.

"That sounds like science fiction," Gentry continued, "which, as you may know, I'm very fond of. However, American doctors, equipped with the finest equipment and best training, are on the verge of detecting damaged DNA at the molecular level and repairing the problem so babies can be born healthy and without a defect that might otherwise be passed on to their children."

More applause. This time, it really sounded authentic, not polite.

"With enough resources and research, I believe it can be reality," the president intoned. "I call on Congress to pass The Rosario Plan to give genetic researchers the resources to achieve this impressive goal."

He gestured toward Rosario, who stood and waved to the audience amid more applause. Kelly recognized the same man he had met in Denver not that long before. He looked a little fatter; the bags under his eyes had multiplied. At the moment, though, his face was glowing.

Response in the media the next day was enthusiastic. Kelly

read an avalanche of editorials and commentaries. Gentry was at the height of his popularity and Congress was in his control. He had engineered three tax cuts in the past five years, and life was clearly better for the average American. Eliminating disease, Gentry noted, would make him perhaps the greatest president since FDR.

On the Tuesday after the speech, Kelly's phone rang again. Thorn wanted to talk to him. In a moment, the familiar voice rang over the line.

"Dr. Kelly," Thorn said without preliminaries, "I want to ask your help."

Kelly almost gasped aloud.

"You understand this material," Thorn continued. "More importantly, I know you speak well. I've set up a meeting with leaders of pharmaceutical companies. If we can get them behind this plan, then Congress will approve it."

*How like Thorn,* Kelly thought. He automatically assumed everyone bought into whatever he proposed. Still, having an inside position could help control the potential abuse. He had no illusions: Thorn wouldn't hesitate to discard him. Still, while he was there, he would have a pulpit that would allow him to address his concerns to the media, even surreptitiously. Instead of sitting home in frustration, anguishing over this proposed plan, he could actually influence it. That's what McKittrick had suggested, he realized.

The meeting was only a month away. After talking with Joan, Kelly agreed to be there and to chair the session. In the interim, he needed to work with Rosario and Thorn to get ready. Thorn said he would be named assistant secretary—Patterson's old position—to give him status at the gathering.

The hospital board was delighted that Kelly had been tapped for such an important post and granted him leave to go. Joan was more skeptical, particularly after Patterson's experience, but understood his reasoning. She just didn't think he could endure the traditional political infighting sure to erupt.

Only Patterson was upset. No, he was furious.

"Is this why you suggested I resign?" he raged over the phone.

Kelly tried to calm him. He pointed out that resignation had been Patterson's idea. "I just wanted you to think about your future," he said.

"You sure it was my future you were so concerned about?" Patterson said furiously. "I had people trying to stab me in the back all the time. I never thought you were armed." He slammed down the phone.

Kelly needed a few minutes to recover. Maybe his friend would understand eventually. He hoped so. This was just a one-time effort to influence what could become one of the most dangerous and intrusive measures ever proposed. Patterson would see: Kelly would be back in the emergency room in a few weeks.

That night, he turned over several times, unable to get comfortable.

"Can't sleep?" Joan asked tenderly. She slid over and rested her head on his chest. "Thinking about John?"

He nodded. "I've known him longer than I've known you," Kelly said. "It's hard to forget the past."

She kissed his cheek. "Pete," she whispered, "you made the correct decision. He'll understand in time."

"Are you sure?"

"Yes." She lay back on her pillow. "Someone needs to be directly involved with this. John wouldn't speak up when the plan goes off the tracks. He was not that type. He doesn't know what moral outrage is. He'd just make a joke about it. And, you know this plan will be different from what's proposed now."

"With Thorn involved, it definitely will."

She caressed his shoulder. "And you'll prevent that."

"But, I have to fly to Washington so often," he pretended to complain.

"Just order more scotch," she suggested.

"I'll miss you," he continued.

"Well," she said, slowly unbuttoning his pajama top, "maybe we need to create some warm memories for the times you have to face off with those big, bad drug companies."

Kelly smiled and took her in his arms. How nice to have a wife who almost seemed to know exactly the right thing to do.

# CHAPTER 11
# PLAN, PLAN, PLAN

Patterson had been so upset, more than Kelly ever recalled. Even the eruption after he and Joan had faked an acceptance letter that offered Patterson a job as president of a big California plumbing concern didn't compare. And, Patterson had carried on for a good twenty minutes after they confessed.

But, Kelly had to put the breakup out of his mind. If he was going to help maintain ethical and moral standards in medicine, he needed to concentrate on the meeting with the pharmaceutical executives. He could not let Patterson distract him.

Still, he often checked his computer and was saddened not to find a light-hearted e-mail from his friend. He wondered if he ever would read one again. Thorn kept sending him information to memorize and questions sure to need answering. Kelly would do his homework, but checked on the mail every now and then. Patterson was still angry; no messages of any kind appeared.

He thought about sending one himself, but refrained. There would be a better time for reconciliation.

Finally, he kissed Joan goodbye and boarded the plane to Washington. He actually was getting used to the short hop. Not enough to ignore his regular scotch, but he could now look across the aisle at the window on the other side without getting nauseous. Looking out his own window, however, was not an option.

No one met him at Dulles. He rode the van back to the gate and caught a taxi to the Grand Diplomat. He was beginning to feel comfortable here, having made this hotel his usual stopover. The clerks didn't recognize him. Another visit or two, maybe they would.

Two mornings later, a limousine brought him to the eleven o'clock meeting with drug company executives he had met at an evening reception the night before. He was getting accustomed to riding in these elongated cars—he didn't get an upset stomach like on an airplane. Still, he really didn't find them comfortable. He was alone on a large couch. Scotch was available, but he didn't help himself. The driver never said anything. Kelly did not start a conversation. He could see out the tinted windows, but no one could see in. So, there was never any communication with people outside. If anything, he was nervous as the huge vehicle maneuvered through traffic or somehow turned tight corners. The driver clearly was comfortable wheeling such a huge car, but Kelly never relaxed.

Rosario met him outside the White House guest entrance—the one that tourists never saw. Kelly endured the usual metal detectors and was led inside. Somehow, none of the decorations or even the aura of history drew his attention. He tried to focus on what was going to happen.

In discussions with Thorn, he worked out a series of talking points. Their goal was to get the drug companies to sign on and cooperate, not compete. Thorn saw that approach as a better way to control everything. Kelly, however, knew he would have a chance to influence decisions with a single leader rather than with a group.

A secondary goal, which always festered in his mind, was to convince Thorn not to say anything about Joan's business. The only way to do that was to put on a false front and seem supportive.

Rosario and Kelly were led by a uniformed officer down a white hallway graced with images of Gentry with many visiting dignitaries and world leaders. They all looked serious; he was grinning.

They came to a large wooden door guarded by another soldier in a fancy uniform. He saluted. Their guide opened the door. Inside the large conference room, five men in suits sat facing a platform and a computer screen.

The executives looked up at Kelly and Rosario with undisguised concern. Kelly smiled reassuringly and shook hands. William Defebbo, CEO of Johnson and Johnson, was the senior man in the group and became the de facto spokesman. He was blunt, confident, and forceful. He was not a man used to listening. In some ways, he reminded Kelly of Wilbur Darby's fierce and focused determination. DeFebbo had already made it clear that he opposed The Rosario Plan, simply because he felt it was too soon to mandate any kind of medical treatment based on incomplete research.

Another strong voice was Thom Sparber, the chief of Pfizer, Inc. He wanted the pharmaceutical companies immunized against any possible lawsuits arising from incorrect test results or faulty treatments. "We can't continue without such carte blanche protection, sir," he intoned over a drink the night before.

Rosario was his usual effusive self, clapping backs, spouting clichés, asking about golf games and promising proper entertainment that evening. Kelly finally walked to the front and sat down in a chair next to an American flag. Behind him and along the sides, the walls were crowded with paintings of patriotic images. President George Washington reigned dourly on one wall; a famed Matthew Brady photo of President Lincoln visiting General Grant was on another. A stenographer sat waiting while a video camera recorded everything. Several White House and media photographers walked around snapping still images sent out almost immediately to the yawning world.

Seated by the dais, Kelly took a moment to look at the somber, stony faces before him. He had a chill, thinking of how far he had come from the day, as a scared young man, he had filed into his first medical school class. Marveling at the change, he dimly heard the snap of cameras and the whirr of the video. He took a sip of water, allowing his pulse to ease. He also stared at the image of stoic George Washington, practicing some meditation techniques.

Rosario finally broke off from glad-handing to welcome the guests. He spent a few minutes boring them with a story about his family and their medical problems. He then showed a video of children stricken with various diseases spliced with comments from doctors talking about new research and hopes for cures.

Finally, Rosario introduced Kelly, "the doctor who was named America's Premier Emergency Room Physician and who is now the assistant secretary overseeing the new plan."

Slowly, in silence broken only by the sound of his chair scraping across the carpet, Kelly stood up and walked to the microphone. Rosario waited a moment in the back and then slipped away. As the highest-ranking government official there, he was supposed to stay, but, as he told Kelly earlier, he had a pressing engagement on the golf course.

Kelly took a deep breath. He knew that, somewhere, Thorn was listening. This was his chance to prove he could handle this assignment, that he was a loyal team player, one that Thorn could trust to run this program. Only then, Kelly knew, could he have the clout to be sure proper standards were in place.

He began by briefly establishing his credibility through his role in what was now known as the Thorn Plan. This meeting, he explained, was to introduce them to a new program. His words appeared on the computer screen in front of him. During his presentation, he only occasionally glanced down. Having practiced enough in front of the bedroom mirror, he felt comfortable without the cues.

"We are looking to identify the 10–15 percent of Americans that harbor the DNA that causes diabetes, premature heart disease, schizophrenia, early Alzheimer's, and, perhaps, mental retardation and common cancers. There are many other rare and devastating diseases that should be identified as well, but we are most interested in the common chronic diseases," he said with words from a Thorn-approved speech. "Our ultimate goal is to harvest a sperm or ovum and 'fix' the DNA, so that the carrier person can have disease-free offspring. First, we have to identify the problem and reduce the number of incidences."

The men were listening intently. "We recognize this is not a simple concept," Kelly said, feeling the stares. Sweat prickled around his collar, but he held his voice steady. "The government has asked Congress to invest billions of dollars to achieve this goal. Your companies will be the chief beneficiaries of that investment."

Each point was emphasized in a computerized show compiled by the White House public relations team. The images flickered on the screen next to Kelly, underlining everything he said with vivid images.

"Sell patriotism," Thorn had ordered.

The pictures did just that.

Kelly waited for his audience to think about the numbers. "We need you and your researchers to develop a reliable genetic screening test that identifies the carriers of the big, *expensive* diseases at an affordable price. The president is prepared to build the world's most advanced genetics lab for the world's leading genetics scientists with an *unprecedented* amount of federal funding. Whether it costs $10 billion or $100 billion, we have the money to spend. And we will keep on spending until the president's goals are achieved."

He paused and scanned faces in the room. "Can you do this," Kelly asked, "or should the president look elsewhere?"

DeFebbo did not hesitate. "Mr. Secretary, you are asking us to make science fiction a reality."

Kelly nodded.

"The submarine, the rocket ship, and the helicopter were once science fiction. So were television, radio, computers, and the Internet." He could see the greedy expression on DeFebbo's sour face. There was no way he was going to turn down this money. "I believe they are all real now."

Heads bobbed up and down.

"If Gentry is really prepared to pursue this concept, then I am sure you have selected the right group," DeFebbo said.

DeFebbo looked around the room to four other heads nodding in agreement.

Kelly smiled. "I was convinced before I came into this room that we had made the right choice," he said. *The scent of money was so alluring,* he thought quietly. "We will need to get this bill through Congress. I expect your help with that. Once the money is authorized, you can turn your scientists to work on creating the solutions the American people expect."

He almost choked when he said that. Is this how Patterson reacted? The words slipped out so easily. He looked around the room. These were intelligent, powerful men who knew full well that the administration was proposing altering the natural condition of humankind—an idea that had in the very recent past been used as justification for government-mandated sterilization, abortion, forced deportations and genocide. Nobody had batted an eye.

Thorn knew their soft spot, Kelly realized. Wave cash and watch them line up. He would not succumb. He would need to have a say in the process to ensure ethical decisions were made. These men wouldn't care. He would have to.

Peter Berg, the chief executive of GlaxoSmithKline, raised his hand like a child at school. Kelly acknowledged him. "Mr. Secretary, how do you envision this coming together with the five of us?"

Kelly smiled. His weeks with Thorn and Rosario had not been wasted. They all knew the question would come.

"We have a proposal to handle that," he said. "We believe you will form a single entity—the Nucleon Company—and contribute your expertise and scientists equally. This will reduce the burden on any one company and eliminate fights over patents likely to increase your costs."

The men considered this option. Thorn said this would be the hardest idea for them to swallow. Each was fiercely independent and used to the daily battles in the business arena. Most did not like their counterparts and thought the other was doing illegal things to get some kind of competitive edge. Sharing was anathema. The American way was to scathingly attack a competitor and deride his products, not to cooperate.

The rest of the day was spent on this topic, even through lunch. The industry leaders had no hesitancy in accepting government handouts to develop new products; they only objected to sharing expertise. However, as Kelly pointed out, such a process would increase efficiency. Each of them could take the knowledge and develop competitive products. He did not tell them that the consortium would increase his chance to influence decisions. Instead of dealing with five corporate cultures and strong-minded CEOs, he could focus on a single entity.

The meeting finally dragged to a close around 4:00 PM—the drug magnates must have developed some special pill for being able to sit for hours on end without discomfort. Kelly wished they would share the secret—he made a brief report about the meeting first to Rosario and then together with the secretary to Thorn. Rosario acted as if he had heard every word spoken during the long discussion, calmly repeating what Kelly had briefed him on without a hint of embarrassment.

At the next meeting of the five executives the following week, Rosario presented a 450-page manuscript that outlined the agreement, set a timetable, and estimated costs. The business leaders countered with a two-thousand-page tome that identified the needs of the physical plant, including every scientist who would be involved and biographies, all the support teams, administrative staff, and every imaginable technical piece of equipment they might need. Rosario barely glanced at it.

The drug lords delineated costs around $2 billion in the first year and rising thereafter. Rosario sniffed at the figure. "That's probably too low," he whispered to Kelly in a way that ensured the audience heard.

With the bill still in committee, the executives nevertheless took home copies of the legal agreement to create Nucleon. Rosario grandly called it the "new Manhattan Project."

"Just so it doesn't blow up in our faces," DeFebbo said.

Each of the five companies would get 20 percent of the Nucleon Company's stock.

The next step was Congress. Pharmaceutical lobbyists were quickly sicced on committee members. They attacked like bulldogs—wining, dining, and burying politicians under mounds of government-funded pamphlets. Scores of patients battling various diseases arduously trekked to the Capitol to demonstrate their diseases and to plead for research funds to cure them. Television and radio hopped on the bandwagon, filling the airwaves and goosing listeners to send supportive letters to their elected representatives. The pressure built.

The bill whisked through committee, then another, and a third. Representatives scrambled to get their fingerprints on what was obviously a popular measure.

Who could oppose funding research that would obliterate such onerous diseases and conditions?

Back home, Kelly watched the cascade with some amusement mixed with concern. He read the proposal carefully. Was there any provision for disallowing government health insurance if a couple was identified to have "bad" DNA, yet still had a baby? Any hint of some unethical or immoral standards? Hardesty's bill didn't address those issues. It simply seemed to provide funding for an all-out assault on devastating illnesses.

He had no concern about that, he told Joan after returning home and resuming work at St. Michael's. Finding such cures would be a boon for everyone. Nevertheless, he scanned the Internet to read reports of the committee debates, testimony from experts and from disease victims, and read everything about the bill he could find. For a while, he was wondering if Thorn was actually doing something that would benefit mankind.

His old friend, Professor McKittrick answered that question. He called Kelly as the bill began to be debated on the House floor. They chatted about their involvement in this historic effort, and then McKittrick asked if Kelly had read an amendment added by Hardesty during the last committee discussion before it was approved and sent to the full House.

"You know," he said, "a lot of provisions get tacked on late in the process."

Kelly didn't realize that. He thought a bill voted out of committee was what the legislators debated and finally gave nay or yea to.

McKittrick had found tucked into an amendment setting up an auditing system, a codicil that authorized the Department of Health and Human Services to create new "regulations" as may be deemed necessary by the president or his delegate, regarding any "discoveries" garnered from the research.

Kelly's eyes widened. He read through a copy of the Bill McKittrick e-mailed him. There it was—bold and clear—yet only a few words. How had he missed that? He was sure that would be Thorn's entry to restrict or eviscerate health coverage. It didn't have to be, of course, but Kelly was sure he had a clear picture of Thorn's hidden agenda.

"Damn," he muttered.

He thanked McKittrick and called his local congressman.

A secretary in Wesley F. Anderson's office was pleased to take a message, but the congressman was tied up in meetings. He never called back. Neither did Thorn, Rosario or anyone else Kelly tried to phone. He also peppered them with e-mails, feeling frustrated and positive that his messages were promptly deleted.

He stared sourly at his computer at the end of the day. Thorn had used him. He was furious. A nurse poked her head into his office, saw his scowl and quickly departed. She closed the door, too, as a warning to others. Kelly didn't care. He pounded his fist into his desk. His hand hurt but not as much as his head.

How could he be so stupid? Kelly asked himself. He thought he was helping to get the plan approved in order to prevent problems. Instead, he had been turned into an instrument of disaster.

What could he do about it?

When Pete returned home for a weekend off, Joan was direct. "You don't have any real position in government," she noted. "As interim assistant secretary, you won't find anyone who wants to talk to you. You have no clout."

"I have a baseball bat," Kelly said glumly.

"And, you are in a small city in Pennsylvania," she continued. "Those people only care about someone in Washington."

"Bring out the scotch," Kelly said. "I'm going back."

"Take the bat, too," Joan suggested.

Kelly wished Patterson could join him. He knew his way around the political labyrinth. However, there was no way to reconcile. Kelly didn't call. Instead, he felt like James Stewart in *Mr. Smith Goes to Washington*, a movie about a naïve man who becomes a senator by a fluke and takes on hardened politicos. Stewart played Jeff Smith, who wanted kids to enjoy some open land near his hometown, while his colleague, Joseph Pain, had other ideas. Kelly had no problem with putting Thorn in the Pain role. He just wondered how much of Hollywood could translate into reality.

He quickly learned the answer: not much.

He may have carried a title, however meaningless, but he had no office. Kathy Watson, Patterson's secretary, was still sitting at her desk, reading a book, but the office she once shared with Patterson was locked. She smiled at him and asked distractedly how Patterson was. Then, she resumed reading.

Rosario was unavailable; so was Thorn. Gentry was too busy entertaining and accepting media plaudits to be approached, not that Kelly had any entrée.

He spent several fruitless days wandering around the capitol. At least Anderson was finally willing to chat with him, although the Congressman gave the impression of being trapped. A pleasant man with graying hair around his temples and a somber expression of implied interest, Anderson fumbled through paperwork while Kelly talked about the need to remove the amendment from the bill.

Every now and then, Anderson would nod as if he actually understood.

Kelly then suggested the creation of a medical panel to oversee the imposition of this new plan.

"Uh, huh," Anderson said, tossing out some paper. Then, he realized Kelly was finished.

"All right," he said with a broad smile. "I'll get my secretary right on it." He stood up and quickly shook hands with properly rehearsed sincerity. He would see that the doctor's "extremely valuable suggestion" reached the proper party officials. "I can't promise that the amendment will be eliminated," he cautioned. "I'm only one vote after all. However, I want my constituents to know that what concerns them concern me."

Unimpressed, Kelly left with no illusions.

Out of options, he went back to see Watson. She seemed happy to have someone to talk to. Based on the pile of books by her chair, she had plenty of time to catch up on the latest romance releases.

He sat down dejected in the chair by her desk. She yawned

at him. He was going to pour out his story. Patterson trusted her; Kelly had no reason not to. However, she seemed lethargic.

"Long day?" he finally asked.

"They are all about the same," she said.

"What are you working on?" he tried.

"Page eighty-seven. I think Prince Rupert is about to have a romantic encounter."

"That's it?"

"It is for me," she answered.

There's not much incentive to do anything, Watson explained. She was secretary to a top official; that gave her certain status and placed her on a high level on the salary scale. She couldn't be lowered, and there were no higher positions available. She could make a stink and maneuver some higher-ranked secretary without as much seniority out of her job, but the lack of stress and the ample time to read really eliminated enthusiasm for skullduggery. She was protected by Civil Service and couldn't be dismissed—even if no one ever used the office again. With any luck, she said cheerfully, the government would forget about her while dutifully sending her checks every two weeks.

Eying her glumly, Kelly finally explained his problem. She actually seemed interested. "You talked to a congressman?" she noted. "Boy, was that a waste of time. You should have talked to his secretary. It wouldn't have done any good either, but at least she would have pretended to listen."

She started drumming her fingers on the desk.

"What we really need to do," she mused, "is get Rosario out of there and you in."

"Like that's going to happen," Kelly scoffed.

"You don't think I can do it?" Watson cocked an eyebrow at him. "Who do you think runs this place?"

Aware of how much nurses did in the ER, Kelly was not about to challenge a secretary. Maybe, he thought, she could do something. Nothing else was working.

"Rosario, Rosario," Watson mused aloud. She made a call and

discussed him with someone. She took a few notes in shorthand. Then, she had Kelly relate everything he was doing for Rosario. Kelly groused that the secretary had missed the big meeting with drug company executives and went to play golf instead, but had little else to add. Finally, Watson waved Kelly away.

At loose ends, he went back to the hotel. While there, he called Erik and filled him in. Erik was not sure that the regulations couldn't be monitored and countered rather than battling with the Congress over the codicil. "After all," he noted, "some regulations have to be written. Dad, maybe you could be in charge of that."

That was a thought.

Two days later, William Rosario resigned after apologizing for using an undocumented alien from the Philippines to caddy for him. According to rumors published as fact in the *Washington Star*, the president had expressed disappointment with Rosario after the secretary skipped a significant, unidentified meeting. Finally, there were suggestions that Rosario may have been carrying on an illicit affair with his office secretary. Of course, no one commented on that beyond the carefully worded innuendo. Rosario went home to Texas, waving a putter defiantly as he boarded the plane. His secretary was paid off by being booted upstairs to a higher-paying position and settled down to write her marginally anticipated memoirs.

Two days later, Kelly was introduced to the media as the nominee to be secretary of the Department of Health and Human Services. He actually got to meet Gentry before the conference and promised to help the president improve his golf game. Gentry had not forgotten that trip to Denver so long before.

"How's the wrist?" he asked.

"Never recovered," Kelly said, looking suitably sad. "Haven't been able to play in years." Gentry seemed genuinely sympathetic.

With Thorn standing behind the curtain, Kelly then told the gathered reporters about his plans to see the newly named Thorn

DNA Plan—the former Rosario Plan—achieve its lofty, ethical goals.

Thorn did not say anything to him when the ordeal ended thirty minutes later.

That night, he got his first e-mail from Patterson in two months. No words: it was an image of two sharp, bloody knives.

# CHAPTER 12
# ON THE INSIDE

For two months, Kelly waited for final congressional approval for his new post. He met key employees in the department, talked with his secretary, and managed to get Kathy Watson transferred to his office. It was a lateral move on the employment chart and acceptable to civil service. Forced by excessive work to put away her romance books, Watson was not overly pleased, noting sourly that this was a fine "thank you" for getting him the job. She was only slightly appeased when informed that Kelly's new salary meant he was losing money compared to working in an emergency room.

While the St. Michael's board was ecstatic at his rise to prominence, Kelly was depressed by the frequent absence from home. Joan could not move to Washington and run her business successfully. A few days away were fine, but not months.

Moreover, her aged father was not feeling well. She spent many weekends with him and finally convinced him to relocate to her brother's home in nearby Allentown.

Kelly was also not happy with the delay in getting approved to officially start his new assignment. Part of the delay came from token opposition and a threat of a filibuster. Several senators were opposed to the current Thorn Plan. States like New York, Pennsylvania, and Florida—crowded with aging populations— had seen a rise in deaths and an increase in fly-by-night health care companies fulfilling the letter of the law, but not the intent.

The threat to hold up the nomination to protest the law led to some internal, lengthy, and eventually successful, negotiations among elected officials.

At the same time, two Supreme Court justices had retired. One died soon after. Gentry moved quickly to nominate two top-ranked judges who had already gone on record supporting the Thorn Plan in written opinions. They won affirmation easily, but the hearings took time and distracted senators and representatives. In a way, the situation eased Kelly's path. Having run through a long set of confirmation hearings, no one wanted a duplicate effort.

Kelly was able to use his luxurious office, but, until Congress voted, he was not officially in charge. When not testifying before one of many congressional committees, Kelly worked on proposals to ensure Thorn's fledgling DNA proposal would arrive with strong ethical and medical criteria. Kelly did not hesitate to include his son in the preparation, but used his own cell phone rather than the office phone. He was sure Thorn would double check any calls he made. In fact, he was positive Thorn wouldn't hesitate to sabotage him. As Kelly listened to the debate over his approval and testified to his strong positions on behalf of the elderly, Erik had a team of ACLU attorneys devise protections, a DNA bill of rights.

Erik's efforts boosted his own position within the civil rights organization. In a short time, Erik became the de facto head of the ACLU's efforts regarding DNA testing. He was already presenting cases involving the Genetic Discrimination Ban law passed under President Bush. As part of his growing expertise, Erik became licensed to practice before the Supreme Court.

His first public effort was to argue in Congress against the two new justices, but he lost. Prior rulings on a law were not uncommon for nominees for the High Court. Besides, as several senators pointed out, most people didn't agree with Erik that the Thorn Plan was a bad idea. After all, as Senator Hardesty noted with ample sarcasm, Erik's father was scheduled to take over the federal department responsible for overseeing the law and had expressed no objection.

Meanwhile, the Nucleon Corporation was becoming a reality. Land had been acquired in some remote hills in North Carolina. The completed lab was up and running within nine months, with construction starting simultaneously with Kelly being confirmed by a 90–10 vote. Scientists and workers alike were required to sign strict confidentiality agreements regarding their work at Nucleon. Corporate officials issued a statement describing its purpose as "a joint effort by the parent companies to pursue specific research of common interest." A few suspicions were raised; watchdog groups and the media could tell something was brewing, but they could hardly report on it without any additional information. Erik even visited the site. He came away both impressed and concerned.

Buoyed by enough cash to raise the Titanic on a bed of fifty dollar bills, Nucleon quickly began to produce results. As Kelly learned the day-to-day operations of his huge department, Nucleon started to turn out results. Several genetic markers were already known to be reliable determinants of specific diseases, but there were many more that had no known markers, only "possible" indicators or, more complicated yet, had a combination of markers. Still, the Nucleon scientists had succeeded in identifying many previously unknown DNA "flaws," and, better yet, they had developed a commercial screening test that could identify the most common genetic faults. The cost was low, only thirty dollars per test. The time period between when the test appeared and when every prospective parent began to be tested took only months.

The next step was, theoretically, fixing the "defect" that could cause each identified disease. Here, progress slowed to a crawl. This was a far more arduous task than simply identifying the defect or defects themselves. It was virtually impossible to determine whether the DNA marker indeed caused the disease or if it was only an indicator that the potential for disease was present. Even if a specific DNA pair was identified as the cause of the disease, it was more than a matter of excising the "faulty" DNA—it had to be repaired or replaced with good DNA. In the absence of extensive human testing—which could not be initiated prior to endless experiments on rats and other animals—no one could speculate what kind of outcome this meddling would yield. There was the other side, too. Sickle-cell anemia, for example, killed young people. However, it also provided immunity to malaria so a victim could live long enough to produce offspring. What if some genetic-related disease actually had a benefit in some inexplicable way?

Although some trifling advances were typically ballyhooed by the Nucleon researchers and augmented by the White House public relations team, most of the scientists felt that marketable "DNA surgery" was many years away—if not a complete impossibility. However, little of this mattered to the employees of the Nucleon Company. The organization was flush with cash, the state-of-the-art facilities were new, and the staff was more than adequately compensated. Even if DNA surgery eventually proved impossible, with no deadline looming and a blank check from the government, the business of correcting DNA began to boom.

When Kelly was finally officially crowned as secretary of Health and Human Services, he received immediate directions from Gentry, delivered personally by Thorn. He was to oversee the development of requirements ensuring the creation of a genetic profile of each individual. Thorn wanted the information placed on a simple I.D. card, like a driver's license, clearly stating any genetic traits that need to be restricted. A couple looking to have a baby need only compare their "gene cards" to know the odds of having a baby with a genetic flaw. If they both have the same defect, the baby is highly likely to have it. If only one partner has a genetic fault, the odds are about 50–50.

He immediately called Erik.

"No such I.D. card exists, and none should ever exist," Erik noted. "Regardless, come up with regulations so strict that they virtually eliminate any chance that this plan will be enacted." He also promised to get information to key senators and representatives who would oppose such a proposal because of abhorrence for national I.D. cards.

To gain time and gather more information, Kelly brought together geneticists like McKittrick and Dr. Stanley Kuchinski, who headed Nucleon, to work out a plan. They did so reluctantly, aware that any proposal would create an enormous outcry. Erik supplied ideas that Kelly brought to the taskforce meetings.

Eventually, the group submitted its proposals to Thorn. He smiled blandly when taking them from Kelly and assured him the concepts would be read very carefully.

Two nights later, in a national media conference broadcast only on C-Span, Gentry described his government's new proposal as part of his re-election plans. At the same time, in a majestic ceremonial media conference with dozens of reporters on hand, Hardesty introduced the Thorn DNA bill into Congress.

Kelly got a copy the next morning in his office. It did not resemble anything remotely close to what his committee had recommended. One section, as Patterson had predicted so many months earlier, said bluntly, "If both partners have a DNA fault on their gene card that was going to result in a severe likelihood of a major inherited disease such as diabetes, cystic fibrosis, sickle-cell anemia, various forms of insanity, multiple sclerosis, lupus, or a host of lesser known genetically inherited diseases, and they were to have an afflicted baby anyway, their child would be barred from receiving Medicare or Medicaid for life."

There was more. "If both partners have the same genetic fault," the Hardesty bill proposed, "they should be advised not to have a baby. If one partner has the fault, testing the fetal DNA could be done in utero. If the genetic fault is present, the pregnancy will be terminated to protect the quality of human life."

Kelly gasped. Abortion! That would fly into the face of pro-life groups everywhere. Abortion had died down as an issue nationally, but this idea would certainly revive it. Opposition had never faded. State legislatures continually looked for ways to counter the Supreme Court's 1973 ruling legalizing abortions.

Moments later, his phone rang. It was Erik.

"I just read the bill myself," Kelly said as his son sputtered his outrage. "Those are not the regulations I proposed."

Erik's voice was already strained. "What's the deal? Are you working in a vacuum over there? How could you not know about this abomination?"

"Whoa, Erik," Kelly said softly. "Calm down. I'm asking myself the same question. If I knew anything about this thing, you would have been the first to know."

There was a moment of silence from Erik. "We've got to get these provisions publicized. Hardesty waited until the last minute to stick this bill in the hopper. I doubt any reporters have picked up on it yet. Gentry made the whole thing seem so innocent. The public needs to be galvanized to fight it."

"Can you beat it?" Kelly asked.

"We have lobbyists," Erik said, "but Gentry is so entrenched with his supporters that we're going to have to battle like hell. There are a lot of congressmen on the fence. We may be able to convince them to vote against a Gentry proposal, but it'll be uphill sledding. If your president wants something bad enough, he usually gets it. Besides, it's part of his re-election campaign. What did he call it, 'the Cornerstone for a Second Term.' Due to his ruthless penny-pinching, Gentry also has access to more funding for pork-barrel projects than probably any president in history, and he uses that money to buy votes."

"That was illegal the last time I checked," Kelly said.

"It is unethical and evil, but technically not unlawful," replied Erik.

"So, now what?" Kelly asked.

"We watch the bill become law and challenge it in court under Equal Protection provisions. I believe the Bill of Rights is still on file somewhere."

That afternoon, Kelly received a note on White House letterhead congratulating him for the fine work he had done on the new DNA proposal, and the creation of the gene card. It was signed by Gentry. It also said that in honor of his hard work, the plan was going to be renamed the Kelly Program.

Thorn did not return several phone calls.

The next morning, most American newspapers ran the full text of the Kelly Program that was before Congress. As written, the legislation was fairly succinct, easily read, and quite straightforward.

Kelly was aghast. The details were dramatically worse than he imagined. And his name was on it.

McKittrick was equally appalled. Could it get congressional approval? McKittrick hoped not, but Kelly's secretary Kathy Watson was more politically astute.

"Sure," she said almost nonchalantly.

"Doesn't that bother you?" Kelly asked.

"Naw," she said. "I don't have kids and am too old to get one. Besides, who needs more handicapped kids anyway?"

Kelly shuddered.

A week after the Kelly Program was unveiled, the American Medical Association unabashedly came out with a placid, middle-of-the-road position statement. The doctors were supportive of DNA research that would eventually be able to eliminate genetically transmitted diseases plaguing the population and only had "reservations" about the proposed rules outlined in the new bill. They made no comment regarding the morals of restricting people's access to health care for their children based on the contents of their gene cards. The AMA director did acknowledge that he was convening an ethics committee to examine the implications of the new bill, but made no reference as to when those conclusions would be announced.

Meanwhile, Congress was abuzz with the details of the Kelly Program. Not that any senator or representative could ignore it. Thorn had already organized extensive lobbying campaigns on Capitol Hill.

The bill was slated to be fast-tracked through the House and Senate. Although the details of the controversial piece of legislation raised much debate and argument, Gentry was optimistic that the "American people would trust his judgment, based on the success of previous actions of the administration." He pointed to the balanced budget, partly the result of immense cost savings from the Thorn Plan.

He made it abundantly obvious that a vote for the plan was an endorsement for his second run for the White House. With popularity polls giving him a nearly 70 percent approval rating, his insistence on passage carried a lot of weight.

Still, questions arose. Conservatives wanted to know if abortion rates were going to go through the roof; liberals demanded to know if children born of these "genetically mismatched" parents were going to be left to suffer and eventually die without health care. Some of the lawmakers suffered from diseases mentioned in the bill, especially diabetes. Under the new rules, they would never have been born. That was a frightening thought.

Surprisingly, there was not a great deal of "grassroots" opposition. Society had grown complacent, trusting. Even pro-life groups couldn't galvanize much of a response. Kelly was frustrated by the lack of outrage. He wished people would read the flyers sent to homes, watch the television accounts, and listen to the debates aired on the internet. Of course, too many were distracted by day-to-day existence issues to care. Some simply couldn't imagine the implications of the Kelly Program. Get rid of disease? Sure, what a great idea. That Gentry has done it again.

*The same kind of thinking led to the passage of the Patriot Act in 2001 and the subsequent erosion of civil rights,* Kelly thought. *Of course,* he reminded himself ruefully, *he hadn't objected to that proposal. Just as that law reassured the jittery public that something was being done to counter terrorism, the Kelly Program was calming fears about diseases and devastating birth defects.*

Gentry kept repeating that Nucleon was making great progress in DNA engineering and would surely soon be able to actually fix the faulty DNA so that nobody would be restricted from the right to have children. He was joined by the Zero Population Growth folks who saw this idea as a great way to hold down childbirth. The pro-choice groups chimed in, too.

By published reports, more than 55 percent of the population favored the proposals after two weeks of public debates. That was up from 48 percent in the first survey. The number of undecided was shrinking rapidly.

The approval figure was higher in Congress. Under Thorn's direction, Gentry added incentives in the form of grants to various districts and states of supportive legislators. One by one, even those senators and representatives who had been on the fence were able to convince themselves that, even if the Kelly Program was not perfect, it would be outweighed by the benefits their home states would experience.

After all the committee meetings and floor discussions, when the vote came, the House passed the Kelly Program by a two–thirds majority. The Senate followed suit with a 58–42 vote. The president wanted to play God, as the *New York Times* put it, and Congress went along "like little angels." In the end, it had only taken Thorn and his cronies three months to push the plan through.

Everyone but the American public was shocked. Most news

commentators and political analysts had expected the vote to be close and did not really expect it to pass at all. The news media was ablaze with the Kelly Program and its details for weeks. Meanwhile, Americans yawned and voraciously read the celebrity gossip or the results from various sporting events instead.

For Kelly, his name now attached to what he considered one of the worst laws ever approved, the abhorrent regulations constantly reminded him of Thorn and the treacherous path that man was following. He seethed with each mention of the plan. He grew angrier with each television report, every flyer, every time it came up in a debate. He received endless e-mails: some threatening him. Many included photos of ill and disabled children. Others praised him. Watson deleted all of them, but the images lingered in his brain.

"We'll challenge this law all the way to the Supreme Court," Erik insisted, representing the ACLU. Naturally, his position created a natural "rivalry" in the media since his father's name was on the program. The two men laughed to themselves as they worked together to gather information for the lawsuit. Erik was focused on the "equal protection" aspect of the Constitution, arguing that children who might be born with diseases were entitled to the same rights as children who showed no signs of an inherited disease or syndrome.

Without any public concern, Erik wondered if the Supreme Court, filled with Gentry appointees, would overturn the law. It had never recognized the rights of an unborn child, he told his father. He would ask the Supreme Court to take the case quickly since so many families would be affected the longer it dragged through the legal process. Regardless, the case promised to be a costly battle and not likely a winning one at that.

Meanwhile, Kelly was caught up in a family problem. Joan's father, Earl, was a sick old man, and for the last several months, had been on the verge of dying, but kept bouncing back. Her brother, Bill, and his wife, were now caring for Earl, who had moved into their home in Allentown.

Less than a month after the Kelly Program became law, Joan called and tearfully told her husband the bad news. Her father had suffered a stroke.

He caught the next plane home and met Joan at Lehigh Valley Hospital that evening. Pale and teary, she was sitting in the cafeteria, nursing some coffee. Several empty cups were on the table. Her brother was up in the room, she explained, but the prognosis was not good.

The CAT scan showed massive bleeding. The doctor held out no hope, but Bill wanted a second opinion, she said listlessly.

Kelly hugged her. There wasn't much else he could do. Slowly, she revealed what had happened. Her father had not been feeling well. Bill and his wife had gone to work. Her father had called 911 and a physician's assistant and a nurse came by almost immediately. The examination revealed "indigestion." They gave him some antacids and helped him into bed. That's where Lisa found him unconscious that afternoon.

Kelly felt sick to his stomach. His father-in-law had indigestion? There were numerous signs of an impending stroke that had no connection to something as innocuous as indigestion. Could Earl have suffered from smaller strokes that had not been detected? Kelly called the 911 supervisor and got the name of the company contacted to send help to his father-in-law.

In a few minutes, he talked to the physician assistant and, shortly afterward, to the nurse.

"He said his stomach hurt," they both insisted. They had checked Earl's blood pressure, which was not strong, but it was adequate enough for an eighty-four-year-old man. He didn't complain or show any other symptoms. He was having a little trouble talking and had some difficulty walking, but they figured, at his age, that was normal. They helped him into bed, concluding that a nice nap would solve the problem. The nurse didn't smell alcohol, but figured Earl was tippling.

"Lots of older people do that," she confided.

"How about numbness in his face, arm, or leg?" Kelly demanded. "Could he see clearly? Was he confused? Dizzy?"

"They didn't see any signs of that," the nurse insisted, now getting defensive.

"How long were you there?" Kelly snapped.

"A good ten minutes," she said. "That's what the regulations mandate. The shorter the visit, the lower the cost."

"He had a stroke," Kelly said angrily.

"He's in his eighties," the physician's assistant replied. "That sort of thing happens. Earl only had indigestion when we were there."

Kelly furiously shut the cell phone and went up to see his father-in-law. The two men had a close relationship, built up during nearly thirty years of marriage to his daughter. Now, the old man was lying quietly in bed, hooked up to machines. All Kelly could do was lean over and kiss a fevered brow.

"He's been unconscious all day," Bill whispered. "They say he's bad, but I don't believe this neurology guy. I asked for a second opinion."

Kelly nodded. He understood the logic, but had to be more realistic. Bill was a high school biology teacher. He wouldn't understand. Kelly looked at the readings. Pulse was weak. Brain wave activity was flat. He would look at the CAT scan reports, but he had no doubt what was going to happen. Joan's dad was dying.

Somehow, he had been put on a ventilator, but his pupils were fixed and dilated. His brain was dead. Kelly decided to keep his mouth shut until he talked to the neurologist, so he asked the nurse to page him. A few minutes later, the doctor called. They talked for a few minutes on the phone. It didn't take long to confirm the diagnosis.

"Bill," Kelly said quietly, taking his brother-in-law into the hallway, "I'm not a neurologist, but I have worked with many emergency room cases tragically similar to your father's situation." Bill looked pale. "If you want a second opinion, please don't hesitate, but, as a physician, I can tell you, he's not going to recover."

Bill stared at him. Kelly could see John Darby's eyes boring into him once again. That experience did not make this situation any easier.

"The neurologist said that the bleed is huge and has already killed his brain," Kelly continued. "A brain wave test was done just two hours ago and it is all flat line. This is not dad anymore."

"What are you trying to say, Pete?" Bill asked hesitantly.

Kelly took a deep breath. He tried to show warmth and understanding. "I'm saying that your dad should not be on this ventilator." He reached out to touch Bill, who avoided contact.

"How could he be dead?" he said. "His heart is still beating."

Kelly looked into Bill's eyes and said, "His heart isn't dead. His brain is."

"But he has to be given a chance! You're not going to turn off this ventilator," Bill replied.

"I'm not going to do anything," Kelly said. "I'm just trying to explain to you what will happen."

Bill was now visibly shaking. "No, Pete, you are the one that did this, with your stupid guidelines," he snapped. "Who are you to play God anyway?"

Turning away, Kelly fought back a retort. "Please talk to your sister," he finally suggested. "She's a nurse."

Bill marched back to the waiting room. Joan hugged him. They talked and agreed to let a second neurologist examine their father. If both doctors said that there was no hope, they would have to accept the decision.

The second doctor would be by later that afternoon. They would all meet the next morning to make a decision. Tearfully, Bill nodded. Lisa came later and took her husband home.

Kelly and Joan followed. There was no reason to stay. At home, Joan quietly let their children know what was happening with their grandfather. The phone calls were brief with the same questions and the same answers.

Diane and Erik planned to be there as soon as possible. Rachel would stay in school for her exams.

Then, Kelly and Joan held hands and sat wordlessly on the couch until late that night.

# CHAPTER 13
# UNEXPECTED CONFLICT

Nobody got much sleep that night. Bill and Lisa were already at the hospital when Kelly and Joan arrived. Bill's eyes were red and puffy. Although obviously reluctant, he listlessly kissed Joan on the cheek and limply shook Kelly's hand. Lisa hugged both of them. She was very fond of her father-in-law and had helped him cope with the loss of his wife a decade earlier. A manager of a furniture store, she usually was businesslike and formal, but showed much-appreciated empathy.

The two women sat together in the small ICU waiting room, whispering between themselves. Bill was quiet, occasionally shooting angry glares toward Kelly, who occupied himself half-heartedly reading a dog-eared, dated copy of *People* magazine. A reporter came by because an important government official was in town, but left with just a brief comment about the need for family privacy. Although a cabinet member, Kelly did not have Secret Service protection, a fact he appreciated. He also had not brought any aides with him, trying to keep the situation personal.

Earl was not a prominent person and had never earned much attention in his life. He was not likely to want any now. However, his death would merit a paragraph because of his association with the secretary of Health and Human Services. Kelly was sorry about that, but knew there was nothing to stop it—even though Earl would have preferred anonymity.

There was little opportunity to even think clearly anyway. The ICU was full and bustling with nurses. Alarm beepers were buzzing everywhere. The decibel level continued to rise.

Around 10:15, a nurse came to lead the family to a private office. The second neurologist was waiting for them there. Kelly had a strange feeling as he followed his family inside. How often he had been the one waiting behind the desk. The doctor identified himself as Paul Alberts and asked them to be seated in the visitor chairs. Bill deliberately sat as far away from Kelly as possible.

Dr. Alberts open a file folder and spread out the CAT scan images in front of him as well as a printout of various brain readings. He passed them over to Kelly as a courtesy. Kelly offered them to Joan, but she declined. Bill took them, but clearly didn't understand what he was looking at.

"What's this mean?" Bill asked sharply, pointing at one printout.

Taking a deep breath, Dr. Alberts said. "I'm sorry. That shows no brain activity." Lisa started to cry.

"I have to agree with your doctor," Dr. Alberts continued softly. "I am sure Dr. Kelly would agree, too, after examining the medical records."

Kelly nodded. He didn't need to make a formal evaluation, not after seeing Earl yesterday.

With a choked voice, Joan asked, "Now what?" Bill simply

stood up and wandered over to a far wall. He seemed to be reading the mounted diplomas.

"There is no reason to keep him on a ventilator," Dr. Alberts continued. "His brain is dead and his EEG is flat." The neurologist paused for this information to sink in. "Perhaps you might want to go to his room to say goodbye."

Lisa tried to take Bill's arm, but he jerked away. Kelly had seen that reaction before. Bill would have to work through his denial. He was younger than Joan was and had lived at home longer. He and his father used to golf on the weekends. Since Earl became ill, he had cared for his father on a daily basis. Bill would need time to recover.

One by one, they trooped to Earl's bedside. Each whispered a few words to the small, still, white-haired figure on the bed. Bill was the last one to go in. He emerged crying. He hugged Lisa, but pointedly not Joan.

"Come on," he said. "We have to make funeral arrangements."

"Bill," Joan tried as the foursome started to walk down the quiet hallway. Her brother ignored her.

"He's upset," Kelly suggested softly. "He'll get over it. Give him time."

Bill whirled. "It's much more than that," he said in a cold, hard voice. Lisa took his arm and tried to get him to move. He fought her off. "Your great idea killed him. And Joan knows what *she* did." He stood glaring. Lisa again tried to get him to leave.

Kelly gave a wan smile. "I can understand you're mad at me, although I believe you're wrong," he said quietly. "But why accuse your sister?"

"Ask her," Bill thundered. His loud voice startled nurses moving through the ICU unit. They stopped. Several heads poked out from rooms.

"Bill, Bill," Lisa urged. She tugged at Bill's arm. Reluctantly, he followed her to the exit. Joan and Kelly waited.

Kelly could feel his pulse racing. He put his arm around Joan's shoulders. "Are you all right?" he asked.

"Yes," she said.

"Do you know what he's talking about?"

She nodded almost imperceptivity. "I'll tell you later," she managed.

They began to walk away slowly. Behind them, two nurses entered Earl's room. In a moment, the hum of the ventilator ceased.

Kelly left his wife alone with her thoughts. He had no idea why Bill was upset with her. He had seen family members lash out at close relatives in such situations. He understood how grief could distort thoughts. Bill would never understand how much Kelly had fought for good standards. He had wanted Earl to be taken care of properly. Clearly, the nurse and the physician assistant had misdiagnosed the problem. But, he asked himself, would the situation have been different if they had recognized the earlier strokes? Earl's brain was damaged either way. No medical intervention could have eliminated the TIAs. Earl was not likely to recover either, certainly would never have enjoyed the same quality of life again. Perhaps better care would have helped, but there was no one to blame. Earl was old and ill. Everyone has a time to go.

The old man left a great legacy. He spent years as a car salesman, a personable, pleasant man who developed a following. His son and daughter had become contributing members of society. He had a lot to be proud of. Now, it was time to say goodbye.

Kelly hoped his wife could recognize that. He could see how distraught she was, sitting next to him, playing with a piece of tissue, dabbing her eyes, and quietly sobbing. Dealing as she did with the elderly through her home-nursing business, she had witnessed this situation repeated many times. She was also strong; she would recover quickly. Still, she seemed very shaken. Her face was wan. Her eyes heavy with tears—even beyond the sadness associated with her father's death.

He hugged her tightly once they got inside the house. She didn't want to let go.

"Pete," she finally said, looking up at him, "that was my nurse and physician assistant." She buried her head in his chest.

"Okay," he started and then stopped. "You sent them to see Earl?"

She nodded. The 911 system operated on a rotating basis, she explained. Her agency was on a list and was contacted for assistance in order. The 911 call from Lisa came in when her agency was next in line, like taxis at the airport. Joan hadn't trained the people. She had expanded and bought several smaller home healthcare businesses in the last year. This was one of them.

"I checked them out. The agency had a good reputation. I thought the people were well educated," she whimpered. "But they didn't even know indigestion from a stroke."

"Don't blame yourself," he consoled her. Blame Thorn, he thought. He's the one who imposed the penny-pinching criteria, the ones Bill blasted him for. The basic concept was good, but sending a nurse and physician assistant worked only if the people who showed up were trained to recognize symptoms. Their job was to perform triage, separating those in desperate need from those with less-serious concerns in situations less obvious than a car crash. If they could not do that, they increased the chance that people needing urgent help would fail to get it.

Kelly was well aware that that was what was happening nationwide. The rising death rates confirmed it. Somehow, he had never expected it to hit home like this.

Joan broke away. "Bill blames me," she said.

"He's blaming everyone," Kelly replied. "Me, too."

Joan slumped on the couch. "I can't check out everyone," she said. "I can't go to every house. I have to rely on what my staff tells me." Kelly sat down next to her.

"Of course," he soothed.

"It's so expensive," she continued, tissue to her eyes. "We're always trying to save money. We should be trying to save lives."

Erik arrived from Baltimore a few minutes later. Diane followed. They consoled each other. Erik, too, was close to his grandfather even after moving away to college and starting a career. He often called him for advice when talking to parents seemed too difficult. All three children spent two weeks almost every summer with their grandparents and were there when grandma had died. Earl often said their presence helped make that awful time more bearable. Moreover, since Bill and Lisa had no children, the trio was Earl's only grandchildren. He doted on them, sending plenty of Christmas presents, remembering birthdays, and attending graduations.

Only later, when on a private walk, did Kelly tell Erik about the nurse and the physician assistant.

Erik listened quietly, as though talking to a client.

"We thought things like this were happening," he said. "We see the statistics, too, but in law there can be coincidences. You have to prove the link, not just guess something's happening."

"It's happening," Kelly said grimly.

They were walking aimlessly through the neighborhood. Tall elm and oak trees lined the street, creating a thinning canopy as the air cooled in preparation for autumn. Many of the trees featured bare limbs. Few birds were about, although an occasional squirrel peered down at them.

"I think Gentry is going to get re-elected easily," Erik said. Kelly nodded. "The Democrats don't seem to have anyone who can beat him." There was nothing to add to that. A bruising series of Democratic primaries had led to the nomination of an avowed liberal—Senator Wayne Brown—from Ohio. His only attribute was his last name, which for some inexplicable reason always attracted a lot of voters in the Buckeye State.

Brown had a narrow constituency and certainly seemed to pose no threat to an incumbent president, even one who had chosen the most unlikely of vice presidents. Thorn had never held elected office before, but, Gentry said, he had been the driving force behind so many of the great programs developed by the administration. As a result, he could not be denied his rightful place among the country's leaders.

There was only token opposition. The Republican delegates knew Gentry was going to win regardless of who shared the ticket. Moreover, Thorn's lack of political experience seemed to curtail any chance he would run for president when Gentry's last term expired. Others with no political experience, such as Dwight Eisenhower, Ulysses Grant, and Zachary Taylor, had run and won the presidency. No one had been elected vice president without serving in some political office before. Thorn, however, Gentry said, was "one of a kind." The country should be proud to have such a man willing to "take up the burden of public life."

Convention delegates didn't hesitate to agree.

At the same time, the move to repeal the Twenty-second Amendment was now rolling along. To most observers, especially media pundits who prided themselves on foresight and analysis, the move was designed to allow Gentry to sit out a term with a caretaker like Thorn, a nonentity, before returning four years later. That possibility had been addressed in an amendment to the bill, specifically allowing Gentry that option. His popularity guaranteed passage. After all, he had a balanced budget with lower taxes and an economy seemingly perking along; he had not started a war nor made any bellicose comments that might start one; even the ongoing war on terrorists seemed finally to be winding down. Gentry had been able to withdraw at least half of the troops scattered all over the globe, with more such maneuvers on the drawing board; and he had charmed most world leaders with his unrefined manners and persistently inept golf game.

Even people opposed to some of his policies personally liked Gentry or "Saint Nick," as some began to call him. Historians were not willing to bless him yet as one of America's foremost presidents, but the public had little doubt. They lapped up stories about his card playing and boisterous behaviors, seeing him as a dear, nonconformist relative with rough edges that everyone adores rather than the nominal architect of the dark, dramatic cultural-changing laws that were evolving.

Both Kelly and Erik agreed there was no way for anyone—Democrat, Independent or from the general public—to overcome that impression.

"Are you staying in office?" Erik finally asked.

"I don't know," his father said. "Thorn will probably dump me anyway." All top officials in the administration had been asked to submit letters of resignation with the president. This was standard procedure so the president would have a free hand choosing his new cabinet. Still, Kelly knew, now that the program bearing his name was in place, Thorn didn't need him.

He felt drained, not just because of Earl's death, but also because of the whole situation. Thorn was going to be vice president, a position that shielded him from administration mistakes while allowing him a free hand. Al Gore had been one of the few vice presidents to handle serious policy decisions, but even that role had not helped him in the 2000 election. That's because, as Kelly knew, few voters recognized that the vice president had anything to do—a view that was usually correct. Now, Thorn could operate in complete isolation from critical comments. After all, Gentry was a lame duck; he'd be an open target for ambitious politicians who could court or attack with ease. Thorn would be ignored, not considered an heir apparent because of his lack of political credentials.

"If you leave, are you going to say anything?" Erik asked.

"Should I?"

Erik nodded. "I would. When else would you get an audience?"

Kelly couldn't argue with that. No one cared what a cabinet member said—especially one who headed a department that attracted little attention in an administration topped by an overwhelming personality. He recalled a treasury chief who attacked George W. Bush's fiscal policies, but that was a one-day wonder. So were comments by James Stockton about

Reagan's "trickle-down" economics. Disgruntled officials were not uncommon and typically passed from the scene with little fanfare or attention.

Moreover, he was not the kind to seek publicity. If anything, Kelly preferred to stay out of any limelight and the glare of media attention. How long could he watch what was happening and not say anything? Could he pretend any more that he could change Thorn's thinking? He knew better than that. He had no real options any more.

"If I go, I won't go quietly," Kelly told Erik.

His son stopped and looked at him. "Thorn will crucify you," he said.

"What can he do?" Kelly asked. "He can't arrest me. We still have the right to express our opinions, don't we?"

Erik nodded. "He can make sure you can't get a job," he said. "Hospitals get a lot of federal money."

Kelly considered that. "I'll retire. Your mother and I have enough set aside. We'll be all right," he said. He didn't say that Joan would have to close down her business or sell it. The link between the Thorn Plan and her success was bound to appear once he left office. Thorn would see to that.

"Not much of a pension," Erik noted. "You haven't been in office long enough."

"We'll move to a deserted island," Kelly said with humor he didn't feel. "That'll keep our expenses down: a hut, coconuts, and an occasional crab."

"You may have to relocate," Erik noted somberly, "but I doubt you can escape Thorn's reach even on a deserted island."

Back home, Joan tearfully reported that her brother would not talk to her. Bill's sorrow had deepened his anger. All Kelly could do was tell her that Bill would calm down eventually and suggest she maintain contact with Lisa.

Kelly stayed home until two days after the funeral. He flew back to Washington ten days before the general election, his mind made up that he would speak out against Thorn and resign.

Instead, he realized that move would have to wait. Thorn had a new idea. This one did not require congressional approval. An executive order allowed doctors to use military personnel in tests conducted by Nucleon. The Department of Health and Human Services would handle responsibility for the process of obtaining soldiers and disseminating results.

Kelly immediately phoned Erik. His son listened to the order somberly.

"That explains it," he said cryptically.

"What?" Kelly asked.

"The timetable for withdrawal of troops has been changed," Erik explained. "The military spokesman made that announcement this morning. Something about increased terrorist activities."

Kelly rubbed his forehead. *What was Thorn up to? Were the decisions related?*

"I'll have to find out what's going on," Kelly said.

Thorn was unavailable.

"Tell him," Kelly grimly informed Thorn's secretary, "that if I don't have a chance to talk to him, I won't be able to implement this directive."

Thorn was in his office fifteen minutes later, sweeping past Watson unannounced and slamming the office door behind him. He stood for a moment, as if deciding what to say, then marched across the carpet. His shoes barely made a sound.

"I would appreciate if you didn't give my secretary orders," he said formally. His voice was clipped and direct; his manner, brusque and cold.

Kelly nodded. "I need questions answered," he said. There was no apology in his tone. "If you don't take calls, I can't do my job."

"What do you *need* to know?"

"Are the soldiers to go to Nucleon or will doctors visit them on the bases?" Kelly began.

Thorn was stiff. "Research will be conducted in the field," he said. "The soldiers are already there."

"Will they be volunteers?" Kelly asked.

"They will be dead," Thorne said. "Researchers are manipulating DNA. We don't need living specimens. We need fresh cadavers. Anything else?"

Kelly shook his head. "No," he said.

"Confine yourself to your work, Dr. Kelly," Thorn snapped. He strode to the door. He looked back. "My condolences on your father-in law."

The door shut loudly.


That evening, Kelly called Erik again and filled him in.

"He's extending the war to get dead bodies for research," Eric decided.

"I don't want to think that," Kelly said. But, he already had.

"Not one commentator, no one, said anything bad after stories appeared today about the use of soldiers as guinea pigs," Erik continued angrily. "Everyone sees this as a way to speed up the research. Soldiers are downright eager to help."

"Do you think they'll be so excited when they find out they have to be dead first?" Kelly asked with equal venom.

Erik was silent for a long time. "Dad, you have to do something. You are in a key position. Try to stall or something."

Kelly nodded to himself. He couldn't resign now. Instead, as if fighting an infection or some disease, he had to confront the situation and deal with it.

From now on, he vowed, Thorn was not going to ride roughshod over anyone anymore.

# CHAPTER 14
# CHANGE IN PLANS

Roused by memories that spiked his emotions, Kelly glanced around the Grand Diplomat lobby. Quietly and efficiently, the Secret Service agents were rechecking identification. In a moment, he was forced to move. The agents simply rounded up anyone in the atrium, including guests, the clerks behind the desks, the bellhops, and the parking valets who were going in and out on a regular basis. The hotel manager, still red-faced, but now looking almost frantic, calmed himself enough to get in line with dour newspaper reporters, bureaucrats in business suits, and women in gowns. They all shuffled along slowly through checkpoints set up by the agents.

Kelly found himself behind a tall woman in a crisp business suit that had been doused with enough perfume to force the evacuation of Lincoln Center. Next to him was a short, balding man who nervously wiped his forehead and stared at the floor as the lines were funneled toward two officious looking agents. Kelly kept steady, moving slowly with his hand over his coat pocket. He didn't want the man next to him to bump into the gun there. He had a permit, so if an agent searched him, he would not be violating any law. He would definitely lose the gun, however, and probably the opportunity to kill Thorn.

He searched faces around him. He didn't recognize anyone, although a few seemed familiar. He had been away from Washington for a year now. A new boatload of people was rapidly seizing spots at the public trough. With the Gentry Administration in its final days, many office holders were resigning. Some would stay, of course, the way, many Reagan holdovers kept their jobs when former Vice President George H. W. Bush succeeded Reagan.

Kelly glanced up at the clock. It was already 1:00 PM. Only two more hours to go. Thorn was punctual; he demanded that in his subordinates. The media had reported his preoccupation with time as though it was an asset. Maybe it was in comparison with Bill Clinton and other presidents who were habitually late. To Kelly, the trait smacked of a rigid attitude and inflexible thinking.

Those in line were mostly quiet, but there was a low hum of voices replacing the music. That had been turned off, too. The atmosphere was as cool and distant as the agents were.

Kelly found himself next in line. He watched as the agent on his side checked paperwork and ran a metal detector over the woman in front of him. The process took only a few seconds. The agent stepped back, stunned perhaps by the overwhelming aroma, and waved the woman on.

He then studied Kelly's face, and took his pass and driver's license. He looked at each carefully, as though he had never seen anything like them before. Kelly waited silently. Beside him, the smaller man brushed past after completing inspection. A quick scan from the metal detector and the second search was over.

"Very good, sir," the agent said crisply. He handed back Kelly's papers.

Kelly took them with a brief smile. He retreated to the side of the entryway. Others who had gone through inspection were not staying, but had gone outside, passing through metal detectors set up by the doors. Kelly paused by the front window. A helicopter zipped by, rattling the glass even at a distance. Several soldiers had taken up positions along the front steps. Everyone looked so tense, arms poised over rifles. Faces were stern, as if they realized that, if Thorn survived this, there would be many more similar situations.

The last president who so divided the voters probably had been Richard Nixon, whose manner and previous campaigns had been calculated only to defeat an opponent, not to please anyone. Thorn was already that kind of polarizing figure. Kelly didn't ask himself how a man like that could get elected. He already knew.

Pausing by the thick front windows, Kelly could see his image reflected in the glass. His hair was turning white and had thinned a little. He did not care about the signs of aging. He knew them well in his patients. What bothered him was his face, which was long and increasingly lined. Maybe the reflection emphasized the incursion age was making in the areas around his eyes and mouth. He shook his head. He looked an awful lot like John Patterson, except his long-time friend had started the aging process a lot sooner.

Security had clearly tightened even after everyone inside the hotel lobby had been checked again. Kelly counted five uniformed D.C. cops now stationed along the walls of the atrium. Arms folded behind them and legs apart, in a sort of military parade rest, they surveyed the room from all directions. The doors to the large conference room were locked. Not even reporters and cameramen with equipment inside were allowed back inside.

The staircase was closed off. The elevators were being monitored. Everyone who stepped out was immediately scanned for weapons.

The hotel manager was now seated behind the front counter, the top of his bald head gleaming under the neon lights. He was staring at the floor. Clerks around him ignored him.

Guests were still checking in. They made it through the gauntlet in front, typically carrying their own bags and worming through security to the front desk. Most talked to the clerks while watching what was going on by the entryway. A few, based on conversations that Kelly overheard, had no idea that President-elect Thorn was coming there. Several said they would have chosen a different hotel, a sentiment that caused the manager to slump even more.

Kelly studied each new arrival with the same intent as the Secret Service agents. Could one of the new guests also be planning to kill Thorn? He looked carefully at faces. The older, chunky man in the brown wool suit didn't look threatening. His tie was askew, and he was breathing heavily from only some mild exertion. *Definitely not a professional athlete,* Kelly thought to himself. *Maybe an accountant or a job applicant, someone who had never held an important position and now, finally, had a scent of a well-paying government post.* The fellow seemed so grateful when a bellhop finally appeared and scurried him off to the elevators.

The woman who came in next did not seem a plausible option either, although her features were hard and cold. Her billowing hair spoke of another era, but her dress was perfect for business. She was either a lobbyist or an attorney. Maybe both, Kelly decided. He had seen too many of that type.

The truth was that anyone or no one could be a killer. What did someone who was planning to pull a trigger look like? From his research, Kelly would say that some of the presidential assassins appeared wild-eyed; others, like Booth, were elegant. Lee Harvey Oswald didn't resemble a parvenu or a madman. He had been casually dressed, maybe a fan on his way to a ballgame. In earlier years, someone with a crazed look might have gotten to the president, joining some receiving line to edge close enough for a fatal shot. In modern times, especially with concern about terrorism, only someone properly dressed and dignified, someone familiar and considered innocuous, could get within shooting distance. That's how Booth managed to kill Lincoln. He was a well-known actor and not out of place in the Ford Theater. The stagehands and other performers ignored him.

Kelly was counting on that same sense of familiarity.

He wanted to be the one to pull the trigger, to stand up for what he knew was right. On the other hand, there was a sense that maybe he could walk away unscathed. Let someone else do the shooting. He could express his shock and hurry home to Joan as if nothing happened.

He gave a wry smile. That would be the easy way, the Patterson approach. He knew it well.

After a few more minutes in the lobby, Kelly decided to return to his room. He simply could not stand for another nearly two hours. Maybe if he were younger. He found it funny to think of his comfort only a short time before he died. What difference did it make? Nevertheless, he walked to the central elevators.

He pressed the up button, feeling eyes bore into his back. The gun in his pocket seemed almost on fire, creating an obvious outline of heat. He stared at the gleaming metal doors, trying to control his trembling.

Finally, the elevator arrived. He walked on slowly. Turning around, he could see the open atrium with the many security officers rushing about. He could watch them through the glass door as the car rose. As the elevator moved away from the lobby, Kelly felt as though he were back in an airplane, looking out the window. His stomach began to churn.

He fled quickly into his room on the seventh floor, closing the door behind him and locking it. Then, almost exhausted, he collapsed on the bed. The gun, he told himself, would have to go. If he waited longer, someone would search him. In fact, he felt caught in pincers. If he had stayed in the lobby, eventually, he was sure to be searched again. The Secret Service would find the gun. When he went back downstairs, he would be checked thoroughly and the agents would locate the gun then. Either way, he was never going to have a chance to use it.

He looked at the weapon. It had not been easy to obtain. A patient was kind enough to make contacts while Kelly pretended to be a collector. Then, he wanted it for protection. Joan felt scared in Washington. He agreed with her, but couldn't picture toting something with a police look. The small, plastic gun seemed ideal, like having a small package of Mace, but with a more lethal impact. He had shot it once at a range. It hardly seemed to produce enough firepower to send a bullet to a nearby target. Now, it didn't matter. Reluctantly, he put the gun back in his suitcase. The police could find it later and wonder.

He took the pen from his pocket. This would have to be his only chance. Would he have time to stab Thorn—assuming he got near enough—and then himself? He didn't know. The idea that he might get this close to fulfilling his goal and not succeed chilled him.

The green pen looked innocuous and worked like a real pen. Kelly clicked it. The tip was sharper than what would typically be expected, but, from even close range, that was hard to tell. Carefully, he returned it to his pocket. One scratch. That's all he needed. Hadn't some Russian been assassinated in England with this stuff strategically placed on the sharp end of an umbrella? He remembered reading something about that. At least he knew the poison worked.

He realized his hands were shaking. He pressed them against the bed. He had operated before, including cases where blood was spurting and death was hovering in the background. This was another medical procedure, nothing more, he told himself. Yet, it would have been so much easier with a gun. Distance was more than yards; it meant a separation from the act of pulling the trigger and Thorn's death. There would be no disguising what was happening with the pen. He would see Thorn's eyes, watch the sweat trickle down his cheek, and taste his fear.

Swallowing hard, Kelly hoped he would be strong enough when the moment came.

And the moment was coming.

He checked the clock by the bed. It was already 1:15. Time was moving forward, slowly but inexorably. He walked to his window and looked out. His room overlooked the parking lot, which had been cleared of cars. Uniformed officers were hurrying about on unknown journeys and striding with complete assurance. In many ways, Kelly felt he was holed up in a fort prior to an attack by some enemy. He could imagine what the front of the hotel looked like.

*What a strange environment to live in,* Kelly thought to himself as he looked around. He was calming down. His strength was returning along with his confidence. It was Washington and he knew its impact on a normal person. That's all it was, he told himself. Not fear. Nothing about living in a small Pennsylvania town could prepare anyone for life in the nation's capitol.

A sharp, ominous knock on a hotel room door startled him. He sat up in bed. He heard the rapping again, this time more urgent and louder. It had a distant sound, as though the pounding was down the hall as opposed to his hotel room door. He got up slowly. Were police searching hotel rooms?

He made a hasty visual survey of his room. Was the gun hidden properly? How about everything that might look suspicious? He shot a furtive glace at his suitcase. It was sitting out on the rack by the bed. He hastily stuffed it under the bed, and then almost tiptoed to the door.

Another rap. It wasn't his door being pummeled.

"Open up," someone barked.

Holding his breath, Kelly slowly squeezed the doorknob. The door clicked loudly as it opened. He peered out. A Secret Service agent was standing across the corridor, hand raised to hit the door again. He turned quickly to see Kelly.

"Is everything all right?" Kelly said in a soft voice.

"Yes, sir," the agent said curtly. "Go back inside."

He waited until Kelly closed the door. Bam! The sound echoed like a cannon shot. The pounding was so loud that a glass sitting on Kelly's dresser rattled. Then, listening carefully, Kelly heard the neighboring door open. Voices were muffled. He couldn't hear what was said. He wondered if guests were being searched in their room or, maybe, someone was being arrested. His heart thumped wildly in his chest.

Calm down, he told himself, staring at a bucolic painting of a farmhouse that hung over his bed. Slowly, he got himself under control. However, he could not blot out a chorus of harsh knocks up and down the corridor. The Secret Service was checking every room.

He pulled his suitcase from under the bed, ruffled through the clothes, and found the gun. He grabbed it, aware of how guilty he would look if the door suddenly opened behind him. Where could he put it? Where wouldn't they look? Permit or no permit, the discovery of the gun could destroy all of his plans before he had a chance. He may be taken away or kept in his room until Thorn had left.

Finally, he shoved it in the back of the closet under the extra blanket. At his height, he could reach there. A shorter man couldn't. Would someone think of that? He didn't know. He stepped back to study the placement. Even there, the small weapon seemed to shout its presence. What else could he do? He didn't know and backed away. He managed to sit down in a chair by the window, all the while straining to hear the sound of approaching footsteps.

Nothing.

Whatever was going on was taking place on the other side of the hallway. He tried to imagine why. Had the Secret Service received a tip about someone on that side of the building? Would the agents handle one side, then the other? That didn't make sense. Why not do both simultaneously?

The whole thing was a puzzle. Kelly tried to focus, but the gun kept advertising its presence. He wished he hadn't brought it. He shuddered. A scotch would be nice, he thought. He would relax, as he did on a plane. He blocked the thought: no alcohol. He was going to be cold sober when Thorn strode into reach. Self-control was more important than dulling his senses.

More doors were banged at the end of the corridor. The sound echoed continually from the opposite side of the hall toward Kelly's room, as if drawn by a magnet. He checked outside again. The parking lot was beginning to fill up, but he saw no unusual activity. What was on the other side, the rooms overlooking the entrance? Was it crowded with cars and people?

That's when Kelly finally realized what was happening in his hallway. He broke into a foolish grin. Of course. The police were making sure that no one could shoot Thorn from one of the rooms. They didn't care about his room, the one with the glorious view of the parking lot. Thorn would be let off in front, emerging from a bulletproof limousine. Only someone with a good view from above would be a threat. *If the Dallas police had been so thorough,* Kelly thought, *President Kennedy would have survived his Texas tour.*

Kelly felt silly. The agents weren't looking for guns. They were taking pre-emptive action.

That also meant they were taking the call about the threat to the life of the president-elect very seriously. The smile faded. There would be a cadre of officers surrounding Thorn, moving as a caterpillar. Thorn would be in a cocoon as he strode like a king through the hotel. He wasn't the kind to shake hands anyway, so that would be no problem for him. He would just march through a human corridor, hemmed in on all sides by people determined to protect him. Kelly's shoulders slumped. How was he going to breach that wall?

He recalled several would-be assassins who had thrust a gun through a crowd, but had their hands hit almost immediately and missed. Despite interference, John Schrank had actually hit Theodore Roosevelt in 1912, but the wound wasn't fatal. On the other hand, Sara Jane Moore missed completely when she tried to kill President Gerald Ford. She was about forty feet away when she shot at Ford. She had little chance through the mass of arms and legs. John Hinckley had the same problem aiming at Reagan.

That was outdoors, however. Thorn would be in a hotel lobby, so Kelly felt he could get closer than Moore managed. Sirhan Sirhan did when he killed Robert Kennedy. The lobby was big, but it still had walls. Moore hadn't been able to get any nearer to Ford because of crowds and security. Kelly would be expected to be in the front row. He was a VIP, after all. Nevertheless, wedged tightly, the pen clasped snugly in his hand, any stabbing would be iffy at best. Spectators would be looking at Thorn, but someone might see him take the pen in hand. Kelly expected to die, but only with Thorn for company. He definitely wasn't going to Valhalla alone.

How could he get close enough to Thorn to succeed? Kelly sat down on the bed. All of his careful planning seemed wasted. He would have to re-think the whole process.

That warning really scared the cops. He damned the person who called in the threat. It was probably just some nut. Thorn was popular enough to be elected easily, although his personality clearly had a dark edge that alienated some people. He avoided most problems simply by not campaigning much, emulating, he said, the "front porch" campaigns of McKinley and other early presidents. Who thought he might be in danger? Nevertheless, the security crackdown was undermining everything.

In a few minutes, the ruckus caused by the Secret Service agents outside his room ceased. Silence filtered through the hallway. Calm again, Kelly lay back on the bed. He let his thoughts cool. He glanced over at the clock. Only an hour. Sixty minutes. That did not seem like much time. Somehow, the long wait to this point had been condensed seemingly into a handful of seconds. He could hear the clock ticking. His pulse seemed to match it.

He was glad to have redone his will. Watterson had been

surprised when he called. Erik's impending marriage had convinced Joan that their will needed updating. Diane had started seeing someone, too, although she was focused on picking up her diploma before donning a wedding ring. In addition, Joan's burgeoning income had also increased investments. As a result, Kelly and his wife had met with the attorney a year earlier to update everything. The process was brief, orderly. Then, suddenly, Kelly was dropping by again. Alone.

"Is something wrong?" Watterson asked. He seemed to be looking for a hint of some illness.

Kelly shook his head. "A premonition," he said.

Watterson managed a shrug. Kelly was not the type to act impulsively on a hunch. But, if he wanted to redo the will for whatever reason, he could. He did not pry. The two men had known each other too long for that. Like many of the prominent figures in the community, they had gone to the same schools, had the same teachers, and, in many ways, shared the same experiences despite minor differences in age. As a result, they communicated well even in silence.

The process didn't take long. Kelly only wanted to make sure that the estate was shielded from any potential lawsuit. He didn't explain why. At that point, with the elections still months away, he was already considering assassination. Thorn had to be elected first. Considering American politics, that wasn't a certainty, only a strong possibility.

Nevertheless, in his thorough manner, Kelly tried to conjure up any possible contingency. One bothered him. He could imagine a Secret Service agent or bystander being hit in the crossfire and suing his estate. Joan would have enough problems without that. Of course, he didn't know if a lawsuit could happen, but couldn't imagine seeking legal advice to find out. What would any attorney tell him? Don't shoot? Kelly couldn't even picture a hypothetical situation he could raise to get a real answer. Better to erase that concern, even if it weren't real.

The solution was easy, even if the explanation wasn't.

Watterson didn't probe beyond learning about the need to protect Joan from the crushing impact of a potential lawsuit. To do that, he simply transferred all of the family assets into Joan's name. Kelly had to sign many forms for the house, bank accounts, and cars. In a few minutes, Kelly owned nothing. In some ways, he felt as though he had disappeared.

How ironic, he thought. In a few months, he could be as infamous as John Wilkes Booth or Lee Harvey Oswald and, yet, legally, he ceased to exist.

He hoped Joan would understand. She was not to know until later, he cautioned the attorney. Watterson didn't argue about that either. Clients had reasons. He wondered if the marriage was having problems. After all, according to local gossip, the two had separated briefly. Nevertheless, he kept the conjectures to himself.

Kelly didn't need to be asked to recognize the question in Watterson's eyes. The attorney had no idea how close he and Joan were now. Except for a brief hiccup, they had been that way almost from the beginning.

When they met, Kelly was still working on his surgical internship, a diabolical training procedure that exchanges sleep for fitful naps on any available flat space and turns brains into mush. He had little time for women. Not yet finished with her nursing degree, Joan, too, hesitated to take any beau seriously.

The conflicting intentions combined with strong feelings to create the usual series of breakups and reunions.

In a nostalgic mood as he lay on his bed in the Grand Diplomat, Kelly pulled out his wallet. It contained a small packet of photos: Erik was there in his guise as a high school senior, with a silly grin and the annoying, parentally condemned stud through his eyebrow. Diane was represented as a college freshman, all business-like with her chin thrust out in firm determination and dark eyes burning through the camera. Rachel didn't like her newer photos and refused to let her father have a recent one. She was still in eighth grade then, ever youthful with ponytails and a wicked grin that implied something naughty was about to take place.

He didn't have many pictures of Joan. They had a formal portrait taken at their 25th anniversary. A copy of that picture was the only one of her in his wallet. He looked at it fondly. She looked so elegant in that beautiful dress she had bought for a night of dinner and dancing at the party the children arranged.

They had endured as a couple despite everything, even the chaotic beginning.

No wedding date had been set. They had decided to marry, but in some distant future. Then came the chance for Kelly to work in the emergency room at St. Michael's. He couldn't refuse. However, Joan had her own apartment; Kelly was still staying with his parents, but he had his own furniture. Joan had a cat; he owned a dog. She also had a decent job working in a doctor's office.

They spent a weekend discussing what to do. In many ways, the decision seemed inevitable. Monday, they filed for the marriage license and completed blood tests. Tuesday, the parents were told. His mother had something of a conniption, but pulled herself together long enough to plan something excessively extravagant. The limited timetable quickly undercut her preparation to her eternal dismay. Years later, she was still reminding Joan of what festivities she missed out on had the affair gone as conceived.

Joan's parents were nonplussed. The father was a car salesman; the mother, a teacher. They were delighted that their daughter had bagged a doctor. Joan's brother was happy for her, but being ten years younger, was only sorting out his own jangled emotions and not ready to acknowledge his sister's. He did take the dog. Her parents accepted the cat.

Wednesday, the couple called friends and family. No invitations went out. On Thursday, Kelly and his instant fiancée drove to Allentown to find an apartment. Friday, they drove back. Saturday, they were married by a justice of peace in the living room of the Kelly home. The justice, a family friend, tossed down too many celebratory drinks and ended up forgetting to file the marriage license. They found out three weeks later when called by a studious city clerk who read the request for a license, but found no evidence that the ceremony had taken place. They honeymooned Saturday night amid boxes ready to be moved, arduously loaded up a U-Haul on Sunday, and moved to the new apartment. Monday, Kelly reported to work. Their eventual honeymoon to Cape Cod would have to wait.

Joan first found a job as a nurse at a retirement center, then, after five years, opened her own homecare business.

Kelly smiled at the picture in his hand. What had she seen in him? She told him once that he was "thoughtful." What did that mean? He asked. "You think about things," she explained. "You don't always respond quickly, but you are able to focus your thoughts on some topic. Then, finally, you come up with an answer. All the doctors I've met always acted so quickly. You're different."

He wondered if that were good or bad, but was so glad she liked that trait. He had met many women—an obvious reality in his line of work—but none like Joan. She was mentally strong with a clear sense of determination. Diane got that part of her personality from her mother. Rachel, like Joan, had a foolish side, a willingness to play a practical joke occasionally or to embellish a story about some situation that turned what should be a serious moment into a hilarious one. She was also able to face something straight on and make the correct decision. Erik inherited that aspect.

No one else, Kelly was sure, could endure having a husband who killed the president.

How had other families reacted? He didn't know. Probably not well. For example, Schrank, the man who wounded Teddy Roosevelt, ended up in jail for decades and was never visited by a single person in all that time. Most of the others, like Guiteau and Booth, didn't survive long enough for their families to show much interest. Oswald's wife became something of a celebrity, but his family never got involved. Moore was released after thirty years in prison, but she was part of the Charles Manson gang of killers. Most of them remained in jail and were never likely to hold a family reunion.

Of all the people who shot at presidents, John Hinckley, who nearly killed Reagan, seemed to be the only one to maintain any kind of family tie. He enjoyed supervised meetings with his parents after being found insane at his trial. Kelly was thankful his parents were dead and wouldn't be faced with such a situation.

Joan was another matter. What would Joan do? Mourn, of course. Ask questions. Yes. But, she'd get on with her life. She'd console their children. Erik should tell her the truth. He definitely would appreciate what happened and why, even if he would reject his father's course.

Should he leave some kind of note? Kelly considered that. He wasn't a writer—nor did he really think he could spell out exactly how he felt. Patterson should be doing that for him. He was always penning mash notes or sending letters to the editor. His political interests were piqued by responses to some of his more outlandish letters. He had a way of massaging sentences. Kelly was just hopeful someone could read his medical scrawl. No, he had decided long before, there would be no suicide note.

He checked the clock. Only forty-five minutes. When should he go downstairs? Not yet. There was no point standing there, getting more anxious.

How odd, he thought. He could take a scalpel and perform an emergency procedure without a second thought. Yet, this simple operation, merely sticking a pen into a cancer, was causing such emotional turmoil. He thought that by now, given all that had happened, he could better control his feelings.

They had gotten him in a lot of trouble before.

# CHAPTER 15
# UNDERCOVER

Kelly had been so angry and upset after realizing what Thorn was doing. The man had no scruples of any kind, no moral compass, no ethical compass, Kelly decided. He had to be stopped. The question was how.

He pulled Watson into his office. She was always full of insider gossip—who was dating whom; who was using drugs; who had signed off on some bill because of under-the-table lobbyist gifts; who was hoping the truth about his immoral activities didn't emerge before the next election; who was dumber than a rock; and the like—but she was no help with Thorn. The man worked long hours and then went home alone, she said. He was not married, but had been seen with Hollywood starlets enough to dispel any gay rumors. He didn't drink, didn't use drugs as far as anyone knew, and didn't accept bribes. His campaign had raised plenty of money and spent less, another sign of frugality Thorn mentioned repeatedly during his vice presidential campaign. He did bet on horses occasionally, but only modestly. That diversion had stopped, however, when Gentry added him to the national ticket. Gentry's poker games were considered frivolous, but the public may not as readily accept more organized gambling. Betting on horses smacked of elitism, and Gentry promoted himself as the "people's president." If Thorn continued putting down two-dollar bets, he did so with discretion.

"There's got to be something," Kelly said.

His secretary cocked an eye at him. "Why? Do you want his job?" she asked mischievously.

Kelly laughed lightly. "Hardly," he said. "I want to stop him. His schemes are hurting millions of people and destroying this country."

Watson shook her head. "That's what *you* think," she said. "He doesn't think that. He thinks he's doing something good for America. Working through Gentry, he's reduced government spending, changed medical treatment, reduced our involvement in wars, and made things better."

"Are you on his side?" Kelly barked.

Watson stood up. "There is no side," she said calmly. "You just have a different perspective."

"There are ethical considerations," Kelly insisted.

"Depends on who decides on the standards," Watson replied. She had drawn herself up like a battleship about to defend itself against boarders.

Kelly stared at her. "He's wrong," he said through clenched lips.

"Someone always is," Watson noted. She marched back to her desk.

He needed several minutes to calm down. Watson was not going to be any help. She had been spoiled by working for the government. Her ethical compass no longer pointed anywhere, he decided.

Erik was next on Kelly's short list to contact. Unlike Watson, his son shared the same concerns with him. Their conversation on the phone was brief. Convinced phone lines were tapped, Kelly asked about a non-existent engagement dinner. Erik understood. His father wanted to meet. He said it was three days from then. Kelly said he could make it. He notified the president in writing that he would be leaving for Baltimore. Gentry didn't respond. He never did. Once Kelly was unable to help his golf game, the president seemed to forget about his existence. Thorn chaired the cabinet meetings anyway. Gentry would listen a few minutes and then nod off. Awake or asleep, he never seemed to miss anything.

Kelly and Erik chose a quiet restaurant in Baltimore's rebuilt Inner Harbor area.

"My boss thinks Thorn has hidden agendas," Erik noted as they sipped wine in a quiet corner of a Japanese restaurant.

"You could say that about any politician, Erik," Kelly replied. "In this case, however, it's true. I don't like Thorn *and* I don't trust him. I'm not in his inner circle, but I'm beginning to see where he's going. It's a left turn from sanity."

Erik nodded. "There's just something about the man that gives me the willies," he agreed.

"You don't know half of it," Kelly said, lowering his voice. There was not a big crowd at Edo Sushi, but he didn't want anyone overhearing. He had to wait as the waiter showed up with a platter of different sushi they had ordered, almost at random: two California Rolls, something called a Boston Roll, an eel and avocado combination that stretched over the platter, a vegetable roll, and a Florida Roll with lobster inside.

As they ate—Kelly had mastered chopsticks, but Erik used his fingers—Kelly described his frustration and his hopes to do something.

"What?" Erik asked.

"I don't care," Kelly muttered. "Somehow, Thorn has to be knocked off his pedestal. He can't be allowed to continue."

160

Startled by the venom, Erik almost dropped a sushi into his mixture of soy sauce and wasabi. "What are you going to do, shoot him?"

Kelly shook his head. That was a last resort. "I figure there must be something in his files or his computer, something so incriminating that he would be forced to resign," he said.

"How are you going to find out?"

Kelly shrugged. "What if someone happened to check his files while he wasn't there?' he asked innocently.

Erik shook his head. "You are talking about something like the Nixon plumbers. They broke into the Watergate and ended up destroying the presidency. Besides, I think he's too clever to keep something incriminating on hand. From what I heard, there's nothing anyway. He isn't Hoover. There are no blackmail files."

"Are you sure?" Kelly asked.

"We'd know," Eric assured him. "That's not something anyone could keep quiet."

Kelly finished the last Boston Roll, which, apparently, was sweet potato inside a rice cocoon and wrapped in nori.

"I was thinking more about planting something rather than exposing it," he finally proposed.

He had been trying to develop a plan since talking with Watson. As Erik knew, Thorn was definitely too smart to keep anything potentially dangerous in his files or in any way linked to him. He wouldn't be caught in the act either. He'd have buffers. Besides, if Watson didn't know of anything, maybe Thorn was avoiding anything that could undermine his position. He wasn't Eliot Spitzer, the once fast-rising New York governor whose political career was eventually torpedoed by the discovery he had hired expensive call girls. Thorn would not do anything like that. His pleasure was screwing people, but legally.

However, Kelly concluded, there's no reason not to create some kind of paper trail leading to something particularly damaging. For example, he told Erik, Americans would be outraged to know the war continued because of the need for cadavers. However, Erik countered, Thorn was shielded by the reporting of increased insurgency. Naturally, more soldiers would die.

What if a letter from Nucleon could be found that outlined the need for bodies and then suggested that Thorn continued to delay troop pullouts until the need was met? Kelly offered. That would be explosive and damning. Or maybe something from a drug company that called on Thorn to funnel money its way in return for political support—and dated just before the Thorn Plan announcement?

It wouldn't have to be planted in Thorn's file, Kelly noted, only made available to the media.

Erik sniffed. Someone would have to forge a letter like that.

Kelly insisted it wouldn't be difficult to pull off something similar. He needed appropriate letterhead, Thorn's signature, and a willing accomplice in the vice president's office to produce a copy. The first two on the list were already in place. Thorn had forwarded plenty of letters from the pharmaceutical companies and Nucleon. Besides, Kelly had written them enough times with copies forwarded to Thorn. Any of them could be easily revised. Maybe Watson could handle placing the letter in the appropriate file or knew someone who could.

The rest would be up to the media and an outraged public. He would also need someone to write it, someone devious enough and outraged enough to join willingly.

Kelly said he already knew someone with that skill and animosity. John Patterson. Unfortunately, he noted, some of his anger was directed at him personally. However, Kelly hoped his friend would reconcile his differences for such an important cause, he explained to Erik.

"Don't count me in," Erik said. "I prefer to rely on the courts."

"Fine," Kelly snapped and almost immediately regretted his reaction after seeing Erik wince. He didn't mean to sound so upset, but the legal system had been no help so far; neither had the media. Thorn had to be confronted. Who knew what idea he'd come up with next?

"Dad," Erik said, looking at his father intently. "Do not do anything that will get you in trouble. You'll destroy your career and yourself. And, you'll boost Thorn at the same time."

Kelly leaned back. He deliberately wiped his lips with a napkin. "I know what I'm doing," he said. "I don't want to jeopardize my career, but I would sacrifice everything to end this man's reign."

Erik shook his head.

"Somehow," Kelly continued slowly and intently, "Thorn has to be brought down. He's having soldiers killed so he'll have enough bodies for experiments. Millions of elderly are dying because his program goes too far in undermining their health care. God knows what monstrosity Nucleon is going to come up with. He can't be allowed to continue."

Erik's face hardened.

"Give the information to your favorite reporter. Let the media handle this. Or resign and tell the world why. Raise the issue." His eyes narrowed. "But don't lower yourself to his level with some mean-spirited scheme. Who will get hurt then? Only you."

Kelly held up a hand. "I think we'd better stop," he said.

"Just don't tell me whatever you decide to do," Erik said.

"How's Julie?" Kelly asked pleasantly.

Erik stared at him for a long time.


Late the next morning, still in Baltimore, Kelly dialed Patterson's cell phone. No one answered, so he left a halting message. That afternoon, he called the house. Terri answered.

She sounded pleasant and even happy to hear from him. John wasn't around, she said. He was doing some consulting work with a local consortium of physician assistant training schools.

"Tell him that the knife has been cleaned and ready for someone else," Kelly suggested. "It's his turn to use it."

Terri dutifully wrote down the message.

Patterson still didn't call back, so Kelly tried again the next day. Still, no response. A week later, he flew directly to Denver. His stomach was churning by the time the plane landed, but airsickness was only part of the problem.

Initially, he had focused on what Erik and his secretary Katie Watson had said. They didn't understand, he told himself. They were no different from the occasional nurse or doctor who challenged him about a diagnosis. After a while, they realized he was right. Erik and Katie would realize it too. Even if they didn't, it wouldn't matter. He didn't need to convince them of anything. He didn't need to convince anyone.

Too often, people refused to act before it was too late. The FBI knew terrorists were going to attack American targets before September 11, 2001, but didn't do anything. The Western powers knew Hitler would not be appeased and ended up with far worse problems during World War II. Similar examples, he knew, littered world history. He would not hesitate. Let history judge him. Eventually, people would see the truth.

Having satisfied himself, Kelly turned his thoughts to his second problem: He had no idea how Patterson would react. Would he understand? The fact that he had not called back indicated he was still upset. Could that anger be redirected? Would Patterson even talk to him? Kelly found that question more upsetting than anything Erik or Katie could possibly say.

He would have preferred to arrive quietly in Denver and essentially sneak up on Patterson. There would be no way that his old friend would slam the door or refuse to talk to him. However, he was an important government official. He could not travel anonymously.

Several reporters met him, responding to his office's news release. While riding cross-country, Kelly had redirected his thoughts away from Patterson by preparing a plausible explanation for his visit. The pilot Thorn Plan program had been conducted there close to eight years earlier, and he had decided to check on the progress. No other community offered that kind of long-term statistics. No, he was not there because of negative reports from the Denver area. Everything so far had been glowing. This was just a fact-finding mission. It had been intended as a surprise so he could get an uninhibited view of any progress.

He watched reporters dutifully take their electronic notes, eyeing with some amusement the two older reporters who still had a pen and paper and recorded the information in cryptic shorthand. He wondered which account would be more accurate: the ones who used a Palm Pilot or those who relied on more traditional recording methods.

His comments and answers to questions became sound bites for radio reporters while television made him walk down the ramp several times and then recorded the few comments made at the impromptu airport media conference. He endured it all in a relaxed manner. The real tension would come later.

The taxi driver knew the area. Once again, Kelly watched as the car climbed toward the blue sky and hurtled past other homes toward the one that seemed to teeter on a mountain ledge.

He saw the Mercedes in the driveway. Patterson had a new roadster. Wealth had some privileges, he thought.

He got out at the end of the driveway and hiked up toward the front door. The walk was longer than he had remembered from years ago and the air thinner. His shoes crunched across the gravel, ending any chance of an unobtrusive arrival. Finally, tired and panting, he paused by the front porch and rested a moment with his hand on the lintel.

The front door opened. Patterson stood there, his face a silhouette created by the screen and the shadow of the heavy wooden door.

Kelly straightened. "I was just checking to see if the house had fallen off the mountainside yet," he said.

"In Arab countries," Patterson replied, "there's a custom that anyone who comes to your tent has to be allowed to enter in peace—even an enemy." He paused. "But, I'm not an Arab." He started to close the door.

Kelly weakly held up a hand. "And I'm not your enemy," he said.

Patterson looked at him. His eyes seemed to mist over. "I guess not," he said quietly. He came outside and deliberately closed the door behind him with a solid thump. "I am still mad at myself for throwing everything away. You are a convenient target." He took Kelly's arm. "You are getting too frail for this, old man," he said.

"I'll be all right," Kelly insisted, as John led him onto the immense front deck, to the chair he had sat in for the first time so many years before. Once again, he almost had his breath taken away a second time by the sheer beauty of the view. "This is better than I remember," he finally said.

"It never gets old," Patterson said.

"We do," Kelly answered. "We're getting far too old for this kind of shit."

Patterson managed a smile. "What's eating you, Pete? Need to go to another sewage convention?"

Kelly nodded. "The garbage keeps rising," he said wearily.

Slowly, he filled Patterson in on the reason for the visit. Patterson listened. "Want a drink?" he asked when Kelly finished.

Kelly nodded. "Just water." He was too lightheaded already for anything alcoholic. How could anyone breathe here? He didn't recall struggling for breath on that initial visit, but he was in his mid-fifties now. The lungs just didn't have the capacity anymore. His heart didn't feel that strong either.

Patterson returned with a large tumbler filled with ice water and a bottle of beer. Kelly sipped. He started to feel better.

"When I first saw you," he said, "I was going to leave you outside. Then, I couldn't. I knew that you hadn't asked me to quit. I quit on my own. I was mad at Thorn—mad at myself for lacking the backbone to stand up to him. You have that. I never did. I just liked the glitter, the excitement of public life. Hell, I wouldn't have cared what program I fronted as long as I was the one getting all the attention."

"Then you're in?" Kelly probed. "You'll help me get rid of him?"

Patterson took a long pull on the bottle. "When I was younger," he said, "I would have jumped in feet first. This would have been a great opportunity. I would have loved every minute of it."

"Now?"

"Pete," Patterson said, "I've made a great discovery." He finished the beer. "I like quiet. I like to sit here and commune with nature. I like to cuddle with Terri and play with the dogs. I don't care if I ever see or hear from a reporter ever again."

Kelly lay back in his chair. The glass felt so cold in his hand that he had to put it down on the wooden deck. Suddenly, the water did not taste good. The afternoon was getting cloudy. "Don't you want to help me?" He asked plaintively. "We're talking about a man who could undermine everything you and I believe in."

Patterson shook his head. "No, I never believed in anything," he admitted. "This country survived Ronald Reagan. It survived George Bush. It'll survive Joseph Thorn. This isn't my battle anymore." He gave a wan smile. "'Home is the sailor home from the sea, and the hunter home from the hill,'" he recited.

Kelly studied his friend. Patterson looked so calm. The lines that furrowed his face were still there, but they had softened. He looked younger and healthier. Glancing to the right, Kelly could see a pile of firewood. That was one way Patterson was keeping himself fit. Walking down the driveway to get his mail had to be another.

"I can't change your mind?" Kelly asked.

Smiling, Patterson shook his head. "I won't even watch the news to find out what happened." He stood up and offered a hand. "Need a ride?"

"No," Kelly said. "I don't want to take you away from here." He used his cell phone to dial the taxi company.

Patterson shrugged. "I really didn't want to leave anyway." He pointed toward a crag. "There's a mother bald eagle up there with two chicks in her aerie." He looked down the side of the mountain. "I saw a family of mule deer moving across the trail below us. I even think I saw a couple of white pelicans flying nearby. They're rare out here." His voice filled with excitement. "Do you know that there are some 113 sport-game species in this state? If you sit right here on the porch, many of them go by. No mountain lions. They're too smart to go into a neighborhood like this, but elk sometimes wander around."

Kelly listened. His friend sounded like he did when expounding on the size of Denver or on the capitol. But, Patterson wasn't the same. What they once had was gone—all that remained were memories.

The taxi inched up the driveway, spitting white stones to the side.

Kelly shook Patterson's hand. "Call me if you need help," Patterson said. "I'm still good for a few things."

Kelly nodded. His mind was elsewhere: Somehow, he was going to have to bag Thorn. Patterson could talk about elk, but Kelly was going for bigger game. And, apparently, he was going to have to do it alone.

# CHAPTER 16
# LOST IN PARADISE

The only question was how to do it. Whatever scheme he developed had to work. There wouldn't be a second chance. The forged letter was intriguing, but the more Kelly mulled it over, the less plausible it sounded. DeFebbo of Johnson & Johnson and Sparber from Pfizer, just to name two, were not going to be cowed by a letter like that. They would deny ever sending it, demand their files be checked, and defuse the whole situation.

Kelly wished Patterson were working with him. He'd come up with some clever idea to undermine Thorn. Watson would have, too, the same way she dethroned Rosario.

As always, Kelly's first approach was to research. What had brought down vice presidents in the past? John C. Calhoun had resigned, but only because of a disagreement over states' rights with President Andrew Jackson. That argument had long since dissipated. Henry Wallace had lost his position under Franklin Roosevelt because of his outspoken views on outlandish subjects. That couldn't happen to Thorn either. Gentry wouldn't send him packing. Gentry would be lost without Thorn.

The best model was Spiro T. Agnew, who resigned as vice president to avoid going to jail after admitting to accepting bribes while in the White House. *That was a possibility,* Kelly thought. *Now, who could bribe Thorn? Would he accept a bribe?*

As Kelly pondered those questions, life intruded and shifted his focus. For starters, Erik and Julie finally got married. The wedding, held in Baltimore, was a festive occasion. Rachel overdid the champagne and spent much of the evening, bottle in hand, alternately sipping and pouring some into the empty glasses of friends. Diane finally took her back to the hotel.

Kelly stayed in the background during the reception. He and his son had not talked much since their Baltimore dinner meeting, although Kelly continued to funnel information to the ACLU regarding possible human rights violations with all the governmental cost-reduction medical plans.

The organization had achieved only limited success in the courts. One small victory had made the DNA cards optional, but only until the individual decided to procreate, then it was a requirement. Nevertheless, most people opted to get one. Not only did the government underwrite the cost—it had a secondary value of computerizing almost everyone in the country, helping both security and law enforcement—but comparisons turned into something of a parlor game. Participants, particularly teens, found they could mix and match, pairing up in cyberspace.

At the same time, doctors found making a diagnosis much easier. A patient whose card indicated a marker for a particular disease could be checked for that ailment first. In many cases, according to the AMA, diseases were detected early enough to introduce treatments in preliminary stages. In some cases, diseases previously thought unstoppable had been restrained, sent into remission, or even cured.

While social libertarians protested the decision not to provide government-funded care to disabled children whose parents had dangerous markers on their gene card, arguing that the laws denied equal protection, the Supreme Court disagreed. Justices pointed to the tobacco rulings as precedent. In those cases, long-time smokers received compensation if they began the noxious habit before the health issues were abundantly clear. However, once cigarettes carried warning labels, smokers used the products at their own risk, the justices ruled. That was true in this case as well. Chief Justice Allan Pietro, who had been named to office by Gentry, ruled that the government had taken every precaution to alert parents, and if they still chose to conceive a child, then the parents were responsible for any subsequent medical costs related to the marked DNA. Of course, parents were not liable should a child arrive with a disability or illness not indicated by their gene card.

That was small comfort to many people who found they could not afford the risk. It also didn't sit well with ardent Catholics, who preferred to leave birth to God and not turn it into a kind of Russian roulette game where only the healthy could give birth. Bishops thundered in pulpits; priests echoed their outrage. Parishioners yawned and checked their gene cards.

On the other hand, the falling birthrate cheered Zero Population Growth people and, surprisingly, pro-life groups. They saw the ruling as a way to reduce unwanted pregnancies and, therefore, abortions. At the same time, child shelters and adoption agencies reported an upsurge in interest as couples who wanted to start families but were deterred by their DNA problems turned to alternatives.

Overall, based on polls, the majority of Americans supported the Kelly Program, the DNA cards (now commonly known as "Dards") and the attached regulations regarding federal assistance.

Buoyed by the surveys, Gentry issued periodic reports, touting the success of this "great leap forward into the brave new world of medicine," as he famously crowed on more than one occasion.

Meanwhile, the Twenty-eighth Amendment to the Constitution began to roll through the states. Republican majorities made passage easy. Two years before the end of Gentry's last term, the Twenty-second Amendment was repealed. A president was no longer limited to eight years in office. Kelly thought the change should have earned a lot of coverage. After all, constitutional amendments were rare. The last one had limited congressional pay raises until after the next election and had been approved in 1992. More ballyhooed proposals, such as the Equal Rights Amendment, got far more attention, but were not ratified. The new one, however, got limited notice in or out of the media and was voted in with little fanfare. The *New York Times* reported the approval by the thirty-eighth state (Ohio) in a small paragraph as part of its national roundup.

Gentry briefly mentioned the passage of the amendment in his State of the Union address the next year, congratulating the American people for the wisdom to erase a law that prevented "the best and the brightest" from remaining in office.

He was getting too old for such an effort, Gentry continued. His goal now was to retire, put his feet up, and enjoy the comforts accrued from a job well done. A man like Vice President Thorn, however, might just be the perfect man to retain power far into the future.

Kelly noted that everyone in Congress applauded. He could not. Finally, he had accumulated enough statistics to prove that Thorn's policies were undermining the health of the elderly. The government was saving billions on Medicare and Medicaid, while older Americans were being systematically under-diagnosed and kept home to die. Even in communities with dedicated doctors, nurse practitioners, and physician assistants, the rate of death had risen rapidly. The policies governing treatment of the elderly, which Thorn had initially proposed and had been written into legal terms by Kevin Delacourt—now the vice president's special assistant and legal counsel—confounded the most sincere efforts to provide quality care.

Yet, there was no outrage. Those dying were old and often infirm. Their deaths came as no surprise, Kelly noted as he grimly sent the figures on to the ACLU. Some of the reports even made the media, but had no impact. The rise in deaths of individuals eighty years old and over was attributed to stress, overmedication, under-medication, lack of medication, limited exercise, or too much reliance on fast food—depending on the source.

The rise in military deaths sparked some concern, albeit limited public reaction. Increased insurgency, as expected, provided a suitable explanation why more soldiers were dying, overshadowing any concern about the need for more corpses to test.

Kelly read each rationalization with disgust, saw each issue disappear as though sinking beneath placid waters, and groaned as each new revelation dissipated like a mirage in the desert. He did what he could to keep his concerns in the forefront. As secretary of the agency that oversaw American health, Kelly continually had his aides send out essays about making good health decisions, what families should do during a health emergency and the like. Some were published. Most were not. Fewer were heeded.

He couldn't resign and speak out. At least his official pronouncements were looked at by the media. As a private doctor, he knew that no one would even open his e-mail or ask for his opinion. Grimly, sadly, he stayed in office.

Meanwhile, more family problems absorbed Kelly's attention. Erik had declined to get a DNA card. Julie, on the other hand, did not hesitate. Nevertheless, when they decided to start a family, they were required to bring their cards in for a medical evaluation.

Erik asked his father to intervene, but Kelly could not. Specialized clinics had been set up—both by public companies as well as by the government—to aid in gene therapy and counseling. Erik and his wife had to visit one of them. There, over his objections, Erik had to supply a sample for testing. The orderly collecting it was shocked by his reluctance.

"Don't you want to know if your child could be handicapped," she asked.

"Even criminals have the right to refuse to give samples of DNA without a court order," Erik informed her.

The orderly simply shook her head and took the sample from the inside of his mouth.

"I felt defiled," Erik told his mother.

"Thank God I never had to do that," Joan told him.

As an attorney, Erik knew full well that he could refuse to provide the sample. On the other hand, he was also aware that state laws now required DNA testing before a marriage license could be issued. That state was well known for liberal marriage laws—no blood test had been required earlier, two-day waiting period only after applying for a marriage license and no residency requirement—but on this subject, Maryland had become rigid. Virtually all other states had followed suit. Even Las Vegas and Reno walk-in marriage chapels were obligated to have Dards checked prior to the ceremony. Many now had a doctor available to conduct the evaluation. With technology available for rapid comparison and heavy fines for misdiagnosis, the results were consistently accurate.

Any couple could still get married, regardless of the Dard information. "This is a free country," Gentry insisted in discussing the issue. "You can marry whoever you want. You just may not want to have children."

He cited numerous statistics showing that more couples than ever were not having children after Dards came into existence. "As always," he boasted, "the Gentry Administration is simply building on what the American people have already decided to do."

Amid the social tranquility, Kelly continued to run his mammoth department. He discovered quickly that his role was merely to help set procedures. Veteran civil servants actually did the work. As a result, until late in his second term, he had few problems. He made speeches, visited new hospitals, made sure annual statistics were gathered on the health and welfare of Americans, and issued reports. A survey of his constituents showed that more than nine of every ten citizens did not know his name. He was in good company: few voters could name any member of Gentry's cabinet.

Kelly went to cabinet meetings, but avoided Thorn. He never saw the president in private, shunned social gatherings where Thorn might appear, and found excuses to return home frequently. Joan did not like Washington and preferred to remain in a familiar setting while keeping her business growing.

Erik called him shortly after Thorn announced his candidacy for the presidency. He was one of four Republicans planning to run; the other three were considered long shots at best. One, a Libertarian at heart, wanted to put natural sites—such as lakes—up for sale to the highest bidder. Another called for comprehensive bombing in Iraq and attacks on Syria and Iran. The other candidate would be eliminated even before the first primary.

At least eight Democrats were already battling each other for media coverage and public attention. None seemed a threat to Thorn, according to columnists, who labeled them the "eight dwarfs."

For Kelly, the idea that Thorn could become president was a nightmare. However, he was not prepared to act. In fact, he saw little he could do except grimace and surreptitiously distribute the latest statistics to Erik.

When Erik phoned, he was feeling depressed. Erik did not help his mood.

"Dad, you have to do something," Erik said, almost shrilly. Kelly was not used to hearing him sound so distraught.

"About what?" Kelly asked without much enthusiasm. He could tell Erik wanted a change in public policy and none was going to be forthcoming. If anything, Thorn was demanding tighter regulations to reduce childbirth further. The United States was now the third most-populous country in the world, straining water and food supplies, not to mention adding pressure on natural resources. Americans would need to conserve and to get by with less. Kelly was in no position to ease regulations.

"Do you want grandchildren?" Erik asked.

"Of course," Kelly replied, hoping that—despite Erik's militant tone—he was going to say Julie was pregnant.

"As you know, I have a Dard," Erik continued, "but I refused to look at the results until Julie and I decided to have children." He paused. "Dad, I have a marker for a Down's syndrome baby."

Kelly sat up in his chair. A child with Down's syndrome had one extra chromosome. It was one of the easier conditions to detect during DNA testing. The syndrome was characterized by mental retardation, a broad, flat face, a small head and ears, and other deformities. Once the second most common birth defect, the incidence had virtually disappeared in the year that the Kelly Program was in place.

"What do you want me to do?" he asked his son.

"You are in charge of the damn program," Erik said. "Can't you do something? I don't care if we have a Down's syndrome baby."

"I wish," Kelly said. He knew what Erik meant. As a youngster, Erik had grown up near a young man named Kirk, who had Downs syndrome. The two got to be very close, although Erik quickly took on the role of the older person in the relationship, even though he was six years younger than Kirk, who had the mental capacity of an eight-year-old throughout his life.

"You mean that you *won't*," Erik snapped. "Like everyone else, you are afraid of Thorn."

Kelly let him vent. Thorn may have initiated the laws, but he wasn't the only problem. The courts and the public had both accepted the new rules. He couldn't counter or circumvent them.

"Erik," he finally said, "if you want to have a child, your mother and I will help you."

"It's not that simple," Erik said. "Julie refuses to have a child who might have Downs syndrome . She's actually grateful that the Dards revealed the possibility." His voice shook. "I am so angry, upset, outraged."

"Please, don't take it out on Julie," Kelly pleaded. His son sounded beyond control.

"No, Dad," Erik assured him. "I would never do that." He took a deep breath. "We're going to try to adopt."

"That's a great idea," Kelly enthused.

"You think? The waiting list in Maryland is six years long," Erik said with resignation in his voice. "Even then, there's no guarantee. We'd both be well over forty by then—and the age limit is forty." He seemed ready to cry. "We want a family, Dad."

"Have you considered international adoption?" Kelly offered. "No other country has adopted Dards."

"Many of them are," Erik reported. "Korea, China, Russia, and Mexico, the four top countries for foreign-born babies, have begun the process." He paused. "Dad, Thorn is going to infect the world with this damn plan."

Kelly felt completely helpless. He wanted to say something, but there was nothing to say. He picked up his letter opener and saw his reflection in its shiny surface. He was old and haggard, with gray hair and deep-set eyes. *He looked like his friend Patterson,* Kelly thought. He also finally understood how his friend got that way.

With a swift move, he drove the opener into his wooden desk. It stood straight up, sparkling under the cold fluorescent lights.

# CHAPTER 17
# GOODBYE, HELLO

Kelly's first thought was not murderous. He simply wanted to get Thorn to resign. The vice president had to be embarrassed and dishonored so that no one would ever respect his opinion on any subject again. Rejection had to be complete.

Unfortunately, Kelly had no inside dirt on Thorn—nor had he hopes of obtaining any. His aides were fiercely loyal. Still, one might be pried loose if opportunity presented itself. That's how Washington worked. Many ambitious men did not hesitate to scramble over the prone bodies of competitors they had subtly and ambitiously undercut—and Kelly thought one of Thorn's minions might have the proper temperament.

Kevin Delacourt had seemed like a soul-less bureaucrat when they met years earlier. After all, Delacourt was willing to write the rules that coldly consigned millions of elderly Americans to an early death. At the time, Kelly was appalled. Now, he wondered if Delacourt didn't have the amoral conscience perfect for undermining Thorn. In fact, the young man might do it without a second thought.

As a precaution, Kelly asked Watson about Delacourt. She shuddered.

"He'd walk over his own grandmother to get a sandwich," she reported. "In fact, I heard he did."

"My kind of guy," Kelly told her.

Contacting Delacourt was not easy. He had neither a connection to Kelly's department nor any reason to visit. Attached to Thorn, he rarely was seen outside the White House. Who knew what kind of devilish work he was accomplishing there? Nevertheless, Kelly decided to call and invite him to visit.

His secretary said he was available a week later. The delay was no surprise to Kelly. He may be secretary of a major department, but he carried little weight in the administration. Everyone knew where he stood in the pecking order and used sly tactics to remind him. Delacourt was not an exception. He was not going to rush over under any circumstances.

The extra days were helpful to give Kelly time to prepare. He also had to find some hours for Joan, who was not feeling well. Stress, she felt, was undermining her health. She was in her mid-fifties now and not feeling as energetic. Kelly promised her quiet times and soon. He was trying to wrap things up and would return home for good. She was relieved. He was so cheerful and the path ahead seemed clear. That, in turn, helped calm her. She went back to Pennsylvania after three days in Washington with new resolve, but her work hours remained long and exhausting. Her business was now one of the largest in Pennsylvania with offices scattered across the state and close to a thousand employees. Every day, she was fielding offers either to buy a home-nursing agency elsewhere or to be bought up by a larger one. She asked Diane to help her, but her daughter wasn't interested. Neither was Rachel, who was now majoring in sociology, a field she found "divine." It was her fourth new subject area in two years.

"I could get stressed out trying to keep track of Rachel alone," Joan moaned to her husband.

"Maybe you should sell the business," he suggested. If she was no longer connected to the company, he could leave office with a loud blast at administration policies without fearing Thorn's retaliation.

Joan, however, declined. "I've worked too hard to get to this point. Besides," she said, "I feel like I'm making a difference." She hugged him. "I even get clients calling me because you are the HHS secretary. I hope you don't quit too soon. The connection is great for business."

Smiling half-heartedly, Kelly did his best to seem delighted to help. Maybe he should have told her, he thought, how her company could be jeopardized by the link to him. However, seeing how exhausted she was, he refrained. Instead, he assured her that he would try to stay on a while longer.

Delacourt was ten minutes late, strolling into Kelly's office with a determined stride and a thick, black briefcase in his left hand. *It was probably empty,* Kelly thought, *but it made any bureaucrat feel important.*

He was a tall, solid man with broad shoulders, although heavier than when they had first met. His carefully tailored suit hid the extra weight well. Kelly extended his right hand. Delacourt had a firm grip, the kind designed to prove strength, not just serve as a greeting. Kelly finally disengaged and sat down behind his large desk. Delacourt settled firmly, almost regally, into a visitor's chair and looked at Kelly with a disinterested expression on his lean face.

"I was thinking of the time we first met," Kelly began. "You wrote those regulations for the mandatory 'Do Not Resuscitate' clause and the treatment guidelines that banned heroic measures." He smiled at Delacourt, who stared back with fiery zeal. His dark eyes burned with energy. His hair had been cropped close, giving him the look of a Marine out of uniform. That alone would have made Kelly laugh. Based on his published government profile, Delacourt had never served in the military.

"I was thinking that you were never really publicly acknowledged for your work," Kelly continued. He thought he detected a slight tremor in Delacourt's face when he heard the comment.

"I'm just doing my job," Delacourt said flatly. "I appreciate coming to the attention of the secretary." His voice remained unchanged by any hint of emotion.

Kelly nodded. "Oh, I notice lots of things," he said. "For example, look at this," he went on, opening a file folder in front of him. It had lots of paper in it, but none related to Delacourt or to anyone else in the administration. He had gathered odds and ends from various reports and simply collected them together. The pile looked very official. Delacourt surreptitiously tried to read the top sheet upside down, but failed. "I found the names of at least ten hard-working, dedicated individuals in the White House who have never earned any real recognition for their work," Kelly noted. He closed the folder.

"I think it's a real shame," Kelly continued, shaking his head. "How is a young man to get a chance to really influence public policy when he can't even get his name on his door?"

That hit home. Kelly knew it would. In his visit to the White House for the meeting with the pharmaceutical leaders, he had noticed that many offices had no nameplates. Watson said that was Thorn's decision. He didn't want any of his subordinates to get swelled heads. At Kelly's request, she had checked the day before; no titles were posted.

Delacourt sat up. "I am sure the vice president has his reasons," he said. He was leaning forward, as clearly interested as a robotic automaton could be.

"Things may happen sooner if the vice president were no longer making those kinds of decisions," Kelly said in a low voice. The words hung over the desk, ominous and clear, like a thundercloud in the distance but inevitable.

Delacourt blinked. He flexed his fingers, the way a wrestler might before a bout. Kelly relaxed. The aide was intrigued. He might be ready to help. What had Roman Emperor Caligula said in a successful effort to diffuse unrest with the Praetorian Guards: "send a dog to eat a dog?" Delacourt had the hungry look of a pit bull.

Finally, Delacourt looked directly at Kelly. "What did you have in mind?"

Kelly didn't answer immediately. Instead, he got up and walked slowly over to his office window. From the Hubert Humphrey Office Building, ironically named for a former vice president, Kelly could look across Independence Avenue toward the U.S. Botanical Gardens. The view was always restful. To the right, he could catch a glimpse of the Capitol, rising over the top of the various buildings. Appropriately, he thought, the White House was not in sight.

"I was just thinking that if Vice President Thorn somehow left office, then many deserving young men, the real backbone of this Administration, would be revealed for the world to see," Kelly said, acting as though he were merely speculating. "Imagine what possibilities would lie ahead for someone in that position. The horizon—he gestured toward the window—would be endless. Chairman of some board, CEO of some Fortune 500 company."

"He's going to run for president," Delacourt said.

"I'm sure you'll be amply rewarded for your help getting him elected," Kelly replied laconically.

He turned around. Delacourt was thinking. He knew how Thorn discarded people without a second thought. His career could be over in a heartbeat. In fact, based on past experience, it probably would be.

"Are you trying to save your job?" Delacourt asked suspiciously.

"No," Kelly admitted honestly. "I am resigning soon and going home. I'm just concerned that some of this country's future leaders will be stifled and passed over by a man who has no ethical standards and no concern about others. He just uses people."

"He does," Delacourt agreed. "I don't believe he will simply walk away."

"I don't want him to," Kelly said. "I want him to crawl."

He sat down at his desk and produced another folder from a side drawer. This one was the real one: in it, were the plans to demean and discard Thorn.

*The concept was relatively simple,* Kelly thought as he opened the folder. He began to read the outline aloud. Delacourt had access to the vice president's files. He would plant a coded sheet with innocuous seeming numbers, but they would correspond to a similar sheet at the office of a defunct Colorado housing contractor, Will Ascivedo. The owner, conveniently at home following a major heart attack, was not likely to testify or even know what was happening. He had worked on single-family homes for Mercy Housing, a Catholic Church-related nonprofit organization that got money through the Department of Housing and Urban Development. The planted files would show Thorn to have been instrumental in the transaction.

Kelly would make a claim to the media, producing the coded list, which would indicate that Thorn received a large "contribution" for the contract. The coded list would be matched by a ledger found inside Ascivedo's house. Kelly would plant the ledger. Checking on health treatments would give him access. Kelly didn't plan to do the actual dirty work. That would be left to Watson, who was supposedly "returning" the doctored records. The family wouldn't know any difference. From all reports, the ex-contractor was failing fast and wouldn't either.

Thorn would never be able to prove that he didn't accept bribes. The figures in the ledger and the planted sheet would match; the corruption would seem obvious. When Kelly finished outlining the plan, he sat back and stared across his desk to the cold young man.

Delacourt had listened carefully. "What kind of timetable do you have?" he asked.

"The ledger will be in place within two weeks," Kelly said. "If you plant the document before then, you'll be set. Be careful not to get fingerprints on it," Delacourt looked impressed. Kelly hid his smile. The hours spent watching CSI were not in vain. He even typed the list on a library typewriter. The minimalistic handwriting would not be traceable. Just to be sure, he discarded the pens.

He placed the letter in a folder, using a handkerchief to wipe the corner where he touched it, and passed the folder across the desk to Delacourt. Kelly thought he spotted a tremor in the young man's hand. "I hope you realize that what you are doing is on par with Nathan Hale," Kelly said.

Delacourt looked at him grimly. "Who?" he asked.

"I regret that I have only …" Kelly started to recite, and then stopped. Delacourt didn't know. Just as well, actually. Hale was a hero of the American Revolution and was hanged by the British as a spy early in the war.

Delacourt placed the folder in his briefcase. He loudly snapped shut the lock. "I will e-mail you with any updates," he said. "What should I tell Mr. Thorn if he asks why we met?"

"Let him know I asked you some questions about the regulations you prepared. You explained and promised to return with some additional information," Kelly suggested.

"You thought of everything," Delacourt said.

"I tried."

Delacourt nodded.

"Kevin," Kelly told him, "you are performing a very important task. People will know your name; I can promise you that."

The door closed with a resounding click. Kelly sat down again. His heart was beating wildly. That went well, he thought. There was actually someone with lower ethics than Thorn, someone so cold and calculating that he could give lessons to Benedict Arnold. He could still see Delacourt's eyes. They had no emotion, but reflected dark wells of nothingness. Kelly shuddered. How evil that man was: no conscience at all to guide him.

Thorn would be stunned. So would Patterson. He'd probably send a third bloody knife. That idea made Kelly laugh. All he could do was wait, but he was going to savor each moment, anticipating the final thud when Thorn's pedestal struck earth.

Delacourt's e-mail arrived on Sunday. "Tuesday meeting set," it read. "Will have file in place. Please confirm."

Kelly smiled at the obvious code. Delacourt had met with him once. Any person who read that simple message would think that he was simply referring to a follow-up session.

The next step was to ask Watson to fly to Denver. The ledger was ready. Kelly had worked carefully on it. He had a faxed copy of paperwork Ascivedo had filled out during one of many hospital visits and which Watson had retrieved. She said she was checking on nursing conditions related to five Denver-area patients. That was natural follow up to the pilot program report filed two years earlier, Kelly imagined. He hadn't focused on Ascivedo. Investigators would have to think that the alleged bribery involving the same man was just a coincidence. Kelly had no illusion that his handwriting mimicked Ascivedo's perfectly, but felt it was close enough.

Watson would go on Wednesday. She was happy to make the trip, although uncertain why. "I don't trust anyone else," Kelly told her.

She seemed happy to hear that. She also had a sister in Colorado and looked forward to a trip there. He gave her the ledger. She placed it in a large envelope without any more questions.

Returning to his office, Kelly was very proud. He had considered every angle and thought of everything.

Tuesday morning, on time, Delacourt arrived. He almost slipped into the office, carefully closing the door quietly as if to avoid any hint of being detected. He laid his big briefcase down by his chair.

"Everything set?" Kelly asked,

"As you requested," Delacourt said in his usual businesslike monotone, "I placed the letter in the vice president's file."

"Which file?" Kelly asked.

"He has a file for older documents that need to be shredded. They are scheduled to be destroyed in a month," Delacourt said. "If you are not able to follow up, the document will be gone. No one will be the wiser."

"Clever," Kelly whistled. He had selected the right man.

"More than you know," Delacourt said.

He stood abruptly, walked over to the office door, and opened it. Instead of leaving, however, he swung the door open and stepped back. A dark, ominous figure was visible, outlined by the light coming into the room. The man was flanked by two soldiers in uniform.

Kelly nearly jumped up. He leaned forward, resting on his hands, trying to see better. Suddenly, he felt weak. He couldn't see clearly. He gaped, trying to focus. His stomach fell; his body followed. He knew exactly who was glaring at him from the doorway.

Thorn was staring at him with hard, angry eyes. His face was hard, like an executioner readying for his disgusting work.

"I asked myself," Delacourt said in his cold, clipped tone, "who was going to be a bigger help to my career: a lame duck secretary about to resign or a man about to be elected president?"

Kelly stared down at his desk. It was polished, reflecting his pale face.

"I also taped our conversation," Delacourt said. "That's what big briefcases are for. You see, I thought of everything, too."

Thorn marched across the room and slapped down a piece of paper in front of Kelly. Taking a deep breath, Kelly glanced at it. His resignation. It was straightforward. One sentence. Cold. Remorseless. "I hereby resign the office of secretary of Health and Human Services, effective immediately." Kelly recognized it. Former vice-president Agnew sent a virtually identical message to the Secretary of State Henry Kissinger when he left office in October 1973.

"Sign it," Thorn ordered.

Kelly complied. His right hand was shaking.

"There will be a news conference at 2:00 PM," the vice president said. "You will not want to watch it."

The soldiers with him stood at either side of the desk in stark attention. Both were big men with broad shoulders. Their faces were impassive. Kelly stood up. His legs shook. He felt as though he were going to his execution. As he walked around the desk, he reached for his photo of Joan.

"Nothing," Thorn ordered.

With the guards beside him, Kelly was marched through the office, walking by Watson, who watched open-mouthed; ushered down the hallway, past secretaries and aides in various offices, who crowded doorways to watch; to the elevator; to the basement parking lot.

Windows were filled with curious eyes as Kelly steered his car toward Independence Avenue, away from the Gardens. Behind him, the Capitol Dome seemed to watch him, glittering, almost mocking him, until he finally disappeared into the maze of streets.

******

Joan was happy to see him, but immediately recognized something was dreadfully wrong. Kelly could not explain. He had no idea how he had managed to get home, but had driven the 140 miles straight through. He didn't remember seeing signs or even traffic. He hadn't turned on the radio and played no music. If he had run out of gas, he wouldn't have realized until the car actually stopped. Instead, he simply pulled into the driveway as if it were seconds from his old office.

He pulled away from Joan, dragged himself upstairs into his bedroom, and collapsed on the bed. His head throbbed. All the way home, he had seen nothing but Thorn's sardonic smile in front of him. Everywhere he looked, no matter what road he followed, Thorn was forever mocking him.

Tears trickled down his face.

He was awakened by the incessant ringing of the telephone. He ignored it. At some point, he heard the front door slam. A car drove away. He looked at his watch. It was 3:00 PM. The phone rang again. He ignored it. He knew reporters would call. He was not going to answer. He wondered what Gentry had said to the media. Secretaries resigned, sometimes under strange circumstances. He recalled that several had been indicted. That thought frightened him. Would Thorn press charges? He doubted it. That would give Kelly the opportunity to testify about everything the vice president was doing. Thorn would prefer silence.

"Joan," Kelly called feebly.

The house was quiet.

He wandered into her office. The computer was turned off. Her desk was empty. No papers littered what had once been Diane's bedroom. Even her closet was strangely neat and almost empty. Kelly finally went downstairs to the kitchen, feeling the silence gather around him like a shroud. A printed sheet of paper lay on the table. He glanced at it and saw his name.

Joan had signed it. He read slowly.

"I am leaving. President Gentry announced your resignation today and said that he ordered the FBI to begin an investigation into whether you and your family (me!) had profited improperly from the medical cost-reduction plans.

"I do not know why you did not tell me. If you do not trust me enough after twenty-nine years of marriage, then you never will.

"I told you I needed to avoid stress. You have doubled it. You have no excuse, no explanation.

"I am sorry my father is no longer alive. I would go home to him. Instead, I will be at Bill and Lisa's. Do not call."

The phone rang again. Kelly slowly sank to the floor. The letter drifted away and settled down beside him. He felt churning emotions sap his strength. One word kept repeating over and over in his head: Thorn, Thorn, Thorn. It synchronized with his pulse and throbbed through his head.

Finally, he stood up. The phone rang again. He steeled himself. He was not going down quietly. He had promised himself to stand up to Thorn. He would. What more could he lose? His career was over. His wife had left him. Thorn was going to pay.

Kelly strode over to the wall phone.

"Yes," he said, half hoping Joan would be on the other end.

"Dr. Kelly," an authoritative female voice said, "this is Lydia Kershaw. I'm a reporter for the *New York Times*."

Kelly interrupted. "Shut up and listen," he growled hoarsely. His right fist was clenched. His heart was racing. "I have a lot to say."

# CHAPTER 18
# RESURRECTION

Eric actually seemed sympathetic on the phone, but did not waste any words. "You knew no one would listen," he said calmly. He sounded so far away. Kelly wished he were in Maryland now, too, but a cell phone was his only link to the outside world. He sat back on the couch in his home amid intense silence. The house phone had been ringing for twenty-four hours after the president's media conference. Even *Golf Digest* called after Gentry made a crack that Kelly lied about his golfing prowess.

After the *New York Times* ran a brief note that Kelly denied any wrongdoing, the phone calls had tailed off. Kelly no longer answered it. No one was the least bit interested in the charges he made against Thorn. Reporters appeared to listen to his detailed explanations, but no one had printed a word or placed them on the Internet.

"I told the reporters so much," Kelly insisted weakly.

Eric's shrug was almost audible. "Sour grapes," he sniffed. "Who is going to believe anything you say after you were fired? All you can do is deny everything, which is what you'd be expected to say. Although I'm not your attorney, I recommend you be quiet."

"I never should have left St. Michael's," Kelly said glumly.

"Dad, you were like a guppy swimming with sharks. What did you think would happen?" Erik said.

"I don't know," Kelly admitted. He wiped his forehead. He felt cold inside, but was sweating.

"I talked with mom," Eric continued. Kelly perked up. "She knows you were trying to protect her, but she's badly hurt." Kelly sunk down in the couch again. "Give her some time."

"Yeah," Kelly agreed.

They chatted for a few more minutes. Erik had come to grips with their inability to have a child. Instead, he and Julie were looking into private adoption. That avenue had become so expensive with the drop in the birthrate, but, with the right connections, anything could be done. However, Erik noted, he may have to shift to some monolithic law firm. The ACLU simply could not pay enough for that kind of expense.

He and Julie were upbeat. Something would work out, he said.

Kelly wasn't so sure and closed the phone with a sense of complete loss. Erik seemed to have recovered. The situation was a lot bleaker for himself. What was he supposed to do now? He was alone; there was no job to go to; no pieces to pick up. Kelly felt completely punctured. Thorn had won. That idea galled him.

Other people had been in this kind of situation, he thought. What did they do? What had Rosario done after he went home? Probably went golfing. The charge about the illegal caddie had been settled amicably. Rosario had apologized. That was the last mention Kelly recalled of him. Other humiliated politicians seemed to have fared well, too. Agnew had pled guilty and then went about publicly as if a criminal record didn't mean anything. Nixon resigned, fled to his California home, and re-emerged as some kind of elder statesman. Jimmy Carter was a failure as president. So, he started Habitat for Humanity and won a Nobel Peace Prize.

Kelly straightened his shoulders and sat up. He was not going to give up. If they could do it—and many others besides—he could, too. No, he decided, pounding his fist into the couch. He was not going to surrender either to depression or to Thorn.

Rejuvenated, he called Watterson. After all, there could be some legal problems. Hadn't Gentry promised a full investigation? Even if that was another lie, Thorn may be more cunning in his approach. Some legal advice could be handy. Watterson wasn't interested in getting involved in any lawsuit outside wills and probate, but suggested a lawyer in Harrisburg who had some government litigation experience. The guy had been an IRS agent. Kelly decided to wait. There would be time enough to spill secrets to a stranger.

Finally, Kelly dialed a familiar number. The phone at the hospital rang twice before the receptionist answered. Kelly didn't give his name, but asked if Dr. Matt Jefferson, his assistant in the emergency room years before, was available.

A moment later, Jefferson was on the line.

Somewhat hesitantly, Kelly identified himself.

Jefferson gave a low chuckle. "Slumming, huh?" he said cheerfully. "Got some free time?"

"Lots," Kelly told him, grateful for a friendly comment rather than a nasty crack.

Jefferson didn't hesitate to invite Kelly to visit the hospital. Kelly wasted less time following up. Walking into the entry and down the hallway to the waiting room was so strange. Kelly had forgotten how innocent everything looked: the bucolic images on the wall; the small children's area with cartoons and toys; the simple metal chairs; the brown tile now worn from so many passing feet. Kelly could smell the familiar aroma of antiseptics.

He could hear the swish of nurses hurrying by. The walls seemed to embrace him. He felt at home.

Jefferson walked out to meet him, smiling broadly, and shaking his hand enthusiastically. He ushered Kelly back to his old office. It was Jefferson's now, but it hadn't changed much. The aged, battered, army surplus file cabinet still sat to one side. Diplomas on the wall were new, but hung where Kelly once posted his.

Only the photos on the desk were different. Jefferson clearly was proud of his family and had five pictures of his son—from his days as a high school athlete to his current status in the military. Kelly remembered Nathan visiting his dad at the hospital. He was two years younger than Rachel was, but the children would play together in the waiting room. Looking at the pictures, Kelly could hardly believe so much time had passed. Nathan was a broad-shouldered man with light hair and a mischievous smile—despite posing in his Marine uniform.

Kelly sat in the visitor's chair. It was the same one John Darby once sat in, he thought.

"Do you have the time?" he asked, not wanting to pull Jefferson away from his duties.

Now with graying hair, but the same pleasant expression, Jefferson waved off the concern. Things weren't so rushed any more, now that the Thorn Plan was in place, he said. He mostly supervised nurses and physician assistants and checked their reports. Of course, he chuckled, there's an occasional weekend warrior who hobbles in after forgetting his age and relying on misremembered days of a supposedly heroic youth. The rest were victims of car crashes and similar traumas. No government policy could end accidents. However, the elderly and indigent who didn't really need emergency care were being kept away, exactly as the plan envisioned.

They talked for a few minutes about families and the hospital. Kelly was glad to chat, to hear a familiar voice without wondering what sinister and/or cynical plot lay behind the gentle words.

Always accommodating, Jefferson never asked about Washington or discussed what had happened. He did wonder if Kelly planned to take a long vacation.

"Actually," Kelly said, "I'd like to get back to work."

"Here?" Jefferson gasped. "I figured you'd be a six-figure consultant or something."

"I prefer the simple life," Kelly said. He almost gave himself away with a smile. Who would hire him as a consultant?

"We could use the help. One doctor left last week for Iraq. Of course," Jefferson noted with a grin, "the director's job is taken."

"I'm happy being an employee," Kelly said.

Jefferson promised to get back to him. Three days later, Kelly was invited to return to St. Michael's. Jefferson reported that Fred Grey, the hospital's chairman of the board, liked the idea of having a former important government official working there. Perhaps Kelly could help get them a few grants, he asked. Kelly agreed, although wondered silently if his name on an application would be more of an anchor than an asset.

News of his hiring merited a small mention in the media. Kelly looked at the paragraph in the Allentown *Morning Call* with bitter amusement. His new job meant nothing compared to what Thorn was doing, yet no one seemed willing to probe that.

The following Monday, Kelly walked into St. Michael's with trepidation, but the nurses welcomed him with professional courtesy. He didn't recognize any of them. He wasn't sure if that was good or bad. He was positive they knew about him from the way several whispered to each other. He kept his head up, looking proud. They must not be allowed to see the pain inside.

When the first patient was wheeled in, he felt rusty and not as confident, but quickly and happily fell back into the old routine. His voice carried assurance, and he felt buoyed and confident.

Jefferson was cheerful as ever, but seemed concerned. Kelly hoped his presence wasn't the problem. During an afternoon break, he stopped by and asked.

Jefferson shook his head. His son was in Iraq. He was

supposed to be rotated home a few months ago, but that plan had been cancelled because of rising terrorist activities. He was now scheduled to return stateside in another week. Kelly listened and felt a chill sweep over him. He wanted to say something, to point a finger at Thorn, but couldn't. Jefferson obviously didn't know what had happened. He clearly believed that increasing rebel attacks had caused the change in military thinking.

"I got something a few months ago," Jefferson continued, "and forgot all about it until I saw you." He ruffled though files on his desk and held out a letter.

Kelly took it. It was from the Department of Health and Human Services. With a start, he immediately saw his familiar signature on the bottom, but didn't recognize the contents. He hadn't written it—he hadn't even *seen* it before. It must have been mailed before he left, but it hadn't gone through his office. Thorn didn't want him somehow interfering. Kelly had an instant headache.

Then, as he read, his knees began to buckle. At one point, he had to lean on Jefferson's desk to maintain his balance.

The letter thanked the families of soldiers for their patriotic support of America's freedom and wanted parents of soldiers to know that, even in death, their sons and daughters could continue to be "true American heroes." It requested permission to allow any soldiers unfortunate enough to die for their country to "live on" by being included in studies that "promise to remake the future of medicine." In that way, no soldier "will have died in vain, but will remain part of the honored roll call of American heroes."

Included was a permission slip that asked that parents agree to allow their child to be recognized "forever" by being involved with Nucleon's "unprecedented research" into human DNA. In small point, the letter noted that parents who did not return the form were assumed to "patriotically" support the concept.

"You always had a way with words," Jefferson said when Kelly finished reading.

"Thanks," Kelly mumbled. "You understand what this letter is asking, right?"

Jefferson nodded. "You want dead soldiers to be used in medical experiments. I think it's a great idea. It's a way to help keep this country strong."

Rubbing his forehead, Kelly handed the letter back. "Are you going to sign it?" he asked.

"I guess. When I have time," Jefferson said. "Back in the Middle Ages, great artists like Michelangelo and Leonardo da Vinci used the bodies of criminals to help them reproduce human anatomy. Better than tossing somebody in a grave where it's no use to anyone."

"Matt," Kelly said slowly, choosing his words carefully, "what if the government changed return orders to make sure that there were enough bodies for experiments?"

Jefferson considered that. "No," he said finally. "No one would have to do that. We're talking about a war. Soldiers die. I'll just ask Nathan when he gets home. I'm sure he would want his buddies to live on this way."

Shaking his head, Kelly left the office. Why was he the only one bothered by this? Everyone seemed to be letting the government do whatever it wanted. Thorn had somehow cowed a country. What would be next? A war against Iran? Casually dropping nuclear bombs on North Korea? Where did it end? Thorn had control of Congress and the Supreme Court. That grasp would get tighter. He was an overwhelming choice to win the election and carry more of his supporters into office. Everyone thought Thorn was a figurehead, continuing Gentry's policies. Voters had no idea that the situation was actually the other way around.

Didn't someone else care?

In dismay, that weekend, Kelly went over to the Lehigh County Democratic Party headquarters. It was located on North 15th Street, ironically across the street from the Highland Memorial Park Cemetery. The presidential election was just two months away and the people there were listless. They could have moved into the cemetery without disturbing anyone. They sat around, glumly looking at posters of their party's presidential nominee, Rhode Island Senator Allan Barberton, who resembled a dour English professor peering over glasses without a hint of empathy.

Every now and then, one of the walking cadavers would share some gallows humor. No one laughed. The biggest topics were Barberton's admitted affair with an aide and his denial that bribes had influenced his efforts to get lucrative contracts for a business in his state. "I would have done anything for my constituents, even without getting something extra," he boomed once in a misguided effort to counteract charges. As it turned out, according to media reports, both objectives seemed to go hand in hand.

Kelly was more convinced that the FBI had been directed to investigate these no-doubt, trumped-up charges. Thorn would not hesitate to pounce on such a situation nor even generate the evidence himself. No one would know. Without even creating a campaign, Thorn was looking like a workaholic saint next to Barberton.

Unfortunately, the Democratic Party could not come up with anyone better. Few political aspirants wanted to run against Thorn. After watching Barberton's daily hosing by the media, fewer still showed the stomach for any kind of confrontation.

The malaise carried over to the various party headquarters. Not one looked up when Kelly entered the office. After a few minutes, a heavy-set young man finally sighed and roused himself enough to get Kelly a brochure.

He read it slowly. No one talked to him. He stayed thirty minutes, weighing whether to volunteer his time or not. Finally, he decided there was no point. The phone didn't ring the entire time he was there. The only signs of life came when someone retrieved a donut or a cup of coffee. Morgues must be more hectic than this, Kelly decided.

At home, plagued by silence and internal anguish, Kelly

paced. He would have to act. No one else would. The country had collapsed into a kind of weightlessness. If nothing were done, a new kind of leader would take over: ruthless and tyrannical. Nixon, at least, had to face a hostile public and, eventually, a cadre of determined senators. Even Franklin Roosevelt, who was elected to four terms, was countered by a stalwart Supreme Court. Washington, beloved as he was, hardly ran roughshod over anyone. He was attacked by opponents. In fact, Kelly couldn't think of any president, no matter how popular, who did not face some opposition. Although not yet in office, Thorn seemed the exception. Those not on his side were ruthlessly eliminated and debased so they could not rise in opposition. Those with him were subservient.

His vice president, naturally, was Senator Jayson Hardesty, a man who already proved to be a lackey. Not that anyone cared. Thorn promised to carry on the policies of his predecessor. Voters were ecstatic.

Kelly was not sure what he was going to do. One man, confronting such an overwhelming force, seemed unlikely to affect any meaningful change. But, as he thought about it, he realized that like any demagogue, Thorn had a chink. He had no successor, certainly not Hardesty. If Thorn were somehow eliminated, Kelly reasoned, his whole edifice would crumble.

It had to be a sudden, complete destruction. Attempts at bribery would not work, not with a man as driven as Thorn. No scandal probably would, Kelly recognized. Even J. Edgar Hoover, the long-time FBI director detested by most presidents he served under, nevertheless defiantly clung to office through the use of subtle threats and secret information. Thorn would not hesitate to stoop to conquer. If he disappeared, however, the three pillars of government would return to proper balance. If he stayed, the administrative arm would dominate unlike ever before.

The unfolding picture made Kelly shudder.

However, he told himself, before proceeding, he would need to resolve the family problems. He did not want anyone to think he acted in reaction to the dissolution of his marriage, because of outrage over his son's blocked ability to start a family, because of his father-in-law's death or his dismissal. The public must recognize that Thorn was the target, and the reasons were valid and honorable. Investigations had to turn up Thorn's nefarious role in so many horrors foisted on the American public.

Kelly knew Joan had to be by his side.

He just was not sure how to accomplish that. How odd, he mused: married for almost thirty years and still not sure how to talk to his wife. He was not much for reading magazines that dealt with such subjects, but, in idle moments, occasionally flipped through *Good Housekeeping, Cosmopolitan,* and other such journals that ended up in the waiting room. He remembered a few stories on the topic of marital communications, but hadn't even skimmed them. Now, he was sorry about that.

There was only one thing to do. He picked up the phone and called his brother-in-law's house.

Lisa answered. She was polite. Joan wasn't there. She had gone to work.

On the weekend?

Every weekend. Revelations about her husband had really hurt the company. Joan had no idea if it would survive. So many clients had left, Lisa said. Her voice was even and unemotional, in the mode of a manager simply reporting the news.

Kelly considered his next move. He could visit Joan directly, but didn't want to make matters worse with an ugly confrontation. She might not let him in the house or even acknowledge his presence. Lisa could continue to insist Joan was not there. Bill may have forgiven his sister, but was unlikely yet to help his brother-in-law.

With that idea gone, Kelly surveyed his remaining options. Only one person he knew had endured multiple scrapes with the opposite sex and survived, even thrived. At least three coeds in college had threatened to emasculate him at one time or another, but, somehow, Kelly would later spot one or another flirting with

Patterson in the student center or on their way to his car with obvious friendly intentions. Maybe Patterson would share some of that expertise.

Patterson listened as Kelly explained the reason for the call.

"Flowers are a start," he suggested. "What's her favorite flower? Roses? Tulips? Carnations?"

Kelly thought a moment. He rarely bought flowers, associating them with visitors bringing them to the hospital. When he did, he simply chose a nice-looking bouquet in the hospital store, relying on the advice of the clerk. He could identify few flowers anyway.

"I don't know," he admitted.

"Maybe candy then. Does she like chocolate?" Patterson tried.

"I'm not sure," Kelly said after a few seconds. "She might nibble some sweets at parties, but we rarely had any at home. We were a little old for Halloween."

"Then maybe buy her some music she likes," Patterson continued. "Does she have a favorite band?"

"She listens to folk rock a little," Kelly said, relieved he knew something. "Of course, she also likes Motown, R & B, and pop tunes." He paused. "That's not much help," he admitted.

"Do you know anything about her?" Patterson asked. "Her favorite food? Favorite color? Type of movie?"

"Not as much as I thought," Kelly conceded ruefully.

"Are you sure you were married to her?" Patterson tried.

"We both led busy lives. We weren't home much. We didn't have a chance to do a lot together," Kelly tried to explain. "She took care of the kids and then started that nursing business. I was in the ER day and night."

Kelly could imagine Patterson shaking his head two thousand miles away. He definitely heard the low sigh.

"Do you love her?" Patterson tried.

"Yes," Kelly said quickly.

"What's love to you?"

Kelly had to think about that. "I guess to cherish, honor, and support someone else, to care about her," he said.

"Those are wedding vows," Patterson interrupted.

"What do you think love is?" Kelly reacted.

"It doesn't matter what I think," Patterson answered quietly. "It's your wife who left, not mine."

Kelly nodded and took a deep breath. "Love," he tried again, "is the recognition of the importance of someone or something else above all others. It can be an idea, an item like a piece of cloth, or a person."

"Go with that," Patterson said. "Tell Joan you love her."

"How? She won't talk to me."

Patterson sniffed. "Come on. You're a former bigwig in government. You can't think of some way to reach her? I could, and, hell, I'm in Colorado."

Kelly tried to focus. He would find her and talk to her. She would listen. He did love her.

"Be yourself," Patterson advised. "That's the person she fell in love with."

"Yeah," Kelly said with little conviction. Did she still love him?

Sunday morning, he realized that she would go to church. She always did. Bill and Lisa belonged to Grace Episcopal Church. If Joan went to church, she would go with them. Kelly instantly felt better. At least he knew something important about her.

He liked the church, having joined his in-laws there when they spent weekends together. It had a homey atmosphere with the old-style steeple, large abstract stained-glass windows, and simple altar. He got into his suit, carefully checked his hair, and tried to smooth away the lines in his face. He wanted her to see him as he once was, not as he was today.

The church parking lot was not full this fall morning. Maybe some people had gone to the Eagles game: they were playing the hated Giants, a football match-up that always drew wide attention. Kelly parked in an empty site a few spots away from the nearest car. He didn't see Bill's Prius and hoped he had not made a mistake.

It was only 9:45; services did not start until 10:00.

He walked inside and after taking a quick survey and not seeing Joan, Kelly sat in the corner of a wooden pew in the back of the church. No one was likely to see him there. Anyone coming in would look straight ahead.

No more than five minutes later, Bill walked in with Lisa. Behind them, Kelly saw Joan. His heart began to pick up its pace. She still moved him. Elegant with her hair carefully trimmed so each hair was in place, her long arms moving in rhythm, Joan walked in with the calm assuredness Kelly remembered so well. Her face had lost some color, yet she seemed as young and enticing as when he first saw her in that clinic more than thirty years ago.

He watched the trio find a seat. Joan entered the pew first. Two other couples sat further to her left. Bill was on the aisle. Kelly waited until they had retrieved their missals, and then moved around to the far side. He excused himself as he moved down the pew and finally wedged himself between Joan and the last couple.

She glanced at him, then away. Then, finally, color draining from her face, she looked at him.

"I have a lot of forgiveness to ask for," he said softly. "This seemed like the best place to start."

He held out his right hand. She looked at it. Tears welled in the corner of her eyes. She put her prayer book in her lap, took his hand, and held it tightly in both of hers. Their hands never moved throughout the entire service.

Lisa noticed; Bill did not until they all went up to receive communion.

At the end, as they stood, Joan turned to Lisa. "It's time for me to go home," she said. Lisa looked at her, then at Kelly. She nodded slowly and, it seemed, with understanding.

They did not talk much in the car. Kelly didn't know what

to say. He felt as though he were on a first date. Joan sat near the door. Once or twice she started to speak, but stopped.

Finally, she asked him if he was all right.

"I'm managing," he told her.

"We'll manage better together," she said.

The answering machine light was on when they walked in. Kelly held Joan's hand and hugged her tightly. She was crying. He almost did.

"I'm sorry," he said.

She nodded. "I am, too." That was all either could say.

She went upstairs to change. He sat on the couch and hit the answering machine button. One call was from Lydia Kershaw, the *New York Times* reporter who had been refreshingly and atypically objective and honest in her reporting. He noted her number on the pad and erased the next two calls from reporters. Both wanted comments on his new job and how it felt to "fall" back to where he started. Actually, one reporter used the word "fall," the other said, "return in humiliation."

The fourth and last call was not from a reporter.

"Pete," a distraught voice said, "it's Matt. I won't be in Monday. I just got called. Nathan was killed in Iraq. He was to be home Thursday." The clink ending the call was loud and cold.

Kelly fell back and stared at the ceiling. Instant anger and disgust swept over him. His eyes narrowed, and he stared outdoors where the cool winds were stripping trees and turning the world to gray.

"Thorn," Kelly seethed, putting all his fury and outrage into a single word.

For a moment, he thought his heart stood still. He slumped onto the couch, panting. He tried to calm himself. His mother had angina; his father died after a heart attack. He needed to be careful.

"Pete," Joan cried, coming down the stairs, "are you all right?"

Kelly nodded weakly. "Overcome with emotion," he whispered.

# CHAPTER 19
# LAY ON, McDUFF

Only thirty-five more minutes. Kelly checked the clock a third time to be sure. The second hand seemed to be crawling around the dial. Still, the time was slowly dwindling.

He felt calm, ready. He had not expected that. He was sure the anger simmering inside for weeks after he heard about Nathan would erupt somehow, like lava from a once-dormant volcano. Instead, he had directed his fury toward accomplishing this goal. Now that the moment was nearing, he was confident and relaxed.

He took several deep breaths and focused on the blank wall. His heart slowed down. That had been a scare when he had heard about Nathan. He thought he might be having a heart attack, but the moment passed.

Joan had taken his blood pressure and said it was normal. She wanted him to get a physical, but he demurred. Later, he said. As a doctor, he knew when something was wrong. Actually, he didn't want anything to interfere with his plans. Medical checkups would have to wait.

Now, two months later, as winter began to settle over the country, he had a sense of a coming end. He had a slight headache and some nausea. He credited that to the situation. He was also sweating more than usual, even though he had turned down the air conditioning.

Only thirty minutes left.

He had even put in a wakeup call for 2:40, just in case he fell asleep. That would not be necessary. He was prepared.

He was also resigned. His choices had vanished. Nothing he could do would bring back Matt's son or help Erik and Julie start a family. Nothing could revive his father-in-law or the hundreds of thousands of Americans who had probably died earlier than they should have because of Thorn's alterations of the original Darby Plan. Nothing could change what was happening at Nucleon, which had long since hurdled any ethical barriers. Now, he knew he had to end this nightmare. Perhaps then, America would wake up.

He went to the closet and retrieved his suit coat. This was the suit he wore when sworn in as secretary of the Department of Health and Human Services. No one else knew that, of course. Thorn would not recognize it and appreciate the irony. However, some historian would. That would help clarify how carefully he had planned for this day.

He checked his pockets, carefully placing a Thorn-Hardesty campaign button on his lapel. The agents with the metal detectors needed to find something.

Patting his chest, Kelly made sure the pen was in his shirt pocket and visible. He wanted the Secret Service to see it, to believe it was innocuous. "Hide in plain sight," Kelly remembered from reading murder mysteries.

Properly dressed, his collar neat and his tie straight, he walked into the bathroom. He peered into the mirror and combed his hair again. There was so much more gray than he recalled. In a few years, he would have resembled his father, who had a shock of white hair. Kelly brushed his teeth and tossed away the brush. He wouldn't be needing it any more.

In the soft light, he could see that his eyes were clear. His face was pale, but that, too, was understandable. Even the slight pain in his left shoulder seemed natural. The cooler air always encouraged his budding arthritis to act up. Still, he felt good. His hip, which had been bothering him lately, seemed to have calmed down. He could walk easily.

Back in the bedroom, Kelly checked around. Historians would want to know every detail. The suitcase was stowed away neatly; the bedclothes were smoothed. That was something Joan always did to help the maids, even though the bed was going to be stripped anyway. Nothing lay on the floor. Dirty clothes had been placed in a bag inside the suitcase. Kelly had paid for one extra day and asked housekeeping not to disturb the room. Police would find his belongings as he left them. He put a ten-dollar tip by the phone for the maid. No reason for her to be shortchanged.

Everything was visible, non-threatening, except the gun, which still sat on the closet shelf behind the blanket. Finding that would be a coup for whoever searched the room.

The clock notched twenty-five minutes. It was time to go.

Idly, Kelly wondered if he should have had a final meal. That's what condemned prisoners had: something special that they could savor one final time. He wouldn't have had to pay for it. How could the hotel collect from a corpse? Joan could ignore the bill—although he was sure she'd write a check.

He was a little hungry. He hadn't had much appetite upon arising and had a piece of toast with coffee for a late breakfast. Maybe he should have had lunch, something to maintain his blood sugar level. What would he have ordered? Probably roast turkey, gravy, sweet potatoes, and corn. That would have been nice, like Thanksgiving. He always liked that holiday. It was his favorite, untainted by religious connotations. No one bought unnecessary gifts or focused on bunny rabbits. Instead, everyone expressed gratitude for whatever bounty had come his way. Kelly decided this day was like Thanksgiving and Christmas together, since he was supplying a great gift for the country.

He had considered calling down to room service and ordering a meal, but eventually decided not to. He had felt his stomach beginning to act up as the time slowly slipped away, as though he were in a plane and looking down from some unseen height. Food never helped, only scotch.

A sudden thought made him smile; his last meal. He hadn't considered that before. Everything he did struck a chord: this would be the last time he combed his hair, the last time he put on a suit jacket, the last time he opened a door, the last time he put his key in his pocket. He doubted any other assassin thought that way. None of them thought about death. Some expected to live, even be honored for killing the president. Booth certainly did. Others were crazy. He was completely rational: he was being a patriot.

What is love? Patterson had asked him. It was the feeling that something was greater than self—the willingness to sacrifice self for another. That was what he was doing. Nathan Hale was no less a patriot, or John Adams, Paul Revere, or Sergeant Alvin York. Kelly hoped he could say something memorable at the proper moment, like Booth's *Sic Semper Tyrannis [thus always to tyrants]*. Maybe future schoolchildren will have to memorize whatever he said.

Kelly opened his cell phone and checked for messages. No one had called. He so wanted to phone Joan but could not. What could he say? His voice would tremble. He was sure he'd cry. That would have alerted her. More, he couldn't bear to say goodbye. She would have to cry for him later. Nor could he call Erik or his daughters. Hearing their voices might chip away his resolve.

They, too, would have to learn the awful truth with the rest of the country.

Finally ready, he surveyed the room one more time and then left. The door closed quietly behind him. The hallway was empty. Several trays crowded with dirty dishes sat in front of doors, but only on the left side. Rooms overlooking the entrance had been evacuated. Most people had vacated the hotel anyway. They might have appreciated the chance to see the president-elect, but not with the suffocating security and inconvenience. They'd all come back to stare in awe at the place where the assassination took place, but only after the echo of the outcry had faded away.

The elevator came quickly. No one was using them. It was as if the whole world had suddenly come to a stop. Kelly rode down silently, watching through the glass as the floor slowly rose to meet him. His stomach began to churn. His pulse picked up. He forced himself to look away, to try to relax. It didn't seem to help.

With twenty minutes to go before Thorn was due, the elevator eased to a stop in the lobby. His heart beating so loudly that he was sure someone would hear, Kelly stepped out. He felt lightheaded.

An agent was waiting for him. A big, burly man with close-cropped hair, he passed the metal detector over Kelly, and then asked him to empty his pockets. Kelly complied, putting his wallet, a handkerchief, hotel card and some loose change into a small basket. Then, almost as an afterthought, the pen went next, casually, without a tremor. Finally, apologizing, Kelly found the campaign button and tossed it casually into the basket, acting as if he had forgotten all about it.

The guard scooped up the button and pinned it on Kelly's lapel.

He then checked Kelly's driver's license and his VIP pass. Watson had gotten that for him. She had not acted surprised to hear from him or even shocked he wanted to attend the first media conference of the president-elect. She was now back at her old position, guarding an empty office and reading her books. It was, she said, "the perfect job."

The agent compared the ID to the pass. He nodded and smiled.

"Nice to see you again, Dr. Kelly," he said.

Kelly looked puzzled. The guard would know his name from the ID, but the "again" part was strange. This was not the same agent who had checked him earlier.

"Markham. George. I was with Vice President Thorn when you left the government," the agent said almost apologetically.

Kelly looked at him closely and realized Markham was one of the two gigantic guards who had accompanied Thorn and led him out of the office. *This must be his reward,* Kelly thought, *promoted to the Secret Service. Thorn always took care of those who helped him.*

Kelly said thanks. His mouth was dry. Slowly, his hand trembling, he retrieved his pen and put it back, then his wallet, hotel keycard, and ID. Markham did not wait, but moved on to the other elevator, which was now opening.

Walking slowly, Kelly moved toward the entrance. The lobby had begun to fill up. Some people had gravitated toward the entryway. Someone had placed a red carpet on the tile flooring. It was held down with metal stanchions. Dark ribbons had been stretched between the stanchions to create a barrier. A row of soldiers, standing at parade rest, had already taken up positions along each side of the carpet.

Kelly checked his watch: fifteen minutes.

He looked around. No one looked familiar. People were standing, chatting, or staring toward the front door with undisguised boredom. Reporters, obvious with notebooks or tape recorders, circulated through the crowd, talking, writing notes, and collecting quotes while munching on doughnuts. The snacks had moved close to the front desk. Occasionally, a strobe flashed. Heavyset men carrying cameras on their shoulders elbowed their way to the edge of the red carpet. They aimed toward the entrance. One intrepid reporter tried to get inside by going under the ribbon, but was quickly removed. He taped his introduction in a cleared area under the alcove.

Kelly wandered over by the front desk. The manager was sitting very still behind the desk. He appeared almost catatonic. The intense security must have overwhelmed him. However, the manager would have been relieved to know Thorn would be killed in his hotel. That would bring gawkers running. Too bad that Thorn hadn't stayed the night, Kelly decided cynically. That room could have been rented for a premium.

Kelly leaned against the desk, grateful for a moment to rest. He felt very tired. The hum of the crowd and the heat from so many people combined to make him feel dizzy. The dull ache in his shoulder returned. He looked around for some water, but did not see anything. Somehow, the coffee and doughnuts seemed too far away.

"Dr. Kelly?" a cool voice next him interrupted his thoughts.

Kelly turned slowly, unsure why anyone was identifying him. He found himself looking into Delacourt's pale blue, deadly serious, eyes. Kelly almost gasped.

"Nice to see you," Delacourt said.

Kelly offered a limp hand. Delacourt shook it unenthusiastically.

"Hot in here," Kelly said.

"Mr. Thorn wanted a big crowd," Delacourt noted. "There are some possible donors we can hit up later."

"What are you doing these days?" Kelly asked, although he really didn't want to know.

"I'm Vice President Hardesty's chief of staff," Delacourt said. He fingered the campaign button on Kelly's lapel. "I'm glad to see you are back on the winning side."

"Always," Kelly replied, checking his watch. Only ten minutes. He did not say goodbye, but walked slowly through the throng to the stanchions. There was little room except toward the back, near the conference room. Kelly managed to squeeze by several people, one of whom looked angrily at him. He gave a wan smile of apology.

He was tall enough to see over many people. To his left, the carpet ran toward the conference room. The podium, clearly visible through the open door, bristled with microphones. To the right, the large door guarding the entrance was manned by two guards. The rotaries on each side had been closed. Beyond the door, Kelly could see a throng of police and military near the circular entrance. The limousine would have to come through there.

Security was overwhelming. Once again, he silently cursed whoever had called in the death threat against Thorn. How much easier this would have been with typical police protection. He would have been able to use the gun. That was far simpler than trying to lure Thorn close enough to stab. The heightened security also added stress, which Kelly could feel starting to weigh down on him. He tried to find some calm image to focus on, but there was none.

*Any minute,* Kelly told himself. He began to breathe very heavily. The ache in his left shoulder increased. He felt as though something was squeezing his stomach, as though he were wearing a cummerbund. Awkwardly, he loosened his belt a notch. That did not help.

Now people were pressing closely against him. They shifted and moved, heedless of whom they bumped into. He felt trapped. He gulped for air, feeling perspiration soak through his shirt.

The clock facing the lobby said 2:55. Would Thorn be there? Kelly tried to control himself. He didn't know how much longer he could stand. His legs ached. Several times, he felt as though he would fall down, but did not because so many people were wedged into such a small area.

He eased his pen from his pocket and palmed it in his left hand. His thumb held it tight. His middle finger covered it. His ring finger helped keep it in place. Kelly was right-handed, but remembered a Bible story about a man who saved his people because he was left-handed. He had killed a Canaanite king because guards only searched his right side. This way, he could reach with an open right hand as though to shake Thorn's hand and stab with the left. He held his left hand by his side. The man to that side pressed up against it. No one could see the pen.

A buzz started as a long, white car with small American flags attached in front slid into view. Heads craned. Conversation picked up and then stopped. Suddenly, the lobby was quiet save for an occasional muffled cough.

Kelly could not see the car door open or really hear anything. He watched the soldiers by the door come to attention. Two men inside held the doors open. Although having trouble seeing clearly, Kelly focused on the men appearing in the doorway. There were several, all in dark suits. *Secret service agents,* Kelly thought. They scanned the crowd, walking slowly like ushers marching unescorted to the altar. Markham was in the lead. Behind them, Kelly could see hands in the air and cheers.

The crowd around him began to applaud. Kelly felt his left arm freed. He raised his right hand and waved.

Thorn stood in the front doorway. His face had a half smile, as though completing some long journey. He turned and spoke to the man next to him. Hardesty, Kelly realized immediately. The one-time reporter would be president next. He had been Thorn's lackey. He wouldn't know what to do. People would see through him immediately. His administration would be in shambles. Soon, all the dismal secrets about Thorn would ooze out.

"Let all the evils in the mud hatch out," Kelly told himself. That's what Claudius said after realizing Nero was going to succeed him as emperor of Rome. These evils were far worse. They would all emerge, once Thorn was gone.

Surprisingly, Thorn was talking to people along the sides as he inched along. Previously, he had been a private man, not willing to greet visitors or supporters. Gentry had handled that task with great glee. Thorn invariably seemed awkward. Yet, he did not hesitate now to exchange handshakes and wave to those behind the front lines. The agents pressed around him, but were powerless to completely protect him. Thorn was smiling, which distorted his usual somber features and seemed painful.

He inched along, nearing Kelly. Kelly felt his pulse shoot up. With his right hand, he carefully pushed up the clasp on the pen. That activated the poison. He kept the tip just above his middle finger. He could stab himself afterward, but not before.

Thorn was close enough now to see clearly. He had gained a few pounds and was adding jowls. His hair was still cut short; his manner, as ever, was firm and confident. His shoulders seemed set by a straightedge.

He talked to people who addressed him. They called him "Mr. President." No one was casual.

"Joe," Kelly said.

Thorn stopped cold and glanced at him. Their eyes met. The agents stiffened. "Dr. Kelly," Thorn said after a pause. "How nice …"

Kelly could stand no more. His legs collapsed. Caught in a fiery grip of something squeezing his chest, he pitched forward. Markham tried to intercept him, but Kelly fell toward Thorn. Thorn put up his hands. The pen penetrated his wrist and slipped from Kelly's limp hand. The president-elect moved away as Kelly collapsed, half in Markham's grasp and half across the ribbon.

People screamed and moved back. Someone grabbed the pen as a souvenir as agents hustled Thorn the rest of the way.

Markham knelt over Kelly and felt his pulse. He picked up his cell phone and dialed 911.

"Possible heart attack," he reported.

Kelly lay limp on the red carpet—hearing noises—but completely unaware of what was happening. He felt his eyes glaze. He stared up at a familiar face. He recognized it, but couldn't put a name with it.

He closed his eyes and felt darkness overwhelm him.

\*\*\*\*\*

He was lying on the floor and could feel the hard tile under him. Someone had unloosened his tie and a cool compress had been placed on his forehead. Water ran slowly down his neck. He felt a tremendous weight on his chest. His breathing was labored. He sucked at the air. He could feel people around him. Voices were talking.

"What happened?"

"Is he all right?"

"He just collapsed right in front of President Thorn."

"Dr. Kelly?" someone asked. Kelly managed to open his eyes. The brightness hurt. He closed his eyes again and slowly reopened them. He could see a familiar face.

"Sir," Markham said. "Do you feel all right?"

Kelly could not answer.

More voices: "The medics are here."

"Move out of the way."

Kelly could see another face. He didn't recognize it. Someone was taking his pulse. A stethoscope was pressed against his chest.

"I've seen this happen a lot," an authoritative voice reported. The stethoscope was removed. "I'll bet he didn't eat before going to see Thorn."

Something tapped his shoulder with a playful nudge. "Right, Dr. Kelly?" Kelly couldn't respond. His mouth seemed filled with cotton. "Sure, he didn't eat. He got lightheaded and fainted."

"It's exciting to see the new president," someone added.

People were agreeing.

Kelly tried to shake his head.

"Just let him lie here a few moments. He can go back to his room in a few minutes. I'm sure he'll be able to walk there on his own power. Can the hotel get him some toast and tea? That would help. He'll be up and about in no time," the voice continued.

*No, no,* Kelly thought urgently. *This was a heart attack.*

Sounds grew louder. Someone was screaming. "Thorn has collapsed," someone shouted.

"Oh, my God."

"What happened?"

"I'll be right there," the authoritative voice said.

Kelly could hear sirens roaring in the distance. Feet pounded across the floor. Suddenly, he was back at St. Michael's, in the emergency room, watching a patient being wheeled in. He slipped on his mask. He was ready. He was home.

# CHAPTER 20
# TOMORROW and TOMORROW

Dr. Peter Kelly's funeral at Grace Episcopal Church was quiet and low key on a sunny, crisp December morning. The minister did not talk long; neither did John Patterson, who represented Kelly's friends. Erik spoke on behalf of the family. All three praised a good man trying to do the right thing in difficult times. All were sure that Dr. Kelly's ideas, which had inspired such progress in medical treatment would continue to be his legacy for millions of Americans yet to be born.

A handful of dignitaries attended, including Dr. John McKittrick, the incoming secretary of the U.S. Department of Health and Human Services, who spoke to Joan and her three children on the way out. John Darby came, too, although he looked pale and sickly from cancer. He said that the chemotherapy was really helping and that he should recover in a month or two.

Dr. Matt Jefferson arrived with his wife and several nurses from the emergency room. He also did not seem healthy, but said he was fine and had recovered from his son's death.

Katie Watson flew in from Washington, D.C. "He was a very good director," she reassured Joan, even though Kelly was more of an absentee landlord.

"He said you were very helpful," Joan replied, although her husband never said a word about his secretary.

Most of the guests were long-time area residents who knew Dr. Kelly from his days at St. Michael's. Patterson thought more political figures could have come, but realized they were preoccupied with the death of President-elect Thorn and the succession of Jayson Hardesty to the White House. The former Colorado senator had already named Kevin Delacourt, a little-known attorney, as his vice president. Delacourt had just turned thirty-five and pundits foresaw a long career in the top echelon of American politics for him.

Patterson stood protectively by Joan in the reception line. Terri held her arm on the other side.

Finally, everyone filed out for the short ride to the cemetery. Erik came up and took her hand. Rachel and Diane walked behind her with Julie.

The graveside ceremony was brief. Kelly would have wanted that. He didn't like fanfare or attention, the minister reminded everyone. "He was a gentle man who would never harm anyone and only wanted what was best for his family, his patients, and his country." He might have said more, but he had never met the deceased.

Finally, everyone left. Joan sat in the back seat and let Erik drive her home. She didn't speak, but stared out the window. Her business was in the process of being sold. She would find something else to keep herself occupied. There must be plenty of activities for widows.

Rachel and Diane busied themselves upstairs, going through old photos and comforting each other. Erik and Julie went back to their motel to change. Terri was in the kitchen, quietly getting together some lunch.

Patterson sat on a chair next to Joan and stroked her hand.

She wasn't sure what to say. Finally, she asked, "Do they know what killed Thorn?"

Patterson shook his head. "I doubt they ever will," he replied. "Hardesty already announced that he doesn't want President Thorn's body defiled by an autopsy."

"I'm just glad he wasn't shot," Joan said.

"Why?"

"Pete had a gun," Joan explained. "He told me he was taking it."

"Pete wouldn't shoot anyone," Patterson assured her.

"Pete was so unhappy," she continued. "Do you think President Hardesty will do anything differently?"

Patterson nodded. "Of course," he said. "Pete was an inspiring model. I hear that Delacourt worked with him. I am sure many of Pete's ideas rubbed off on him."

She managed an uncertain smile.

"Are you sure that's what you want to talk about?" he asked.

"No," Joan admitted. "I was thinking about all the stress that day. Maybe it damaged his heart."

"I doubt it," Patterson replied calmly. "Pete had a checkup before he left for D.C."

Joan looked at him with a puzzled expression. "Are you sure?" she asked. "I asked him to, but he didn't want to."

"Oh, Pete didn't want you to worry," he lied smoothly, as always. "He told me about it. Called me from his hotel room. Told me he felt great and was so glad to get past what had happened. He thought that seeing Thorn would bring him closure."

"Thank you for telling me," Joan whispered.

"He was healthy as a horse," Patterson continued. "It was just some freak thing."

She nodded. "It's so like him to want to make up with Thorn.

Pete was such a loving man. He never would have hurt anyone. I just hope people remember all the good he did."

They sat in silence, broken only by the sound of dishes being moved in the kitchen. Finally, Joan said, "I thought I killed him." She looked at Patterson with red-rimmed eyes and a mournful expression.

"Don't torture yourself," he soothed. "You aren't responsible." She shook her head. "You were home. You couldn't help him."

She stared at the carpet.

"John," Joan whispered. "I'm the one who called in the warning about the death threat."

Patterson sat up. "Why?"

"I was worried. He took the gun. I know how angry he was. I just didn't want him to do anything," she whimpered. "All that security must have overwhelmed him."

Patterson immediately disagreed. "No," he insisted quickly, telling another lie. "I'm sure that had nothing to do with it."

*It's hard,* he thought, rocking Joan as she wept, *to hold onto the truth.* He had asked Pete what love was once. He should have asked a much bigger question. What was truth? The problem was, he decided, it's unlikely anyone knew what the truth was anymore.

-End-